Fran Annaford works in the entertainment industry. Enforced idleness during the corona pandemic led to increased activity on the laptop, and the eight volume 'Starnberg Set' series was conceived and written.

If Time Were Not a Moving Thing is the first part, and You *Don't Own Me*, the second. The third volume in the series is entitled *Give Me Time*.

Fran travels extensively in the course of her work. Home is wherever her partner and animals happen to be.

For my partner. An inspiration to many.

Fran Annaford

STARNBERG SERIES: BOOK 2 - YOU DON'T OWN ME

AUSTIN MACAULEY PUBLISHERS™
LONDON * CAMBRIDGE * NEW YORK * SHARJAH

Copyright © Fran Annaford 2023

The right of Fran Annaford to be identified as author of this work has been asserted by the author in accordance with sections 77 and 78 of the Copyright, Designs and Patents Act 1988.

All rights reserved. No part of this publication may be reproduced, stored in a retrieval system, or transmitted in any form or by any means, electronic, mechanical, photocopying, recording, or otherwise, without the prior permission of the publishers.

Any person who commits any unauthorised act in relation to this publication may be liable to criminal prosecution and civil claims for damages.

This is a work of fiction. Names, characters, businesses, places, events, locales, and incidents are either the products of the author's imagination or used in a fictitious manner. Any resemblance to actual persons, living or dead, or actual events is purely coincidental.

A CIP catalogue record for this title is available from the British Library.

ISBN 9781528926874 (Paperback)
ISBN 9781528927642 (Hardback)
ISBN 9781528927925 (ePub e-book)

www.austinmacauley.com

First Published 2023
Austin Macauley Publishers Ltd®
1 Canada Square
Canary Wharf
London
E14 5AA

My thanks to all at Austin Macauley for their continued support.

"Thorsten, did you hear that? Arabella said *my wife!*"

Her husband grunted and walked ahead through the open gates. Juliette Simon had decided this morning to make the introductory visit to their next-door neighbours when she happened to look out of her tower window and noticed the gates stood open and a large SUV parked in the driveway. Whether the unfettered access was by accident or design, she couldn't know. After installing a high security barrier at the entrance to their private road, replete with cameras, she figured out the four villa owners in the cul-de-sac felt it was now safe to leave their property unprotected. At least during the daytime. This wealthy area of upper Bavaria was a magnet for criminal gangs, although in Juliette's case, her fear of paparazzi and stalking fans outweighed her fear of being burgled. She had taken with her a good bottle of wine from her native Veneto region of northern Italy.

"A good fuck would cure them of that." He smirked.

And you consider yourself just the man for the job. Although you sure as hell don't satisfy me. They returned to their own closed gate, and with unnecessary force, he punched in the code to open it. The building in front of them was twice as large as their neighbours, and modern, whereas the neighbours was probably seventy or eighty years old.

Juliette spent months with the architects designing her new house and garden. It was not the first piece of real estate she purchased after her career took off nine years previously, but it was the first residence to be built to her own specifications, and she loved it already. Although it had three and a half floors and a sunken basement, it did not sit higher than Marie and Arabella Cooper-Nyman's next-door villa. Theirs was built into a slight hill, which rose from the hedge border of the adjoining properties. The older established garden sloped much more steeply down to the lake than hers did.

Her husband punched another code into the front door. It opened onto a wide hallway, which had windows onto their drive. They were all securely barred. At the end of the hall, on the left, was a lift. On the right, a broad staircase stretched to the upper levels. Juliette walked into her office, the room next to the stairs, to deactivate the alarm. Thorsten sauntered into the lounge. It was an expansive L shaped room, into which the second door of the office opened. The glass doors along the inner L led onto a wide terrace, with a freshly planted pergola at the far end. Another glass door led into the dining room, which in turn backed onto the massive kitchen, from which double doors could be opened back into the living room. Seen from above, the house, which faced directly onto Lake Starnberg, was built in the shape of an E, without the middle tongue, or a C with ninety-degree angles.

Juliette walked into the lounge from her office. "I'm hot. I'm going up to change. I can make lunch, or would you rather go out?"

He muttered something she couldn't decipher, and opened a door onto the terrace, going outside to flop on a lounger.

She took the stairs. The lift was intended for her parents when they visited. They weren't yet old enough to need it, but Juliette built this house aiming to live in it for many years, and one day they would be grateful. Who knows, one day maybe she would be too, especially if she continued with her backbreaking stage routines. She occasionally felt a twinge in her left knee, the result of a fall four years ago when a fellow dancer dropped her.

She walked into the master bedroom, and on into the enormous connecting dressing room. It stretched the entire length and width of the L part of the lounge and office underneath and was windowless but air conditioned. Racks of stage costumes filled three walls. On the rear wall, tiers of shoes stretched up to the ceiling.

The section nearest the door contained her more modest private clothes, and she slipped out of her jeans and into linen capris. She pulled a sloppy cotton hoody over her head, went into the bathroom and splashed water over her face. She pulled her dark blond hair onto her head in a messy high bun, fanning her neck to cool it, before going back into the bedroom, where she opened the French doors onto the balcony. It jutted out over the terrace, so she couldn't see Thorsten. She looked over to her right, but the high hedge blocked her view of the neighbouring garden. Peering up she could just see the windows of the neighbours' top floor. A hand reached out to open a window, and she caught the sound of voices, but could not make out the conversation. That might be the bedroom. What were they doing in there? She felt a tug in her core. *What?* She shook her head quickly and looked over to her left side. The next door led into Thorsten's bedroom, situated over the dining room. Further along, above the kitchen, was a child's bedroom, bathroom and playroom. When she showed her parents the designs during the planning stage, her mother urged her to incorporate the little suite. She shrugged and conceded.

Her husband's room had its own terrace, separated from hers. She sometimes wondered why she designed it this way. Why she wanted the only access to her bedroom to be through a door she could lock. When she invested in the property two years previously, their marriage had been intact. *More or less.*

On the floor above were three ensuite guest rooms, each opening onto a long communal balcony. The last one in the row was a larger self-contained apartment with a small kitchen.

Situated above her dressing room was her music room with its own terrace. Built into the rear corner of the long room was a spiral staircase leading to her tower room where she kept her books and her most personal possessions. There was a comfortable sofa on which she could rest, and a small shower bathroom. Nobody was allowed in, not even Thorsten. *Especially not Thorsten.* She cleaned it herself. It was where she wound down, and where she went for inspiration.

She would love to go up there now, and think about the strange visit next door, but Thorsten called out.

"Why are you taking so long? Didn't you say something about food?"

She walked slowly down the stairs, prepared a salad for herself and a steak for him.

***

After lunch, he wanted to take a nap and suggested she come upstairs with him, but she shook her head and said she had to work off the salad. He rolled his eyes.

She went down into the basement, not going straight to the pool or the spacious and fantastically well-equipped gym, but instead into her sound studio under the living room. She put on headphones and began to listen to the first cut of her new album, before she turned it off, dissatisfied. She didn't yet have enough distance to be objective. The sessions finished only a fortnight ago. Her arranger and the composer of many of her hits had sent the CD over. She could have downloaded it from Dropbox, but she preferred to hold the physical manifestation of her work in her hands. She pushed down an icon on her smartphone.

"Bert, hi. Thanks for the CD. I haven't listened yet. It's too soon, but I will by the end of the week. Could you then come over and we can talk about what I think needs changing."

"I'll be there. Let me know when you're ready."

She nearly told him she had visited the neighbours, but something held her back. Bert composed and arranged some of the songs on the crossover album that had earned them a platinum disc. At least she presumed it must have been for the album *Cooper-Nyman Rock*. She couldn't imagine a classical recording having sold a million copies. Juliette had collected two platinum and three gold discs for her recording sales which, among her other earnings, enabled her to pay for this house and the three luxurious cars standing in the four-car garage.

Her wealth also allowed her parents to move out of their small apartment in the middle of Lazize on Lake Garda in the north of Italy, and into a new home with pool in an enclosed and secure neighbourhood overlooking the lake.

Her parents sacrificed a great deal when at the age of twelve her extraordinarily mature voice became apparent. The first thing they did was to send her to a private Liceo where she learnt to speak English and German. She was touched to learn they were taking evening classes, so that they could all practise speaking together. After she obtained her maturità, they made it possible for her to attend the musical academy in Munich. She won a scholarship to study, but they continued to pay for her living expenses until she began getting small concerts and gigs and could support herself.

She would be forever grateful, hence the lift in her house. She was quite determined that they would move in with her when they could no longer care for themselves. It was the Italian way to take personal care of parents at the end of their lives.

Juliette was restless and went out into the garden. As she wandered over to check on the freshly planted rose bed next to the hedge, she was aware of sounds from next door. She moved into the shadow of the hedge.

She heard panting, then a wail, "Bella, darling, please…deeper. Oh sweetheart."

Now she couldn't ignore her own throbbing core. She thought about joining Thorsten in his bedroom, grimaced, and went to the indoor pool instead. It was filtering, and she stood in front of one of the jets so that the water pushed between the tops of her legs. She held on tightly to the edge of the pool. It took barely a minute before she felt it coming, and she climaxed with a power she rarely experienced. She put her head on the edge of the pool as the after waves pulsed through her. When she recovered, she swam forty lengths, showered, worked out for an hour, showered again, and still couldn't get Marie Nyman's sighs of ecstasy out of her head.

***

Bert came over ten days later. After a detailed working session in which they hammered out changes she wanted made during the next part of the editing process, they relaxed with a cup of tea on the terrace. Thorsten was out somewhere. He rarely told her where he was going, and she was increasingly uninterested in asking him.

"Bert, you never told me they are…um…gay. Next door I mean. We went to say hello."

Bert laughed. "I thought you knew. Everybody does."

"Not me. I don't move in their exalted world, you know. And I don't read gossip magazines anymore. They write such crap about me, it's unbearable."

"And…were they nice?"

"Yes, very, though I thought Marie Nyman looked at me a bit suspiciously."

"She's a rather reserved Swede. They call her the Ice Queen." He sighed. "But I would leave my wife for her."

"Not for Arabella Cooper?"

He raised an eyebrow. "She more your type?" Juliette felt herself blushing. He laughed. "Annette's too. She said she would quite happily desert me if Arabella crooked her finger. Juliette…don't look at me like that, and don't get paranoid if you feel a pull in that direction. You do know that only a tiny percentage of people are entirely hetero, don't you? Most of us are on a sliding scale between 90/10 and 50/50. And in the case of Cooper-Nyman, I haven't yet met anybody, male or female, who doesn't find them the hottest couple on four legs. Lovely legs they have too. They are both so beautiful." He sighed deeply.

"Yes, they are. But how do you know about their legs?"

He laughed again. "We made that double album in August. Neither of them wore much in the studio."

She struggled not to let Bert see her swallowing at the image. Her mouth was quite dry. She took a long gulp of her tea.

"Talking of which. Arabella and I wrote one of the numbers together. They won't be releasing singles, so it did cross my mind it would be a good one for you. It's called *How could you leave me*. I'll mail you the album and you can listen to it and tell me what you think. And I'll send you a CD as well. The photos of them in the booklet are steamy." He winked.

***

There was a Saturday night TV special coming up. They were advertised as going out live, but of course, they didn't. They were rehearsed and filmed over two days in a large conference facility in a changing roster of German cities. This one would take place in Hannover. Juliette was beginning to get bored with the format and if she had to be really honest, with the fairly mindless songs she had to sing. But folksy pop is what had made her a superstar, and that was her fan base. She was gradually pulling them towards soft pop, with an occasional hint of rock, but she and the team around her, principally her omnipotent manager, Andreas Meyer, put the brakes on her ambition to go further. Only Bert Schmidt sympathised, and some of the songs he wrote for her were becoming increasingly complex. But they both knew she would have to ease them carefully into her albums and her live shows. Huge swathes of her record buying public were of the dirndl and lederhosen wearing variety.

Bert sent her the *Cooper-Nyman Rock* double album, and she listened to it with astonishment. That an operatic soprano could sing like that left her speechless. She thumbed through the accompanying booklet several times. He was right. The photos were erotic, particularly Arabella in that tux adaptation. She phoned her dress designer and ordered a version for herself. The way Marie was dressed was the way she herself often went out on stage, short leather skirt and corsage. Marie's breasts were more voluptuous than her own. She stared at her cleavage, and her nipples hardened.

She knew as soon as she heard it, she was going to record *How could you leave me*. It was a heart-breaking ballad and she loved it, although she knew it was going to be difficult to get it past Andreas Meyer. Her public expected only happy songs from her. She talked to Bert and asked him to get Arabella Cooper's agreement. Somehow, she would make it work.

Having enjoyed three precious weeks at home, she now had to gear herself up again to being the Juliette Simon the public expected to see. Thorsten would come with her to Hannover, but he wasn't dancing in the show. The TV company had not asked him to. They hadn't asked him for the last three shows as it happened. He was lazy and getting lazier, and she saw he was growing heavier. She wouldn't tell him. He didn't want to hear it, and she couldn't face the shouting match. He justified the lack of an invitation by saying the show's director was jealous. Juliette's relationship before Thorsten had been with Leon Hoffmann, but it was long over before Thorsten caught her eye. Leon was now married, and not at all jealous. She knew that for certain. She suspected Leon thought Thorsten a brainless idiot but would have had no problem having him in the show if he had been dancing to his previous form. He wasn't.

But he would come with her, because he loved the attention and the photographers, and Andreas liked having him around, to cement her happy-couple-image. There would undoubtedly be a half dozen magazine articles following the TV special. At least the rumours the previous week in five of them, claiming yet again she was pregnant and taking time out to be a mother, would be allayed by her super sleek appearance. She had been working out hard for a month, and was femininely muscular, without an ounce of surplus fat on her body.

***

Juliette was scheduled to be the final act on the show. She had held on to this top of the bill status for the last four years. She would sing two songs, the first a ballad, followed by an up-tempo dance number.

The show's choreographer sent her a film, herself dancing the routine Juliette was required to learn. The dance troupe had already rehearsed. After studying the choreography and practising it alone in the gym, she felt it was a little more complicated than usual, and she asked for an additional day's rehearsal. It was agreed and she left for Hannover.

In the small rehearsal studio, she wore just her dance gear without makeup. She looked like any other member of the troupe, most of whom she knew. They had a hard session, and she needed a shower afterwards. They all did. There was only a communal shower in the girl's dressing room, but that didn't bother Juliette. They were all colleagues. The seven of them stood under the jets.

Normally, she would have been oblivious, but she found herself taking an interest in the naked bodies. She looked at the long legs and muscular abs around her but registered nothing more than an aesthetic admiration for beautiful bodies. She felt nothing else. Slightly puzzled but relieved, she dried herself off, dressed, this time applying make-up, and went to meet Thorsten in an expensive restaurant in the city. They would be mobbed when she was recognised, and she needed the protection of full slap.

"Lucky I'm not hungry." They had been photographed from the moment they got into the restaurant, and to her annoyance, the staff did not even attempt to help. They seemed to actively encourage the other diners to come up to them, holding out scraps of paper for autographs, even as her fork was on its way to her mouth.

"They mean well, and they buy your recordings," Thorsten said out of the side of his mouth, as a particularly insistent and overweight couple tried to stand behind her while they asked him to take a photo.

"Come on, I've had enough for today." They stood, and he was chivalry itself, guiding her arm, and holding doors for her, until they reached their hotel suite, where he put his arms around her waist, holding her tight.

"No, Thorsten, please no." He brought her hand to his hard dick. She tried to pull away, but he made her hand stroke him. Being the centre of attention excited him.

"It's been over two months. You used to be gagging for me." *It depends on what you mean by gagging.* And it wasn't true anyway. She sighed. But as he was already hard, it wouldn't take him long. *Better to get it over with, and then I can dodge it for another month...or three.*

They got undressed quickly, and he reached into his suitcase for the lube. She had needed it after the first month of their marriage. He coated himself, and climbed on to her, slipping in immediately. It still hurt, and she grimaced. He started pumping. She closed her eyes. Usually, she would go through song lyrics in her head, but she suddenly had an image of Arabella on top of her; of holding onto her smooth muscular back and looking into her amazing blue eyes. She pushed her hips up. Thorsten sensed it and thrust harder. As he came close, he lifted his hips to give her space for her own hand to rub her clit. He had finally accepted that he couldn't make her climax on his own, and after some clumsy attempts to touch her, he had resigned himself to this solution. She put her hand down, imagining it was Arabella's pianist's fingers stroking her. She felt her orgasm coming, and she climaxed before he did. He rolled off her panting.

"Well, that was a nice change." She was as surprised as he was, and she now wanted desperately to be alone to process what had happened.

They were in a two-bedroom suite. She insisted on sleeping alone when she was performing. Without saying a word, she took her clothes and her luggage, went into the other room and closed the door. She took a shower, letting the hot water run over her for many minutes. What had just happened? The dancers' bodies had done nothing for her at all. Two hours later, she orgasmed while fantasising about being under a woman. She climbed into bed, feeling hungry but too lazy to call room service. She lay awake, confused.

She heard Thorsten go out. He was presumably being considerate not waking her to tell her where he was going. She wouldn't give a damn if he stayed out for the length of their stay in Hannover.

How could she find herself in a loveless marriage after only three years? And why did she ever marry him in the first place?

She had made the decision herself and she couldn't blame anybody else, but everybody around her had certainly encouraged her, from Andreas down to breathlessly romantic make-up girls. Only her parents were wary when they met him, but she was fulfilled by the upturn in her career, and it felt good to have his model good looks by her side. They were never out of the press, and her albums climbed immediately to the top of the charts.

Her first attraction had been to his name. She sometimes felt a longing for her homeland, and when this handsome dancer called Thorsten De Luca was introduced, she gave him a second and then a third look. Only later did it become clear that he had hardly ever been to Italy and certainly didn't speak more than three words of the language, but by then observant members of her team had seen her interest, the press was somehow notified, and they were constantly photographed together. The whole thing spun out of control. She knew immediately that he was not especially intelligent, but he had charm. He was as lithe as a panther while dancing, and exuded an animalism, which had the fans in the audience screaming for him. They began to be booked together, and her segments in the TV shows got longer, and involved more dance numbers. The music was still folksy pop, but with clever choreography, it was possible to make even the most anodyne number exciting.

Andreas sat her down one day.

"You are gaining a new audience of younger fans, but you are also losing a lot of older ones. My focus group research indicates that there is an element of disapproval about your relationship with Thorsten."

"What relationship? You know it's all for the photos and magazine articles. We haven't even had sex."

"That's not what your fans in the mountains and valleys think. I wouldn't either, the way you look at each other."

"I went to acting school, don't forget."

"Listen, Juliette. You have two gold albums, which is a phenomenal achievement in this genre. I really think we can go for platinum on the next one, but we can't afford to lose fans, especially as those fans…the mums and dads, buy a lot of old-fashioned CDs."

"What do you suggest? That I marry him?"

"Exactly."

"No…I'm not in love with him. With his face and his body maybe a little bit. With his mind most definitely not."

"Think about it."

She did. Juliette knew herself to be ruthlessly ambitious and career orientated. She had never been in love. Except with performing and singing. She supposed she loved her screaming fans, who made possible all that she craved. Would it be so awful to have Thorsten as a husband? It would stop other men hitting on her, which was boring and energy sapping. But what about sex? Did she really feel that kind of attraction to him?

They went out to dinner, and she invited him to her apartment. They drank a bottle of wine. *He is gorgeous to look at.* She convinced herself. She let him take her to bed. The wine had made her relaxed, and she stroked his muscles and abs. She felt her arousal flow, and when he entered her, she pushed up her hips to meet his. She had never had an orgasm from sex with anyone, but this was better than a lot of other times. He was gentle at first. She asked him to go faster, hoping it might increase her desire. It didn't, so she faked it, as she always did. He climaxed and slumped on her.

"Juliette, that was fantastic. We make beautiful music together." She flinched. *Surely, he can't be that unoriginal.* But of course, he was.

They announced their wedding. The press went wild, the fans too, and the platinum disc was assured.

***

Juliette had a rough night. She slept but was aware of half waking up every hour or so. Typically, she was at last in a deep sleep when the alarm shrilled at eight. She felt groggy, and needed a cold, or at least a lukewarm shower. It helped. Thorsten's door was closed. She had not heard him come in. Perhaps he hadn't. She shrugged. Breakfast for one then. She ordered it to be sent up. She had eaten almost nothing in the restaurant last night and worked off a lot of calories in the dance studio, so she spoiled herself with muesli, scrambled egg, bacon, toast and fruit salad. She drank her coffee black, which she always did when she had to sing, as milk clogged her mucus membranes, but she pulled a face as she dropped two sweeteners into it. Milky coffee in the morning was her passion.

She dressed in slim jeans, a top, and an elegantly cut jacket. She dressed her hair, putting it up with a clip, and donned light make-up. Stilettos completed the look. In her large dancer's bag, she had her training clothes and shoes, which she would put on for the dance number, but first she knew she would be meeting a lot of people, and there would most probably be unofficial photos. Juliette Simon had arrived in Hannover, and she would have to play the part.

A large black Mercedes waited for her in front of the hotel entrance, as did two dozen fans. She pushed her sunglasses onto her head and signed autographs. Her image was the glamorous girl-next-door, and she had played the part so often she couldn't tell if she was or wasn't. She did genuinely like and appreciate her fans, which made her interaction with them seem real. They thought so anyway.

She got into the car, waving cheerfully, and sighed. She had a drive of about twenty minutes before it would happen again at the other end.

"Do you think you could take me down the ramp today?"

"I have instructions to bring you to the artists' entrance."

"I know, but I'm running late. I don't have time for another horde."

"Herr Meyer said…"

"Fuck, Herr Meyer," she said it under her breath.

She took out her smartphone and punched on Andreas's icon. The driver had really pissed her off. Did she put her ass on the line at every show, or did Andreas Meyer?

"Andreas, good morning, I'm late, I didn't sleep, I got held up at the hotel with fans. How did they know I'm living there? Oh, never mind. I want to go down the ramp…now. The driver quoted your orders…"

"Of course, that's fine. I'll call him." At least, he knew when he was beaten.

On the dashboard, the mounted phone rang.

"Yes, yes, of course." The altercation had taken most of the drive. Instead of having a moment to gather her thoughts and calm down, she was really riled up. The driver veered off before he reached the artists entrance where she saw a group of at least fifty people waiting and drove into the loading bay of the conference centre. She didn't wait for him to open the door, but jumped out, and grabbed a girl with a tablet wearing a headset.

"Where are the dressing rooms?"

"Oh, Miss Simon, oh yes, sorry, I wasn't expecting you here. Let me bring you to your room." Juliette felt sorry for the girl. It wasn't her fault. She shouldered her bag and followed. When she got into her room and dropped the heavy bag with a clunk, the girl put her hand to her mouth.

"I'm so sorry, I should have carried your bag." She looked as if she was about to cry.

"No problem. Just tell my team that I'm here please."

She shut the door, but Juliette opened it again. She felt too irritated to have to listen to nervous door knocks. She was very rarely bad tempered, but when she was, she knew her team would tiptoe around her, and she did not want that either. She sighed. She just wanted to get out on the stage, do her rehearsal, go back to the hotel, perhaps enjoy a leisurely workout, followed by a quiet evening on her own. With a book. And without her husband.

Her stylist Jamie, and make-up artist Petra arrived. She would try not to take it out on them. She loved them both. It was Andreas she was gunning for, but he knew to stay clear of her for the moment. *Coward.* Jamie had her costumes hanging on the rack. For the ballad, she would wear a slim gold sheath, showing plenty of cleavage. She would change for the dance number. The choreography was Bob Fosse inspired, so her costume bore a faint resemblance to Liza Minnelli's in the film *Cabaret*, complete with stockings, straps, and stilettos. She and Jamie had kept it away from Andreas who would be very unhappy. The way she felt about him at the moment, she relished the fight. Her blue grey eyes glinted in the mirror.

But for now, it was just a rehearsal, without costume, and she waited to be called to go on. She would stay in her jeans for the ballad.

The nervous tablet girl came to collect her. Juliette touched her arm reassuringly. She was Italian and tactile. The gesture had sometimes been misinterpreted by a man. The girl blushed. *Why?*

She was led onto the performing area, which was built out into the gigantic arena. There was a stage at one end, on one side of which the orchestra were taking up about a third of the available space. The rest was divided into two. During the show recording, one half would be in use, while the other one was prepared for the next number, with different props, or musical instruments if it was a band.

Jutting out from the middle of the stage was a twenty-metre-long runway, about four metres wide. In the middle of it was a platform, seven by seven metres. On each side were hidden pyro points, where fireballs would be sent into the air during some of the numbers. Thick tape on the floor showed the studio audience how near to the runway they were allowed to stand. This protected the artists from being groped, and their own eyebrows from getting singed.

For the ballad, she would enter from the back of the stage, and with her trademark golden microphone, would gradually walk down the runway until she reached the platform. The microphone was more or less for show. She would also wear a micro-port in her hair, which would pick up a much better sound.

A sound technician fitted her ear monitors and her battery pack, as well as the micro-port. The orchestra were taking a short break before her number, but the conductor was sitting at his desk, looking at his music. It was dark, as the bright lights were dimmed in an attempt to reduce the temperature. Juliette made her way towards the conductor and tripped over something lying directly in her path.

"Merdata!" She just managed to avoid falling on her face, but a second later was almost sent flying again by a figure springing up from underneath her. They gripped each other for support.

"Oh god, I'm so sorry. I thought it was a break. I was just easing my back." The voice was unmistakably American. She spoke English.

"Of all the stupid places to lie down. I could have broken my neck."

"I've said I'm sorry. Why are you creeping about in the dark anyway?"

There was an icy silence. "I think I have every right to be here."

They heard voices, and the lights came back on. They were still clutching each other but broke apart. Juliette looked up slightly at a woman a good two inches taller than her own five foot seven. She wore her thick hair in a long unruly pixie cut, and had enormous dark brown eyes, which widened as they looked at her. Her features were perfect in her slim face. She was remarkably beautiful.

"Oh my god, no, please not." She now spoke accent free German.

"What?"

"You're Juliette Simon, aren't you?"

"And you are?" Juliette's eyes were gimlet hard.

"Jodie…Sanchez."

"Well, Miss Sanchez, I still don't know what you are doing here, but I have to rehearse. You will excuse me."

Jodie stumbled as Juliette's hand pushed her lightly to the side on her way over to the conductor. She said over her shoulder.

"Rather too clumsy to be around a film set I think." There was a veiled hint behind the words and Jodie swallowed hard. It was her first day in her new job. And this had to happen. She had nearly maimed the show's star. She scuttled behind Juliette, giving her a wide berth and took up her position on a high stool behind a music stand, just as she was joined by her two colleagues, who had been to drink a coffee in the break. Her throat was dry, and she didn't have a water bottle with her. *Could she sing?* She cleared her throat. Sadie took a small box of pastilles off her stand and wordlessly handed Jodie one.

"Lifesaver."

"We might be in for a bumpy ride today. I heard in the canteen that Madam is in a terrible mood. She nearly got one of the runners sacked."

Claudia laughed. "Sadie, don't believe everything the girls in make-up tell you. The runner herself told me that it's not true. She was actually nice to her, though she definitely is in an awful temper."

"I don't think I've helped much. She fell over me in the dark."

"You're kidding. How did that happen?"

"I was stretched out on the floor over there. She was on her way to the conductor. She moves like a leopard. I didn't hear her."

"Keep your head down behind your score. Does she know who you are?"

"Not yet."

"Miss Simon, would you please take up your entrance position. We'll run the ballad."

The disembodied voice came over the loudspeakers. The director, Leon was in the broadcast van outside.

"No, I want to run it with the orchestra first," she shouted into the vacuum.

"Juliette, I can hear you fine. Ok, we'll record it then. Just for fun."

Juliette scowled. She moved away from the orchestra to avoid feedback. The conductor gave the downbeat and the orchestra started to play. Juliette began to sing and relaxed visibly. The backing singers joined in. Suddenly, Jodie was not together with them. She stopped singing and looked at her music. She couldn't understand it. She had sung exactly what was written.

"Ritardando," breathed Claudia. That meant she should have slowed down on a certain bar, but the marking was not in her music. Somehow, she had caused a traffic-jam, and they were all out of sync as a result. The conductor stopped.

"Who did that?" Juliette shouted exasperated. "Was it the ritardando? I always sing it like that." She looked accusingly at the conductor, who shrugged. Jodie put up her hand.

"I'm terribly sorry. It was my fault."

"You! How many times are you going to fuck up today?"

"I don't have a rit mark in my music."

"Where's the other girl? Claudia and Sadie, where is Alex?"

"She left to go back to Australia. Jodie joined us today. It's my fault, Juliette. She has completely new music here, because Alex forgot to give hers back. I should have checked."

"Yes, you should have done," her tone was biting. "Ok, let's try again. Jodie, there's another one on the refrain."

This time, the number was perfect. Juliette wandered over to the backing singers during the second verse and stood next to them listening. It was unnerving, and all three were glad when she moved away.

"That was great. Are you ready to do it with action?"

"Yeah. Leon, keep an ear on the backing singers please. I don't think the balance is quite right. What's her name...Jodie...is too loud."

They rehearsed the number half a dozen times. The director was satisfied after three runs, but Juliette wasn't. She called her dresser to bring her shoes and rehearsed again in the stilettos which made her legs even longer and the muscles in her calves tighten. She glanced once at the singers and saw Jodie staring at her legs. She felt hot. Yes, it was time to get out of the shoes and into her dance clothes.

***

She kicked off her stilettos in her dressing room. Jamie picked them up.

"Sorry, Jamie. That wasn't directed at you, or the shoes. I can't seem to shake off this mood today. Have you seen that new backing singer? She nearly broke my neck, and then she fucked up a take. Good voice though."

"Did she sing solo?"

"No, but I could hear her above Sadie and Claudia. She can't really blend in because her voice is so much bigger and better. I hope the conductor can do something about it, otherwise it sounds as if she and I are singing a duet, instead of me being backed. They aren't in the next number, which is a relief."

She drank a small bottle of water, changed into her dance clothes, and went out to rehearse the number.

"The dancers will be waiting for you down on the platform. You make your entrance at the top of the stairs, then come to join them for the chorus."

"I know Leon, we rehearsed yesterday."

"Whenever you are ready then."

The orchestra began, she moved into position and began the number, dancing down the runway to reach the troupe. They sat on chairs. She joined them. On a certain bar, they opened their legs suggestively, and their hips undulated on the seats. Juliette noticed a figure standing watching from where the public would be grouped. The woman had her mouth open.

They did the routine three times, and the troupe collapsed on their chairs.

"Can I have my shoes and a bottle of water please?"

There was a piercingly loud whining sound, and the dancers covered their ears.

"Who the hell has an open mike out there?"

It got worse as Jodie held out a water bottle to Juliette.

"Move back. You're causing the feedback. Get behind us, or somebody turn her off."

The sound stopped.

"Miss Sanchez, third time lucky today. You practically kill me; you cause orchestra overtime and now you have probably blown the sound system." Juliette glared at the girl. She was pale and looked as if she might pass out. "But thanks for the water."

Jodie moved backwards, nearly falling over a chair, at which some of the dancers sniggered. Juliette felt a pang of sympathy.

"Try getting out of bed the other side tomorrow," she called to her retreating back. Now the orchestra joined in the laughter. Juliette cringed. She hadn't meant to cause that.

Her shoes arrived, and they rehearsed the number until they were covered in sweat.

Juliette made her way back to her dressing room. There was a knock on the door. Leon came in. "Hi." He was a good-looking man, not nearly as handsome as Thorsten, but extremely attractive. She thought she had been in love with him during their three years together, but when he admitted that he was having an affair with someone else, she felt strangely indifferent. However, she was very concerned about how it would look being left for someone else, and Leon appreciated this. The end of the relationship was engineered so that she left him. He then kept his new alliance a secret for six months. He and his wife Angela had a daughter. Juliette was a godmother. She looked at him now and re-imagined them having sex together. He was a considerate lover, but as with Thorsten, she found it very difficult to climax. Sex had dwindled in their time together to almost nothing, and she was not at all surprised he needed somebody else.

She blamed her lack of interest on her driving ambition, but it was no different with Thorsten, although by now she had reached super stardom status and it was a question more of maintaining her position than reaching up for further accolades.

"Do you want me to change that backing singer? She's a disaster."

"Yeah, but she has a good voice. It wouldn't be fair. Let her stay, at least until the show tomorrow. If she fucks up again, I'll get her changed for my next album."

"I haven't seen Andreas today."

"No, he's keeping out of my way. We had a bit of an altercation on the phone this morning."

"Does he know about the Fosse number in all its glory?"

"Not exactly. So, it's a good thing he isn't here."

"You'll have hell to pay tomorrow."

She sighed. "I know. But, Leon, I have to move on a bit from my squeaky-clean image. It's getting stale."

"I'm with you, if you want help. Any other problems with the two numbers?"

"No, I think we've ironed out the kinks."

She showered, dressed and asked for her car to be brought around to the artist's entrance. This time, she braved the fans, some of whom had been waiting all day. She was especially nice and took time giving selfies and signing.

There was no sign of Thorsten when she got back to the hotel room. She ordered room service. Her thoughts were busy with the choreography. Then she saw a vision of Jodie's horrified expression, which morphed into her look when Juliette had opened her legs. She felt a slight spasm in her core. *The dance is meant to be erotic after all, but should I be turning herself on?* Or was it the thought of those big brown eyes, which looked almost black. She shook her head, undressed and went to bed. She heard Thorsten stumbling over furniture in the middle of the night. Great, he was drunk again. His hangover had better not be too bad. He had to play the big stud tomorrow, on view to the public and the cameras. Not for the first time she wondered if she needed him in her life. She would be much happier alone. But then she would constantly be hit on. And anyway, Andreas would not allow it. She sighed and slept again.

***

Jamie and Petra arrived in her hotel suite at ten o'clock. She and Thorsten would be filmed arriving at the conference centre and followed with a camera until they entered her dressing room. Which meant carefully chosen casual clothes and full make-up. By mid-day, they were ready to leave the hotel. Thorsten hardly said a word and needed almost more attention from Petra than she did. He wore tight leather trousers and a jacket, which showed his muscular torso. Juliette wore designer jeans and a black leather jacket. Her hair was pinned into a chignon. They looked fantastic together. She put on her sunglasses as they climbed out of the car at the artists' entrance. There were no fans waiting as they already packed the auditorium waiting for the taping to begin. Andreas stood at the door and handed her a large bouquet of amber roses.

"Long time no see," she said out of the side of her mouth so the microphone couldn't pick it up. His mouth smiled at her. It didn't reach his eyes.

Thorsten slumped onto the couch in her dressing room and closed his eyes.

"Where were you?"

"Out."

She shrugged. She didn't care. "You know you have to come out of the audience at the end and kiss me?"

"Looking forward to it."

She bit off her retort as Jamie and Petra came in to dress her for the first number. She sat facing the mirror, and noticed in front of her a small, wrapped package. Gifts were not unusual. She almost didn't open it, and then thought she might have to thank someone she would meet. She unwrapped it. Inside was a small box. *Not jewellery please.* Janina, her secretary always sent that back to the giver. Wrapped carefully in cotton wool was a small bone-China monkey with his hands over his mouth, and a guilty looking expression on his face. On a string attached to his arm was a visiting card, *Jodie Sanchez*, with a printed email address. *Sorry, I'm a clumsy idiot. I'll do my best to keep out of your way.*

She turned the monkey over. It was Meissen China. Expensive. A backing singer didn't earn much. She would send it back. There was no postal address, but Janina would get it from Andreas.

It was a sweet gesture though, and she was touched.

When she was in her costume and ready to go, the sound technician came in and wired her up. She had done her vocal warm up in the hotel, and now repeated a few exercises.

She was always nervous, but the advantage of this pre-recorded show was that although she was singing live and not to playback, if anything went wrong, she could do the number again. It was more than likely that a couple of the other performers had already done just that. And as a further aid, the song texts were flashed up simultaneously on large monitors around the arena, unseen by the cameras, but easily visible to the artist and the audience. As they then mouthed along with the songs, it gave the impression that they all bought the albums and heard the numbers so often they had memorised the texts. And of course, the artist could avoid a text black out if for any reason memory failed them.

As Juliette waited to be announced, she looked over to where she could see the orchestra. The backing singers were to the left of them. They looked cute in black slacks and fitted shirts. Jodie's was stretched tight across her full breasts, and she was nervously flipping the pages of her music back and forth.

Then Juliette was on to ear-splitting applause and screams. She pressed the hand not holding her golden microphone onto her ear monitor so that she could hear the orchestra better. Luckily the song had a long introduction, and the screaming died down before she sang. It was a good take and would not need redoing. As she acknowledged the applause, she turned in a circle. The audience were sitting or standing on all sides of the enormous arena. There were easily five thousand there. She looked over at the backing singers. Claudia was gently rubbing Jodie's back and they were smiling at each other. She felt a pang of annoyance as she left the stage, to be met by two runners with tablets. She was hurried to her dressing room for her quick change into the costume for the second number. Her hair, which had been loose on her shoulders for the ballad, was pinned up into a chignon again. Her make-up was darkened, and her lipstick changed to a much darker red. She looked at herself in the mirror and took a deep breath. *This was going to cause a social media storm, one way or the other.*

The dancers were already in position, the orchestra began, and she made her entrance, this time without a hand microphone. There were gasps, and the applause was even louder than for her first appearance. The whistling was almost painful, and the audience wouldn't stop. The conductor put up his hand. It was pointless continuing. Not even the best sound system in the world could compete. The show's compere came back on.

"Miss Simon is thrilled with your reaction, but we need you to tone it down a little. We'll do the entrance again. Please be enthusiastic but stop before she has to sing. Thanks."

This time, it worked according to plan, and she joined the dancers on the platform in the middle of the arena. They all wore the same costume. Short black leather skirt and bustier with stockings, suspenders and stilettos. As they opened their legs and gyrated on the chairs, there was a collective intake of breath.

At the end of the number, people were screaming again and stamping their feet. She hoped the building was statically sound. Thorsten jumped up onto the runway, and they kissed, which only increased the volume. They walked arm in arm back up to the main stage. Juliette glanced to her right. Orchestra and backing singers were applauding. Jodie had shining eyes. She was sweet. *Maybe she would keep the little monkey.*

She got out of her costume quickly and into her jeans and t-shirt. She brushed out her hair and Petra toned down the make-up. Jamie was packing the costumes into their dress bags. There was a loud knocking at the door. Juliette sighed and rolled her eyes at Petra.

"Come in." Andreas and Thorsten walked in.

"Have you two finished?" They had, and scurried out, giving Juliette a sympathetic look.

"Are you completely crazy? You've lost thousands of fans tonight."

"And perhaps won a few new ones."

"You have to speak to Leon. We will have to cut the number from the broadcast. It will be all over social media, but at least the fans from the valleys won't get to actually see it."

"I will do no such thing, Andreas. If I lose fans, then I lose them. It's my risk, not yours. Do I have to keep reminding you that's it me out there, not you? I know I have to thank you for a great deal. You tell me often enough, and it's true, but I know I am going to have to change and grow as an artist. I can't keep doing the same stuff. Vivienne and Sabine are coming up fast behind me, and they already have a much younger image than I have. They don't have my sales yet, not by a long way, but if I don't keep ahead, they will eventually overtake me. Do you think I haven't given this a great deal of thought? It was a risk tonight, but I hope it will be worth it. That's my last word on the subject. I am going to go out and do the meet and greet, and we will know more after we see the reaction. Are you both coming with me?"

She put on her jacket and was almost out of the door, when she saw the little monkey on her dressing table. She carefully repacked it and slipped the box into the inner pocket of her jacket, zipping it up.

There were hundreds of fans waiting and they were almost hysterical.

"I'll organise the car." Andreas disappeared.

The fans looked a little younger than usual, although her base had a wide age spectrum, from teenies to great grandparents. As she signed there was not one critical comment. They were wildly enthusiastic. It took well over an hour before the crowd thinned out. She got into the car with Thorsten, and it moved off, fans still pressing their faces to the windows.

Thorsten looked sceptical. "It was hot, I won't deny it, but the fans just now were all youngish. You might have lost some tonight, as Andreas says."

"So be it."

***

Shortly before they reached the hotel, Juliette turned to her husband. "I think I want to go home tonight. I don't feel like another night in the hotel or the flight tomorrow morning." She spoke to the driver. "Are you fresh enough to drive me down to Munich Airport?"

He gulped. It was over six hundred and fifty kilometres. "Yes, I think so."

"Then drive now into the garage. I'll pack quickly and be down in half an hour. Are you coming with me?"

"No, I don't think so. The drive is too long. I'll take the flight tomorrow morning."

"I'm going to pick up my car at the airport. You'll have to take a taxi."

"No problem. I have something to do in Munich anyway." It didn't even occur to her to ask what.

She sent a quick text to Andreas with her change of plan. It wouldn't surprise him. After ten years of constant travelling, it was understandable. The hotel didn't need to know as Thorsten was staying in his room. The lift went straight up from the garage to the suite, and twenty minutes later she was back in the car.

"Sorry about the change of plan."

"It's no problem." She settled back in the car, sighing contentedly at being alone. She checked her messages, replying only to her mother's question about how it had gone.

She knew social media would be buzzing, but she didn't look. Andreas would tell her in the morning. She felt the box in her jacket pocket and took it out. Whether she gave it back or not, she would have to thank Jodie. She started to write a mail on her official address, and then stopped. For a reason, she didn't understand, she didn't want Andreas or Janina, her secretary, to read it. She changed over to her personal address: * 'What a sweet gesture. Thanks very much. I think I will have to give it back to you, as it's much too expensive. You obviously did get out of bed on the other side today. You didn't fuck up. Congratulations. Juliette. Oh, and please don't give anyone this address. It's very private. I'm trusting you!'

Was that a bit flirtatious? *What the hell.* She sent it. Her phone pinged. An emoji of the three monkeys, *hear, see and speak no evil* came back, a wink and a kiss. * 'Jodie.'

Juliette saved the address in her contacts.

They reached the airport soon after midnight. The drive had taken only six hours.

"Shall I book you an airport hotel room?"

"No, thanks. I'm ok. I'll be on my way back. If I get too tired, I'll pull over and sleep a while."

"Let Andreas know when you are back in Hannover. And thanks again." She collected her white Porsche SUV from the garage, and he helped her with her luggage. They both drove off. The roads were clear, and she pulled through her gates at one thirty. She pushed the code, disabled the alarm, and went into the living room. She would unpack the car in the morning. She enjoyed the peace and quiet as she looked over the lake in the moonlight and drank a beer. Then she went to her bedroom. She pulled the box out of her jacket pocket and took the little monkey out. On impulse, she threw the box away and put the China ornament on her dressing table. She would keep it after all.

***

She woke at nine. The sun shone behind the curtains. She got out of bed. She had slept naked but had no fear as she pulled back the drapes and looked out over the lake. Her bedroom and dressing room, and the music room above with its tower room were fitted with a special glass, which allowed her a clear view, but from the outside looking in they were opaque. She was under no illusions about the possibility of paparazzi or fans training a telescopic lens on the house from the lake. So far, her new address didn't seem to be in the public domain, but it would only be a matter of time. The local authority allowed her to build a palisade in the lake, so that no uninvited boat could moor at her jetty, but camera lenses could not be kept out. She dressed in jogging clothes and went down to the kitchen. She was very hungry, not having eaten anything except a sandwich for twenty-four hours. She made yoghurt and fruit salad and fried two eggs with bacon. She had every intention of a good work out today so did not have a guilty conscience. She took her breakfast onto the terrace and sat in the sun. Sipping at her second mug of latte, she took a deep breath and pressed Andreas's icon on her smartphone.

"Good morning. Have you heard from my driver? Is he back?"

"Good morning. Yes, he called an hour ago. The traffic was light, so he drove through."

"Good. And…tell me the worst. Am I going to have to sell my house, and perhaps Thorsten as well?" she sniggered. Thorsten first and then the house would be infinitely preferable.

"It's hard to say until the show actually airs the day after tomorrow. There are some wobbly handheld smartphone videos doing the rounds."

"And? Are the silly thumbs pointing up or down?" She hated that about face book. It was so infantile.

"Overwhelmingly up." His tone was grudging.

"Anything else?"

"The streaming downloads of your last album have gone through the roof. But we will still have to wait until Saturday to see if the damage doesn't outweigh the positive trend."

"Andreas…do you think those folk music fans are going to climb onto their tractors and lynch me? I know I'll lose some, but I told you yesterday I have to move on. By the way, I have my new single. It's a song Bert wrote for Cooper-Nyman. It's on their double album if you want to listen."

"They won't allow that."

"Bert has already cleared it with them. Arabella Cooper wrote the lyrics. It's no problem. They are my neighbours by the way."

"Yes, I know. Juliette, please don't be seen with them in public. You do know they are…queer, don't you? We might weather this storm, but a public association with those two would definitely be the end of your career."

Anger boiled up in her.

"They won a platinum disc for fucks sake. It hasn't hurt their image."

"You and they live in completely different worlds. There is zero tolerance for homosexuality in folk music. Either here or in the States. And unless you have forgotten, we are going to try to launch you in the States with your new album."

Juliette didn't trust herself to speak further. "Andreas, I have to go…someone at the door…speak to you later."

Her heart hammered. Not for years could she remember being so angry. It made it worse to know he spoke the truth. No other folk singer had ever come out. She knew of two gay men who were forced to live deep in the closet. Statistically, it was unlikely there was no woman or girl out there terrified to reveal who they really were, and who they loved. But there were no rumours she had ever heard.

Quite why she was so furious she couldn't explain to herself. *I'm married to a beautiful man, even if he is only a muscled jerk on an E-bike.* The fans couldn't get enough of their pictures and interviews. That seemed to prove Andreas' case.

On the other hand, she had seen many unmistakably gay couples in her audiences, men and women. There were some fan exceptions it seemed. She shrugged. It was irrelevant. *I'm not gay.* Jodie Sanchez flashed into her subconscious. She pictured her dark brown almost black eyes and remembered the warmth of her body as they had clutched at each other when she nearly fell. When her thoughts drifted to a shirt stretched tautly across generous breasts, she went down to the gym and pounded the treadmill for an hour.

***

Thorsten came home late that night. Juliette was in her music room learning songs when her smart phone gave her the warning that someone had come into the house. Unhurriedly, she went downstairs. He was in the kitchen, drinking a bottle of water. His eyes were glassy.

"This is happening a lot lately."

"Shut up. It's none of your business." *Except that you don't earn a damn cent anymore and I am actually paying for your habit.* But he was sometimes aggressive when he had had too many, and she wasn't going to get into a fight.

"Good night then. Can you turn off the lights down here?"

"I'll see you later," he leered.

"I don't think so."

"You're my wife. You should do your duty more often." She shivered. He had once before forced himself on her, then apologised profusely afterwards. She walked up to her bedroom and locked the door. She heard him come up later, but he didn't try to come into her room. She needed to talk to somebody, but it was too late to call her mother. Anyway, there were limits as to what they could discuss, though Anna-Maria Simon didn't like Thorsten and would be sympathetic.

She had no real friends she could trust with her deepest feelings. The temptation for them to talk to the press was too great. How she envied the women next door. They had not only each other, but a host of friends. As the weather got warmer, she often heard men's and women's voices and laughter in the garden.

Bert had told her that it took Marie two years to come out and be honest about herself, but now they were open about their marriage. After the first sensation died down, the press left them alone. *Bert, I could talk to Bert*, but it was well after midnight. *Too late*. She put in earplugs and selected *Cooper-Nyman Rock*. She needed to listen again to *How could you leave me*. Instead, she chose *You don't own me*, Leslie Gore's great feminist hit from the nineteen sixties. Maybe she should sing this as well. Andreas would freak.

***

She seldom watched the transmission of her TV shows, but Thorsten always did, so on Saturday evening she sat with him. He made comments about the other performers. He knew them all from his time as a dancer on the show. Sometimes he was amusing, sometimes he told her unpleasant stories about them. He was becoming bitter.

The regular entertainment shows lasted for nearly three hours. This one seemed interminable, but eventually her first number came up. She looked and sounded good and was quite happy with the result. Her sharp ears thought she could hear Jodie above the other backing singers. She would have to check that later. If the girl was going to continue to back her, the sound technicians would have to solve the problem. She did want her to continue, Juliette realised when for a brief shot the camera caught the three of them. *I only want to thank her personally for my little monkey.*

"That new backing singer is hot." Thorsten made a show of licking his lips.

"You think so?"

"Especially in that shirt. Looks like someone for the dykes next door."

Juliette felt her stomach lurch.

"I wouldn't know about that, would I?"

The duet between her two appearances ended and the compere announced her. They had edited the film so that the full extent of the applause greeted her, then they faded out before she sang. She held her breath. It was even more daring than she expected it to be. That dance sequence on the chairs was like nothing this type of programme had ever seen. The number ended, and she watched Thorsten as he admired his own brief appearance.

"Phew. Well, it's done. Too late now. I'm going up to bed. I don't have the nerve to look at what social media is doing. Good night."

She went out on to her balcony to get some fresh air. Lights were still on next door. She could see them through the hedge. She wondered if they had been watching. It was not very likely. *Why would they watch TV if they could be making love?*

***

The show had the best ratings ever. Leon called her to tell her.

"What about the reactions?"

"Five complaints, and hundreds of *wows!* I think we can all live with that. Listen, Juliette, I know I haven't booked you for the summer broadcast from the lake. You know the one from the Chiemsee, but is there any chance you could do it? I know it is very opportunist of me, but the exposure wouldn't do you any harm either. When is your next album due?"

"Sometime after Christmas, to time with my special on the other channel. I haven't started recording yet. Not until September. I wanted to get going in August, but Bert has promised Cooper-Nyman he'll work with them, and they can only do August because of orchestra availability. It's ok though. We still have time to turn mine around before the end of December."

"I will regret until the end of time that the other channel got your New Year's Special before we did."

"I know. I wish you were my director, but with them I am much freer with the content of the show. I can sing musical numbers. And my guests don't have to be exclusively folksy. Actually, I was thinking of asking Cooper-Nyman. And I want a slot for a young talent. But I don't know who that will be yet."

He sighed. "Sounds like heaven."

"Yeah, I'm looking forward to it. How are Angela and Sarah?"

"Fine. Don't tell anyone but I think Sarah will be getting a new brother or sister soon."

"Leon, that's wonderful."

"And how about you? The fans are convinced…again…that you are pregnant. The loving kiss with Thorsten has set them off, for about the hundredth time."

"I know. I heard. You know the answer."

"I would be very surprised if there was something in the rumour. I know you, don't forget."

"Hullo…I have nothing against kids, or even having one…one day. Just not with Thorsten."

He laughed. "I bet you end up with a donor."

They ended the call, after she promised to talk to Andreas about the Chiemsee show. She was thoughtful. Perhaps a donor would be an option. She was going to have to face the fact that she and Thorsten were running out of road. But then there would have to be someone to take his place. She groaned.

***

She agreed to do the summer show. It was now the beginning of July, and it would be recorded in two weeks' time. The weather turned warm, and everyone was crossing his or her fingers that it would continue until then.

Thorsten was in bathing trunks lying on the terrace. Juliette couldn't risk sunburn from the strong July sun, though she would love to tan a little more. But any blotches or strap marks were impossible to disguise from the merciless scrutiny of television camera close-up. She went upstairs to her tower room and read an Italian book. Something made her look up from the biography in which she was engrossed. She walked over to the window. Down on the jetty next door, Marie and Arabella sat, dangling their feet in the water. Marie fed a pair of swans with what looked like a handful of grain. They both wore bikinis. Arabella was a gorgeous deep golden colour. Marie was paler, though an even tan indicated they spent time in the garden. Juliette gaped at her deep cleavage and perfectly flat stomach. She could be a model. Arabella was slimmer and more athletic, with broad shoulders, but her figure was unmistakeably feminine. The swans floated off when it was obvious Marie had no more food. Arabella dipped her hand into a large straw basket and took out sun block, which she massaged into Marie's shoulders and back, before her hand slipped into the top of her bikini and massaged her breasts. It was very sensuous, and Juliette's breath hitched. Arabella was *the man* she supposed. It looked like it. Then they were kissing, and Marie pushed Arabella onto her back. She climbed onto her. Arabella wound her legs around Marie's back as Marie ground their centres together. Juliette had trouble breathing, and she could feel how wet she was, which was a miracle in itself. Then Marie looked out onto the lake, they both stood up and, holding hands, ran out of sight in the direction of their house. She was so turned on; by watching two women. *No!* She had to stop whatever this was. She ran down the stairs and onto the terrace, where Thorsten lay half asleep. She straddled him and stroked him hard. She tore at his trunks and took him out, pushing aside her briefs under her short skirt. He entered her and she pushed herself up and down. He recovered his surprise and thrust hard. She put down her hand and rubbed her clit and came almost before he did. It had taken only three or four minutes which was fortunate as she saw a ship, still someway off, but it would soon pass the garden. She slid off him panting and fell onto a lounger a few feet away. He looked at her in amazement.

"No lube? Have you suddenly realised how attractive I am?"

She groaned. "I'm sorry. It must be the sun. The heat. But thank you."

She wanted to dive into the pool downstairs. "I need a swim to cool off."

He laughed but seemed very pleased with himself. "You want me to join you?" He smirked.

"No, you carry on doing whatever you were doing. Shall we go out to eat?"

"That's on the menu too, is it?"

She closed her eyes and went to swim. Were Arabella and Marie still making love? So, it wasn't as simple as Arabella *being the man*. Either Marie's appearance belied her tendencies, or it was an equal partnership. She felt down to her folds under the water. She was still sticky. She knew she could come a second time. She turned to the water jet and let it push between her legs. She forgot Thorsten completely. Her mind was a whirl. Marie, Arabella, and with those huge near black eyes Jodie, all flashed across her vision. The orgasm when it crashed over her was entirely satisfactory.

***

The stage was built out on a platform in the water, adjoining the dock which served the medium sized ships taking tourists around Germany's biggest lake. The small orchestra and band were on the platform. There would be no dancers, as the stage was not strong enough to support the weight of rhythmic movement. It would cause structural problems.

She was going to sing three of her hits. She was notified the rehearsal would take place the evening before the performance, which would be filmed, and transmitted two days later. The rehearsal happened at night, because the lighting had to be the same as it would be during the taping.

The Chiemsee and Lake Starnberg are only about seventy kilometres apart as the crow flies, but it took much longer by road. For Juliette, it meant either going into and through Munich on the autobahns, or taking a more direct country route, which was picturesque but tedious if you got stuck behind a slow vehicle. As it was impossible to say when the rehearsal would end, Juliette reluctantly decided to stay in a hotel with the rest of the artists. She knew she would get the best room, but it would almost certainly have only one bed which she had no intention of sharing with her husband. She wanted no rumours spread about she and Thorsten having separate rooms. Not that she could care, but Andreas Meyer strongly opposed anything that might suggest they didn't sleep wrapped around each other like Hänsel and Gretel. The usual two-roomed suites in five-star hotels were booked on the assumption that one was her dressing room, although she presumed the luxury hotels couldn't care one way or the other. Discretion was part of the service when so much money was being paid out. But there was no five-star where the filming took place. She persuaded Thorsten to come over only for the performance the following day. He seemed happy enough to hear her suggestion.

She drove her Mercedes convertible, tying up her hair in a scarf and driving the car open on the country roads. She was stared at all the way, but with her sunglasses on she didn't think many actually recognised her. They just appreciated the car and the girl. She checked in and went up to her room. It was good enough, had a large bathroom with a modern shower, but as she suspected, contained only one bed, and she breathed a sigh of relief that she was alone. She opened a window and heard voices in the small garden directly below. She leaned out. Jodie and Claudia were sitting on a bench with their backs resting on the warm wall. She couldn't hear what they were saying, but she had a good view of Jodie's long tanned legs in shorts, her shiny dark brown hair and a deep cleavage under a tight sleeveless t-shirt. *Another model figure to appreciate.* After the shock of her voyeuristic staring at Marie and Arabella, and the resulting sex with Thorsten, she hadn't expected to see another one quite so soon. In fact, she had tried hard to rid her mind of all thoughts of women's bodies, setting herself a punishing work out regime.

She wanted to step back and stop watching, but her gaze lingered just a little longer on the curve of Jodie's breasts, as they undulated gently with each breath. Her mouth went dry. The two girls got up suddenly, and she leapt back, stumbling so that she fell back onto the bed. The shock made her nipples hard. She stroked one and smothered a groan. She definitely did not have time for that now. She took a shower and dressed in a smart linen dress with stiletto sandals. They wouldn't be able to block off the public watching the rehearsal, so she would be on display. She wandered down into the foyer. Nobody had told her how she would get to the stage area, but she presumed a car was organised.

There were three minivans and several cast members waiting, including Claudia, Sadie and Jodie. They had changed into jeans and hoodies and had coats over their arms. A runner, clutching a tablet was checking people off.

"Miss Simon, your car will be here any minute." She waited, trying not to look at Jodie, but not succeeding. The limousine didn't arrive. The runner telephoned.

"I'm so sorry. It seems someone else took your transport."

She shrugged. "Then I'll go on the bus. I have something to say to my backing group anyway." The runner looked grateful. "Come on, girls. Let's take the first bus." The back row had four seats, two and two with the aisle in the middle. Juliette climbed in first and took the furthest window seat. Sadie pushed Jodie who almost crashed into her as she landed on the second seat.

"You are incredibly clumsy," Juliette said laughing.

Jodie glared at Sadie. "Sometimes, it's my fault, and sometimes, it isn't. I'm so sorry."

"Do you think you could be near me for a full half hour without saying sorry?"

"I'm so…"

Juliette took in Jodie's warmth next to her. The girl was trying to keep as far away as possible, but the seats were narrow. She breathed in her scent. It was tangy and she wondered if it was a man's perfume. It suited her, and Juliette allowed herself to inhale deeply, hoping she wouldn't notice. The bus started and was rather loud. The noise level rose.

She said softly, "Thank you again for the little monkey. I have it on my dressing table at home. He is adorable." She stopped the sentence right there before she said what was in her mind, *just like you*. There was a sudden sharp curve as they came into the harbour area. Jodie fell against her. It had happened to everyone in the bus, so nobody noticed when Juliette put her hand on Jodie's arm to steady her. There was an electric spark and they both jumped, wide eyed.

"I'm so…it must be this coat."

Juliette looked into her eyes. Her voice was husky. "Probably." Rather unlikely in high summer.

They climbed out of the small bus and began the rehearsal. As she had feared, the conditions outside complicated everything technical. The evening was never-ending. They were provided with drinks and sandwiches, but the dressing rooms were communal and cramped, and Juliette preferred to stay outside, sitting in the shadow of the TV trucks where she was protected from the public's prying eyes.

The girls had a tough evening. They were backing almost all the other singers. Juliette noticed that Jodie had settled in and often surreptitiously conducted the others. She was obviously musically well trained.

She sang her three numbers dispersed throughout the evening, or at least she marked them an octave lower. She was concerned about the acoustic. They were all miked, but she had a feeling there was an echo coming from somewhere and it was disturbing. She looked at the three girls.

"Claudia, can you just come here to my position and sing a bit. I want to check something." Claudia looked panicked.

"Will I do instead?" Jodie stepped forward carrying the music. Claudia put her hand to her heart, mouthing, "Thank you."

"Go from the top please. Sing the first verse. And move around while you sing until I ask you to stand still."

Juliette wasn't surprised about what happened next. She had been expecting it, having picked Jodie's voice out within the group. But everybody else stopped their whispering and whatever else they were doing and listened open mouthed. Her voice was totally unlike Juliette's. It was much deeper and fuller bodied. In fact, the song didn't suit her at all. None of Juliette's songs would, but given the right material she would sound amazing. She knew without a doubt she had her new young artist for the Christmas show. Jodie moved around until Juliette put her hand up to stop her and sang to the end of the verse in that position.

"Thanks, Jodie. Can somebody please mark the spot where she's standing? That will be my position for my numbers."

The car took her back to the hotel, but she wasn't tired, being wired from the coffee. The night was still warm. She knew she wouldn't sleep yet. She walked into the garden until she found the spot under her window. The wall was warm to her touch, and she pushed her back into it. It relieved her sore muscles. She opened her eyes. Jodie stood in front of her.

"I'm sor...I didn't expect to find anyone out here."

"The bench is long enough for two. If you go and get us two beers, putting it on my bill, you can share it with me."

She was back quickly.

"I didn't say you had to bring back a mass!" The large glasses held a litre each.

"They are closing the bar. I didn't know how thirsty you would be."

"I'll do my best. *Prost.* We had better talk quietly. The windows are open, and people will want to sleep. My room above is empty, but the others probably not."

They both drank deeply. The beer was delicious. "So, tell me, Miss Sanchez, what are you, an American, with a voice like that, doing in a backing group singing folk music in Germany?"

"I'm only part American. My father is Spanish. My mother is half German, half American. They are both simultaneous translators at the UN. I grew up trilingual, for which I am now very grateful, and I have a Spanish passport for which I am even more grateful. I studied at a musical school in New York, but I always wanted to work in Europe. I just happened to be in the right place at the right time for this job. And I'm really loving it…except for all the anguish I cause you."

Their heads were close because they were whispering. Juliette breathed in her scent again which was now mixed with a slight hint of sweat after seven hours on the stage under the hot lights. She must have made a slight sound, because Jodie leapt up.

"Oh God, I must stink. How embarrassing."

"Come back here. I trained as a dancer. Do you really think good honest sweat offends me? We have to finish these beers. Sit down."

It took a while. They both became drowsy, from the late hour and the strong beer on empty stomachs.

Juliette yawned. "This has done me good. I never would have slept without it. Let's go in. Which floor are you one?"

"The second, the top."

"Me too, shhhh." They tiptoed over the noisy gravel and into the hotel. The night porter barely gave them a look until he recognised Juliette. He looked as if he was about to salute. Struggling with giggles, they climbed the stairs. Juliette arrived at her door but had difficulty getting the cardkey to work. Jodie leaned over her shoulder and pressed her hand more firmly onto the contact. The green light came on, and Juliette turned to say goodnight. Their eyes met, then their lips, and suddenly they were kissing. It was unlike any sensation she had ever experienced. Jodie's lips were so soft and her breath so sweet, with a lingering taste of the bitter beer. She pressed harder and opened her lips as she felt Jodie's tongue tentatively asking for permission. She groaned and moved closer, feeling their breasts touch. She couldn't hold back. Her hips moved to make contact, as she deepened the kiss and their tongues clashed. The door to the next room opened and Leon put his head out. Jodie leapt away and disappeared down the corridor, turning the corner, and was out of sight. Juliette slumped against her door.

"Shhh. Juliette, you'll wake the whole hotel. Come in here quickly." She followed him blindly into his room and fell into a chair, touching her hot and swollen mouth.

"Leon. Fuck, fuck, fuck. I'm drunk. I must be. I don't know what just happened. Help me, please." She felt close to tears.

"Juliette, darling, do you really not know what happened? Don't you know it has been waiting to happen for years?"

"No, Leon, no, no. I'm not like that. I've never looked at a woman that way. I'm a dancer. I've seen women's bodies since I was a child. I never looked twice at anyone."

"I'm sure you're right. But have you ever stopped to consider why you get no pleasure from sex with a man. No… don't interrupt. I thought it was me for a long time, until I read an article about relationships like ours, and everything clicked into place. You certainly don't have to tell me, but I am willing to bet that it's no different with that brainless but Adonis-like husband of yours."

Juliette wanted to protest, but she couldn't. She nodded. "Much worse," she mumbled.

"And your sudden interest in Cooper-Nyman this year finally convinced me I'm right."

"But they are my neighbours."

"Seeing them together has made you think though, hasn't it?"

"Andreas told me if I'm even seen with them in public, it will be the end of my career."

"Andreas is awful, and I wish you would kick him out one day, but at this stage of your career and with your sort of audiences he unfortunately has a point. You are going to have to become another kind of singer with another kind of audience before you can hope to live any sort of open life."

"Leon, I'm not going to live a different life. We just kissed. We were tipsy, and tired. It was a long evening. It's not going to happen again."

"If you say so, darling. Now, get some rest, or do you want to go to her?"

For a split-second, Juliette was torn. "Of course not. I don't even know which room she's in."

He smiled knowingly. "She's most probably sharing anyway."

"Leon, what's wrong with me?"

"Nothing at all is wrong with you. She is a gorgeous young woman, and as we heard tonight, pretty talented. Juliette, I hope you can be happy one day, with or without Jodie. You deserve to be." He kissed her gently and watched while she opened her door and slipped inside.

***

She woke late, with a slight headache, and stretched. Her mouth felt sore. Then she remembered and a cold sweat trickled down between her breasts. She felt faint. How was she going to face Jodie today? And what if she told the other girls? Or sold her story to a newspaper. What if she had already done both? She had to do something. She started to almost hyperventilate, then calmed herself down with a deep breathing exercise. She had to talk to her. Offer her money to keep quiet. She sent a text, before she was really aware what she was doing.

* *'Could you please come to my room. There is something I need to discuss. In half an hour?'*

She ran into the bathroom and stood under the shower. She wouldn't have time to dry her hair properly. Why had she said only half an hour? She threw on a linen dress and sneakers, along with a minimum of eye shadow and mascara. Her lips were not visibly swollen, thank god. Lip-gloss gave her confidence. There was a knock on the door. She opened it. There was nobody other than Jodie in the corridor. She pulled her in.

"Sit down please. I won't keep you long. It's now my turn to apologise. I'm afraid I was much drunker than I realised. We should have eaten something with the beer."

"That's my fault again. I'm sor…"

"No, it's not. It was fun talking to you. And that's where it should have ended. It's not me. I'm married. I'm not into women. I'm asking you to forget it ever happened. I'm asking for your discretion, if it's not too late. I'll pay you whatever you would get for selling the story."

There was silence in the room. Then Jodie looked up. Her dark eyes were glinting. Was it anger, or tears?

"Did you really just say that? Do you really think I would sell that to the press? Do you really think I would ever tell anyone? It surprised me just as much as it surprised you. I am also not into women. Or so I thought…not anymore. Don't worry. I'll do this gig tonight because they won't be able to find anyone else, then I'll leave the group. I do seem to cause you anguish, and I respect you far too much as an artist to cause you any more problems." She got up and walked to the door.

"Jodie, wait." Juliette reached out and turned her round. She took her face in her long fingers and kissed her gently. Then she couldn't help herself. She pushed her tongue into a mouth tasting deliciously of toothpaste. Jodie moaned and nipped at her bottom lip. One hand pushed into the thick brown pixie cut, with the other she reached under Jodie's t-shirt. She cupped a generous breast and felt the nipple tighten. She felt the gush of arousal in her own thong. That brought her to her senses. She whispered into Jodie's mouth.

"I can't tell you how much I want you, but my husband could arrive any minute. I don't know how or when, or even why, but I want this to be a rain check."

Jodie nodded and stepped out of the embrace. She ran a hand through her dishevelled hair and licked off Juliette's lip-gloss.

"Don't do that, or I can't let you leave this room."

"I'll see you later."

The corridor was empty, and she rounded the corner to her room without anybody seeing them. Juliette stripped off her clothes, throwing the sopping wet thong into the basin to rinse it, and got under the shower. She had to attend to herself. Her clit was swollen and throbbing. She directed a jet of water on it and felt the orgasm coming almost immediately. She imagined Jodie's tongue in her mouth and bit on her lip to stifle the wail as it hit. She stood twitching as the after waves pulsed. If that was possible just thinking about her, what would it be like when Jodie's fingers were actually on her and perhaps in her? Because they would be. She had made her decision. And sooner rather than later.

***

"You deserve to be happy." Leon's words played on a loop in her subconscious. And she wasn't, she knew it now. Professionally, it was another matter. Her success made her happy. But she was lonely and had been for years. She was a high earning star. She had reached a plateau where it was hard to know if she could climb any higher, and the only person she could share a portion of her real feelings with was her mother. She was married to a vain idiot, who, in private at least, she spent as much time as possible actively avoiding. Otherwise, she lived in her own head.

She stood in her ivory tower looking over into Marie and Arabella's garden. It was empty, or at least the part she could see was. The clouds were low, and the lake an uninviting grey soup. They would be cuddled together on a sofa, or they would be in bed. She wanted to experience their happiness. Bert said their journey had not been smooth. Marie had had a hard fight with herself, but she had always known she loved women, and had only to find the courage to openly admit it. For Juliette, it was new. And she still didn't know if it was real. All she knew was that she desired Jodie all her waking hours.

But two weeks had gone by and she could find no way to be together with her. Thorsten was around the house all the time, and Andreas kept her busy with interviews and costume fittings. Her secretary was agitating for more hours to answer fan mail.

Jodie shared an apartment with two other people, so she couldn't go there even if she had the courage. She thought about going to a hotel, but the risk of her being recognised was too great. Here she was, with more money than she would ever need, a large house, and she couldn't even find a space to take a girl to for a few hours. *A girl.* Would it be any different if it was a man? Not really. She sighed and went downstairs. Thorsten was staring at the rain now lashing against the terrace. He had a glass of whisky in his hand. She looked at him. He was definitely getting heavier. Was that the first hint of a pouch under his tightfitting shirt?

"Shall we go out for lunch?"

"No, I'm going down for my work out." She looked pointedly in the direction of his gut, but he didn't notice. Or pretended not to.

"Afterwards, I'm going to see Bert." She needed to get out of the house.

"Why can't he come here? He usually does."

"He's really busy at the moment. His new project starts recording next week."

"I thought you were his priority, and he had to drop everything when you crook your little finger."

"He does, but when the last recording with them earned him a platinum, I don't have a problem, and am quite willing to go over."

"Ah, the dykes next door." She cringed. There was so much contempt in his voice. *That's the problem*. Him, and millions of others. She thought of Jodie and felt a twinge in her sex. Shit, but she was going at least to try it. She had to still this ache. It was painful. She had never felt it with any of her men. The tell-tale wetness filled her thong. "What have you got against them? We don't see or hear anything from next door. They are the perfect neighbours."

"But they can't possibly satisfy each other. Perhaps I should go over and donate my services. Or do you know what they do in bed? You are into self-service yourself, after all."

He was disgusting. She turned and left the room.

***

Bert said he should be finished with his arranging when she arrived, but as she drew up to his house in her Porsche, there was a large cream coloured Audi in the drive. There was no room for her, but luckily there was a space on the street. It had stopped raining. She parked and rang the bell.

"Juliette, sorry. We are just finishing. Come on in. You know Arabella." He winked.

"Hi. I'm off now. Oh, I'm sorry. I've blocked the drive, haven't I?"

"I parked outside. No problem."

"We really must have you both over to dinner. It's been months since you visited us. I don't have your number though. Do you think we could exchange? No problem if you don't want to. Your number must be one of the best kept secrets in the world."

Arabella's voice was full of respect.

"Yes, and yes. I could say the same about you both. I saw that interview with Marie…Miss Nyman on TV last week. She is a world star. I'm only known in this bit of Europe."

"Oh, come on. You two. This is taking the mutual admiration society a bit far. Exchange numbers and Arabella can be on her way. Marie rang over an hour ago to ask where you are."

Arabella handed over her phone and Juliette typed in her number and private mail address. She handed it back. Her phone pinged: * 'Next week perhaps?'

Juliette made a new contact. She was surprised at the thrill she got from writing *Arabella Cooper*.

Arabella left.

"Still smitten?"

"What? Bert, shut up. No, I'm not. Those two are so out of my league anyway."

"That's an interesting way of putting it. I agree you could never come between them, but why should you want to?"

"Don't twist my words. I didn't mean it like that. But I do want to talk to you about someone. One of my backing singers, Jodie Sanchez."

"You're digging the hole deeper."

She felt herself reddening and put her hand to her mouth.

"You're as bad as Leon." This was not getting any better.

"I see." He took pity. "Anyway, what about Miss Sanchez? I do know who she is by the way. This business is small, and when a potential talent emerges, I get to hear about it."

"Yes, she has an unusual voice, and I want to give her a chance on my New Year show. But her voice needs a totally different kind of song to mine, which is good. I thought you might have some suggestions."

"I would have to hear her live. Maybe she can inspire me to write something for her."

"I'll see if I can arrange something. Talking of new songs, that's why I'm here. You wanted to show me something."

***

* 'Would you be free to come to dinner next Friday? We have some good friends staying who would love to meet you. And we can invite Bert and his wife.'

Shit, shit, shit. Thorsten had announced he wanted to go up to visit his parents in Dortmund and to watch an important international football match. He would be away from Friday until Sunday morning. She immediately texted Jodie and arranged to collect her from the station after Thorsten's departure. But she very much wanted to accept the invitation. It was unlikely to be repeated any time soon. Their schedules were too difficult to align.

She drew a deep breath and texted back: * 'My husband will be away, but may I bring a colleague who I will be working with over the weekend?'

* 'It will be a pleasure. Is he vegetarian by any chance?'

* 'It's a she, and I don't think so.' She noticed Jodie taking a ham sandwich from the buffet that night at the Chiemsee. She shivered at the memory of those soft lips and perfect teeth biting into the bread. *Mmmmm.*

* 'Six o'clock? Let's hope for nice weather.'

She avoided Thorsten all week, meeting up only for a late lunch, which she cooked. She was either memorising songs in her music room or studio, or she was in the basement swimming and working out. He seldom entered the gym; only occasionally pounding the treadmill after an evening spent drinking.

Juliette preferred not to eat dinner when she was at home. It definitely put on weight sleeping soon after eating. Thorsten was resigned to this, and fixed himself something in the kitchen. Juliette had the feeling he was now more often than not drinking his calories.

This couldn't go on. As lazy as he was, being a kept man, which had seemed to be his life's ambition at the beginning of their relationship, was taking its toll. She sighed. She would have to face the inevitable, despite the repercussions.

She was not going to think about it for now. For once in her life, she was going to be selfish, and take what she wanted. *Am I going to take Jodie?* What did that mean exactly? Was Jodie more experienced and would know what to do? *Oh god, I'm nervous.*

***

Thorsten left an hour later than planned. Juliette wanted to scream. Jodie would have to wait at the station. She sent a text: * 'Be there as soon as I can. Sorry.' At last, he was ready. She left with him, saying she was going shopping. He took the turning towards the autobahn, and she continued into the town. Jodie was standing in the sun outside the station. She was more tanned than ever, and the sun had brought out some highlights in her dark brown hair. Or the hairdresser had. She looked stunning wearing her low-waisted jeans and a tight t-shirt over perfect sized breasts. Juliette felt the twinge in her core, and her briefs dampened.

She pulled in and leant over to open the door. Jodie smiled.

"Throw your things on the back seat. Let's get out of here before somebody sees me and wants a selfie."

"Does that happen to you wherever you go?"

"Pretty much so. And the fans have started to realise that I live here. I will have to change the car, or at least its colour."

"I can't imagine the pressure."

"Maybe you will someday, when your career takes off."

Jodie laughed. "I don't think so."

"I think it will."

They stopped at a traffic light.

"I want to kiss you so badly."

Jodie looked at her, her eyes darkening. "The feeling is very mutual." She leant across the wide middle console, and put her hand on Juliette's thigh, pushing slightly between her legs.

"Whoa, you'll cause us to crash." Jodie took her hand away, but Juliette stopped her and put it back, even closer to her crotch. She squeezed her legs and Jodie gasped.

"Um…I have to ask you an embarrassing question. I have never been with a woman. Have you?"

"Yes."

"I thought you said you weren't into women?"

"That was not exactly the truth. I have been with men for the last four years, but before that I was in a relationship with a girl in college. She…she rather broke my heart, and I turned to men after that. I…I don't get so involved."

"How old are you? I don't even know that about you."

"Twenty-six."

They arrived at the house. Juliette pressed the fob, and drove in.

"Welcome to my house. At last."

Jodie could barely contain her whistle.

Juliette took her hand, and they went inside. Jodie pushed her against the door, and they kissed frantically.

"Can we please go to bed? The last three weeks have been an extended foreplay. I can't wait any longer." She pulled her up the stairs and into the bedroom. They tore off each other's clothes, and Juliette pushed Jodie down onto the bed.

"Let me." Jodie turned her round more gently and climbed on top. She straightened her arms out, and pushed their centres together, grinding with her hips. Juliette came up to meet her.

"Oh god."

But now Jodie slowed, and leaned down to kiss her gently, running her tongue over her lips. Juliette moaned, and her hips bucked.

"Wait."

Jodie kissed down her neck, and her tongue circled her nipple. It was already hard, and almost painful, and she cried out as it was bitten gently.

"You are so gorgeous. I've already seen a lot of you in your stage clothes, but nothing prepared me for this." She continued down to her hard abdominal muscles and moaned in appreciation.

"Now that's what I call a six pack." Her tongue entered her navel, and she sucked it gently. Juliette squirmed so much that Jodie needed all her strength to hold her down.

"You are killing me," she gasped.

Jodie slid back up and kissed her deeply. Her right hand gently stroked her slick folds. "Oh my god. You are so wet." Her hand hovered in front of Juliette's entrance. "May I?"

"I'll go crazy if you don't."

She thrust in with two fingers, harder than Juliette was expecting. She gasped.

"Am I hurting you?"

"No, please, deeper." Jodie pumped slowly. Juliette felt herself starting to melt.

"Faster." She was panting. Jodie curled her fingers and pressed her thumb hard down on her nub. Her climax was shattering, and for a few seconds she thought she had gone blind. Then Jodie was kissing her gently and she focused on the kind brown eyes. She felt a tear drip down her nose. Jodie licked it gently and held her tightly. Juliette's breathing slowed. She felt as if her limbs were made of rubber, and she closed her eyes.

Jodie climbed off her and lay by her side. They gazed at each other. She didn't know what to say. Her heart was so full. She had known for three weeks that it would be good, but nothing had prepared her for this. Her walls were still pulsing.

She cupped her hand around Jodie's breast and flicked her nipple with her thumb. It immediately hardened, and she felt her own arousal again.

"You don't have to." Jodie stilled her hand.

"But I want to." Her eyes raked the young woman's body. She was not as well trained, but her stomach was flat, and her breasts were gorgeous. So unlike the dancers' bodies she had seen so often. And her golden-brown tanned skin was a huge turn-on. Juliette leant on her elbows and brushed her lips over a breast. She groaned. The skin was soft, like velvet. She licked up to Jodie's collarbone and sucked on the hollow, then bit her gently. It would leave a mark, but she wanted to do that. She wanted to claim possession of this gorgeous creature.

"I told you, I've never done this, so you must please tell me what you want."

"You're doing fine." Jodie's voice was husky. They kissed and Juliette nibbled on her earlobe, which seemed to be an erogenous zone. Jodie's hips moved, and her legs opened. Juliette continued nibbling down the golden body until she reached her stomach, which clenched as she sucked on the soft skin. She could smell Jodie's musky scent, and she suddenly knew what she wanted.

She slipped between her legs, opening them wider. Jodie's sex glistened, and her hips bucked. She kissed the inside of her thighs, just breathing gently on the swollen clit in passing. Jodie let out a low guttural moan, at least an octave lower than her own voice. She took a deep breath and ran her tongue the length of her folds. It tasted salty and sweet at the same time. She pressed in deeper and knew instinctively that Jodie was close. She was panting and whimpering. She took her clit in her mouth and circled it with her tongue, then sucked on it hard. Jodie stiffened and let out a long wail, holding Juliette's head, and pressing it to her sex. She twitched irregularly, her stomach clenching and unclenching. Juliette slid up her body, pushing their breasts together, then their lips met in a deep lingering kiss.

"Are you sure you've never done this before? That was the best orgasm ever." She twitched again, and Juliette rolled them both over.

"You're not serious. Again?"

"Oh yes, I am. But later. I think we need to shower, unless we want to go out smelling like this, so that everybody knows exactly what we've been doing. The invitation is for six o'clock. And it's already twenty past five."

***

They were late. Fifteen minutes by the time they arrived and rang the bell.

"Sorry. Isn't it typical to be late when you live next door?"

"It's no problem at all." Marie ushered them in. She wore a beautiful soft dark blue jersey dress, which clung to her ample bosom. Juliette fought not to blush. *I'm underdressed.* She had on black designer jeans and a full silk blouse with a gypsy neck, which showed the tops of her well-trained arms. *What is wrong with me?* She set her own fashion, and never normally cared what people thought. Jodie wore white jeans and a linen jacket. Arabella joined them and Juliette breathed again. She had on dark red skin-tight capris and a sleeveless black t-shirt. Her biceps held up silver arm bangles. Marie immediately caressed her arms.

"This is Jodie. We work together. She's one of my backing singers. We are um…working on new material."

Their welcome was warm.

"Come on in. We're in the garden. And aren't we lucky with the weather." Instead of going down inside the house to the music room as she had on the first occasion, Arabella led them straight ahead to a huge, curved room with panorama windows, looking out onto the lake. They crossed it and went through triple glazed glass doors onto a stone balcony. There were steps leading down onto the lawn adjacent to the music room windows. To the right was an enormous wooden deck, built around an old oak tree. It obviously provided perfect natural shade in the summer months. A man and two women were sitting, holding drinks. Juliette felt Jodie take a nervous breath and she took her hand. It felt the most natural thing in the world to do, and she didn't let go as they approached Bert and his wife. He stood as they walked onto the deck.

"I'm not sure who knows who here. Suzanne Weigl, this is Juliette Simon, and Jodie…"

"Sanchez, a colleague of mine. I am so thrilled to meet you…*Suzanne*?"

"Yes, please do…*Juliette*. The pleasure's all mine I can assure you. I'm a big fan of yours."

Juliette looked in awe at the stunning woman with soft dark curly hair, with a white streak brushed back from her forehead.

"At the risk of sounding like a spotty teenager, may I return the compliment? I grew up with your recordings. My mother adores you."

"You make me sound terribly old, but I did start singing very young." She was in her mid-forties, and still at the height of her career as a leading mezzo-soprano. She sang her most famous role, Oktavian in *Der Rosenkavalier* in every great opera house worldwide. Juliette's mother had a DVD, which she had watched with fascination, and she only now realised, more than just a passing interest in the love scenes between the three women protagonists. Something clicked in her head.

"So, for the moment, you all know who is who."

"Not quite. Bert and Annette don't know Jodie."

Bert stepped forward and shook her hand. "But I've heard about her, and you promised me, I could hear her sing. Perhaps later?"

Jodie shrank back a step.

"That's a great idea. We need to get down to choosing a song for her."

"Arabella knows a lot about voices. How about now, before we eat and drink and are too full to even know our own names."

Jodie looked panic stricken, but Juliette pressed her hand.

"Arabella, if you would play, I can listen better."

"Sure."

"But I haven't got any music."

"I'm sure we have something you know. Do you read music?" Jodie nodded.

The four of them moved back towards the music room. Suzanne and Annette stayed where they were.

"Leave the door open. We are interested too."

They went into the cool room. "She has a dark voice."

"Marie sings all this type of music in her chest voice, but I can transpose if necessary."

Bert picked up a pile of songs. "Do you know the old Lesley Gore classic *You don't own me?*"

"Only vaguely, but I can sight read it."

Juliette nodded. "That's a good idea, Bert. I heard it on your record, Arabella. I'm going to sing it someday."

Arabella played the introduction. Jodie came in on her bar, but it wasn't her natural voice. Arabella heard that immediately and stopped.

"Down a tone I think." She started again. Now, it was right. Jodie began tentatively, then gained confidence and soon her rich voice was belting out the song. She was a little out of breath at the end.

Arabella turned away from the piano. "Well done. That key change is tricky if you don't know the song, but it's what makes it such a great number." She looked at her approvingly. "We should go upstairs; I think dinner is probably about to be served."

They went up, to where Suzanne and Annette were just coming from the living room.

Suzanne clapped enthusiastically. "That was really something. I'll definitely buy your record when it comes out."

Jodie blushed. "Don't start saving up just yet."

Suzanne put her arm around her. "I'm not so sure it will be a long wait," she said in her deep speaking voice. Juliette scowled at her.

"Oh, I see." Suzanne grinned. Luckily, they were interrupted by a beautiful young woman with long snow-white hair, coming out of what had to be the kitchen. Suzanne pulled her in and kissed her on the lips.

"I've missed you."

"I've been in the kitchen for less than an hour."

"This is my wife, Beth. Jodie is American, a fellow colonial. Beth comes from New Zealand."

"Only a quarter. Colonial, I mean. My father's Spanish, and my mother half German, but I did grow up in New York."

Marie joined them. "Arabella, darling, please get everyone seated. Put Bert at the end of the table. I'm really sorry, Bert, but originally, we thought Thorsten would be here."

Annette prodded his arm. "He's in seventh heaven, or should I say harem."

They groaned at the weak pun and went into the dining room, which backed onto Juliette's garden hedge. She moved over to the window. By looking up, she could see her tower room, but as there were no windows on the side, it wasn't possible to look in.

The long dining table was surrounded by shelves on all the walls, filled from floor to ceiling with books. It was a great idea.

Marie came in and saw her looking.

"Bella had a room just like this in her London house. I loved the idea and couldn't wait to copy it when we bought this house."

They sat. Juliette was next to Jodie who immediately pressed their thighs together. She drew in a breath. She thought Suzanne noticed. *I think she's guessed. I hope she is discreet.* This evening was very risky.

A woman brought in a tray with two covered serving bowls and put them on the table in front of Marie.

"Everybody, this is Wiebke, without whom we would be entirely lost. Wiebke runs our household."

Juliette guessed that Wiebke came from the village and cleaned the house. It was clever and generous to elevate her position. Wiebke smiled. Marie served piping hot and perfectly cooked saffron risotto with grilled prawns. There were bowls of green salad for them to help themselves. The accompanying white burgundy was delicious. Arabella drank only water she noticed. Roast duck with an expensive Chianti followed, then cheese and fruit. The conversation wove around music, but also ranged over politics, literature and cooking. Beth and Marie were sharing kitchen duty tonight, but Arabella also cooked regularly, as did Bert, Jodie and Juliette. Suzanne and Annette not as often, they admitted. Juliette's Italian childhood had prepared her somewhat differently. Her father hardly ever entered the kitchen. She was grateful her mother had taught her well, and she was an accomplished and enthusiastic cook. She looked forward to extending a return invitation.

Juliette looked around the table. Why was she so guilty of stereotypical thinking? Here at least there was none. Suzanne wore a summer dress, which showed off legs made famous by spending half her life portraying boys on stage, whereas Beth wore slacks and a blazer. She had expected them to dress the other way round. Arabella stayed true to type with her slightly gothic look, heightened by the kohl she always wore around her stunning blue eyes, but Juliette remembered seeing them on the jetty. Marie had most definitely been the active partner. She felt a twinge in her sex and put her hand high up Jodie's thigh. Jodie pressed her legs together.

"Let's have coffee on the deck. It's still warm, and we are not going to disturb the neighbours tonight."

They gradually wandered out into the garden, after using the various bathrooms.

There were three double loungers and several single ones. Bert and Annette were in one and Suzanne and Beth in another. Marie sat at the table busy with the coffee. Juliette hesitated then sat in a single, Jodie next to her. The sun was just out of sight, and the water looked silvery as the moon came up.

"That's a watery moon. I think we are in for bad weather." Marie said as she poured coffee to everyone's specifications. "It's sultry as well. Could be a thunderstorm brewing."

Annette sighed, "We must get going as soon as we've finished coffee. It was a lovely evening and Bert would stay forever, but I know he has a full day of arranging tomorrow before the sessions begin on Monday."

Marie groaned. "Don't remind me."

"Darling, you are totally prepared. If you are as fast as you were last year, we'll be finished in ten days…or less."

"I'm much more concerned about you, than me. We will need to take it easy." She looked at Arabella meaningfully.

Juliette made to stand as Bert and Annette took their leave.

"Please stay just a little longer. It's horrible when everybody leaves at once." She remained standing as farewells were said.

"Jodie, I think I may have an idea for a new song for you. I'll be in touch."

Arabella took the Schmidts around the house to their car.

Suzanne looked at Beth who shrugged. "Juliette, why don't you both sit on the double?" Jodie looked horrified and moved away. Juliette took her hand and brought her to the lounger. They sat, and then lay back together, their bodies touching.

Marie spoke evenly. "Juliette, I was in the same situation once. Suzanne and Beth guessed, just as we have tonight. It was wonderful to be able to be myself, at least in their company."

"I have so much to lose. It would mean the end of my career."

"I thought that too. My husband and I were known as the golden couple. Our pictures were on all the newsstands. Just as yours are."

"But the folk/pop world is the most unforgiving of all. My manager wants to launch me in the States. It's even worse over there. I have a girl-next-door image. It's what sells my records."

"Understood. Perhaps you can change that image one day."

"Perhaps." She knew it would be a relief. She bought Jodie's head down onto her shoulder and kissed her hair. Arabella returned. Marie tenderly helped her into the lounger and stroked her face.

"This is very new for me. I never suspected it about myself, although when I look back, there were probably signs that I didn't know what to make of. Watching your *Rosenkavalier,* for example. I dreamt about those scenes." She sighed. "But for now, I have a husband. And according to at least three of the worst magazines, I get pregnant every week."

Marie took Arabella's hand and brought it to her lips. "That's where we are now, we hope. Arabella is pregnant."

Juliette nearly dropped her cup.

"But I'm going to carry our child. If all goes well, next month, her egg will be transferred into my womb. It's a risky technique, but I want to have *our* baby."

"Friends of my parents used the same method." Jodie spoke softly.

"And did it work?"

"After a few attempts, yes. They have a gorgeous little boy."

Marie and Arabella smiled at each other.

Juliette looked at Jodie in amazement as she said, "But now I think we really should be going. I want to get this newbie into bed."

Juliette blushed as the others laughed. "You will be discreet, won't you? My world would come crashing down."

Suzanne hugged her. "Please don't worry."

***

There were sounds of thunder in the far distance as they got back into the house. The short walk had taken ten minutes as they kept stopping to kiss.

"I'm sticky. I think I need a shower." Juliette led her into the bathroom and turned on the rainbow shower. They undressed each other, more slowly this time. Juliette stroked Jodie's back, moving around to cup her breast.

"Your skin is like velvet. I never even thought about a woman's skin before, but it's a revelation, and such a turn on." She took a nipple in her mouth. Jodie drew in a breath.

"Let's get under the water. Maybe a cold shower would be the best. I have been wet for you all evening."

"Mmm, you say the nicest things."

They soaped each other gently. Jodie turned her so that her back pressed into her breasts where she could feel the hard nipples. She had one arm around her waist. The other one tickled the inside of Juliette's inner thighs. She opened her legs, and Jodie caressed her folds. Her legs shook.

"Please, Jodie." She was entered with two fingers. She opened her legs wider. "More." Jodie added a finger and thrust faster, grinding her hips against her butt. She exploded. Jodie held her tightly as she went limp, then turned her around, and ground their centres together. Jodie leant down and sucked her nipple, panting.

"Oh god, I don't think I'm finished." She felt a second surge deep in her core. Jodie entered her again.

"I need your hand," she gasped. Juliette reached down and ran her fingers through Jodie's folds, then rubbed hard on her swollen clit.

"Yeees." She stiffened. Juliette pushed her fingers in and felt her walls undulating. That pushed her over the edge, and she climaxed for the second time. They leant against each other, breathing heavily.

"That was fantastic. And feeling you come was wonderful. I never knew. I've only ever given myself an orgasm."

Jodie kissed her gently. They got out of the shower and dried themselves tenderly. Both of them were still sensitive. They got into bed and cuddled. *This is a miracle.* Her eyes closed as she couldn't fight sleep any longer.

***

She woke to the sounds of crashing thunder and lightning lit up the curtains. The storm must be directly overhead. Jodie was looking at her, her eyes wide. She cringed as another lightning flash illuminated the room.

"Darling, are you scared?"

"A little bit." She clenched her teeth together.

Juliette pulled her in close and stroked her hair. She was aroused again but clamped her legs together. It would not be fair. Jodie clung to her.

She was almost overcome with feelings of tenderness. "This house is built to withstand earthquakes, don't worry. But I know the storms here are violent. They build up over the lake, and then keep circling. It will go away eventually." Jodie's teeth were chattering. She kissed her gently and rubbed her back. Gradually, Jodie relaxed and snuggled into her. As the storm receded, she fell asleep. *What am I going to do?* She looked at the long eyelashes and the perfect eyebrows. *I don't want to give this up. This is me. I've come home.*

She wanted to talk to her mother, but her stomach clenched with fear. Her parents were not staunch Catholics. Just typical Italian ones, which meant that they unquestionably followed what they had been taught and went to mass on all the Christian holy days. Homosexuality was a sin. Even the present Pope, liberal as he seemed to be, had not changed the standing of LGBT people. Some of the bishops in Germany were kicking against this, more or less openly, and there were many priests who offered gay believers the sacraments, although it was forbidden to do so.

The folk music fans were almost exclusively catholic. She thought back on the evening. Wiebke must also be one. She had the features of a typical Bavarian village woman. She cleaned the house, so she must know about the sleeping arrangements. The way she smiled at Marie held no condemnation. But Juliette knew she couldn't rely on people like Wiebke if she dropped a bombshell like this. She shuddered at the thought. And what was she going to do about Thorsten? She didn't want him anywhere near her anymore. She must get him out of the house. His drinking was getting much worse, and that itself could be a liability. It didn't go down well with the fans either. Jodie put her arm out and it fell across her stomach. She continued to breathe softly and evenly. Juliette closed her eyes again and drifted back to sleep.

***

She woke, and tried to stretch, but her legs were held down. Then they were pushed open, and teeth nibbled slowly up her inner thigh. She groaned. She was aroused and her hips moved automatically. Jodie's hands reached up and caught hold of hers.

"What are you doing?"

"Having an early breakfast." She felt a soft breath on her clit, and with a cry she bucked her hips up to meet Jodie's mouth. Her swollen and sensitive clit was circled, and then sucked. With a wail she came, clutching Jodie's hands until her spasms stopped. Jodie slipped up her body and nuzzled a nipple. She pulled her head up and kissed her, nibbling on her bottom lip. Jodie pressed into her, and she slipped her hand down and stroked the slick folds. Jodie moaned and she rubbed harder, slipping into her as she felt her come. Again, the sensation of Jodie's contractions was a wonder.

"It gives a new meaning to breakfast in bed. I'm shy to admit it, but I've had more orgasms in…a little more than twelve hours…than I've had all this year."

"Don't you and your husband…? Sorry, none of my business."

"Only when I really have to. You won't believe it, but I never self-lubricate, and even when he smears himself, it still hurts." She shuddered. "The way I'm feeling at the moment, I never want to have sex with him again. In fact, I don't think I will."

"You don't have a happy marriage? But what about all the magazines, and the blogs and Instagram?"

"As I frequently tell Thorsten, I trained as an actress, and I'm rather a good one."

"But you do…did love him?"

"Never. I was infatuated with his good looks and his body, which incidentally are beginning to wane, and the press more or less threw us together. My manager urged me on, as the publicity was overwhelming, and anyway, if it is known I'm single, I get inundated with crank messages. I would need twenty-four-hour security to ward off stalkers. Germany's answer to Schwarzenegger seemed preferable to all that. Although the thing I am most ashamed of, because it is so idiotic, is that I actually wanted to become Mrs. De Luca. I was homesick at the time. Having an Italian married name seemed like a solution. So, I, and everyone surrounding me, with the exception of my parents, encouraged me and I married him. And now I have to live with the consequences." She sighed. "Would you like to swim? And then work out a little? I need to after dinner last night, which was wonderful, but it needs to be sweated away."

They spent a couple of hours down in the basement. Jodie couldn't keep up with Juliette, but she was fit. Her long lean legs were muscular from jogging. She ran frequently. Juliette ogled her.

After a breakfast of fruit, muesli and a great deal of milky coffee, they lay on the terrace. The sun was hot, and the sky a clear cloudless blue after the storm. Juliette had to move into the shade of a large umbrella, but Jodie spent a good half hour longer deepening her golden tan.

"Let me show you the house. We are doing everything backwards. The bedroom is not usually the first room to be acquainted with when you visit."

They wandered hand in hand through the rooms, taking their time, Juliette explaining why she had made this or that decision. They ended up in her tower sanctity.

"I love this."

"So, do I. It's my ivory tower. Thorsten has never been up here."

Jodie took her hand. "Thank you for trusting me."

She was pulled down onto the wide, soft leather couch, and the next hour was a blur of limbs.

"That sated my appetite…for the time being, but I feel the need of some protein. How about you? I would prefer if we don't go out to eat, and the fridge is full. May I cook for you? Or we can try together."

They had no difficulty working together in the kitchen. Jodie prepared verdure cotta, while Juliette smacked two chicken halves onto the worktop, and grilled the flat pieces in the Italian way. They ate under the pergola, which, although freshly planted and bare of shadow, was now no longer in the full sun. It was beginning to sink over the lake. They wandered hand in hand down to the jetty and sat for a while with their feet in the water. Juliette looked up to the next-door house. She could see no movement, but she wondered if Marie and Arabella were watching as she had watched them. She shivered as she remembered how she had run down to Thorsten to get some relief. It was definitely the last time that would happen.

"It's getting chilly, and the grass is still damp after the rain. I don't want either of us to get sick before the album sessions begin. Let's go back to the house. Do you play the piano by the way? You are obviously very musical."

"A little."

"Then you can help me with something."

They went into the studio. Juliette spread music onto the piano.

"It's a song Bert and Arabella wrote together. It's on their album, but they have given me permission, and I want it to be my next single. It's much more complex than the stuff I usually sing. Marie makes it sound as easy as *three blind mice*, but the rhythms and key changes are hard for me. I will never have Marie's talent."

"Unless I am much mistaken, I sincerely doubt she can dance like you can. Each to his own. Let me try it alone first. This is not going to sound like Arabella. The way she can transpose, and sight read is phenomenal. I wish." She played.

"Don't put yourself down. You are a really good pianist. That's fantastic. Now help me."

They worked on the song for an hour, and Juliette finally felt confident. "That's great. I'm so relieved. I had almost decided to tell Bert we would have to drop the idea. You could play and sing at the same time, as talented as you are."

"Actually, that's what I would like to do. I have written some of my own stuff." She was shy.

"Let me hear something…please."

Jodie played and sang two hauntingly beautiful melodies. Juliette looked at her thoughtfully.

"I don't know why we are bothering trying to find you material to sing. You are going to perform these on my New Year's Special. They are fabulous. Could you write us a duet?"

"I'll try."

"Now, I think it's our bedtime, don't you?"

They went upstairs and took their time exploring each other's bodies, until sated, they fell asleep, wrapped around each other.

***

They woke late.

Juliette was agitated. "I'm sorry, I can't relax any more. I doubt very much if Thorsten will be home soon, but I can't bear the thought of him walking in on us. Let's have brunch and I'll drive you back."

Jodie kissed her gently. "I understand. Don't worry. I can get a taxi to the station. We don't have to stop to eat."

"Don't say that. Let's just get dressed, and if he comes in, you have been helping me with the new song. It's really great that you are such a good pianist. I can see that being useful in the future."

Jodie looked at her with her huge brown eyes. They were wary. "Is there a future? Are you sure you didn't just want to try this out?"

"My angel, yes I did, I admit it, but if you think I can keep out of your pants after these two days, then you are mistaken. We just have to be discreet. Unless of course you don't want to continue, which I would have to understand." She sounded slightly panicky, even to her own ears.

Jodie ran the tip of her tongue over her upper lip. "What do you think?"

Juliette groaned. "Let's have some eggs and toast and coffee, and we can get going."

She backed the Porsche out of the garage and Jodie threw in her bag. The car had smoked windows, and some measure of privacy. She punched the address into the sat-nav, and they drove into Munich.

"Stop here. At least, let me walk the last few streets. Just in case."

Juliette stopped in the shade of a large chestnut tree. It was quiet, and nobody was about on a hot Sunday afternoon. They kissed for a long time, until they were almost at the point of no return.

Juliette pulled away breathing heavily. "I'll see you at the first session. It won't be possible before that. I have a lot to do. But I'll text. Take care, Jodie…and…thank you."

She did a U-turn and drove back the way they had come. Jodie watched until she was out of sight, then walked back to her apartment. She hoped she would be alone. Her carefully prepared lie about where she had been would hardly be convincing with her kiss-bruised lips. And she needed time on her own.

Juliette breathed a sigh of relief when she saw the empty drive. Thorsten did not get back until late evening, by which time she had changed her sheets and remade her bed, cleared up the kitchen and put away all the plates and glasses. It was impossible to know that somebody had been in the house, except in her tower room. She kept the window closed for as long as possible to preserve the smell of sex, which pervaded the sofa and cushions.

***

The weather was dull and cool.

"You look good. I would almost say well fucked unless I knew better."

She prayed she wouldn't blush as she carried on chewing.

"This is nice too. Guilty conscience?" Perhaps it was. She cooked Scaloppini al Limone for lunch.

"Who was at the dyke's dinner?"

"Suzanne Weigl and her wife, Bert and Annette."

"Not very pleasant for Bert. So much diesel power."

"You were invited, you remember. He wouldn't have been the only man. Bert didn't seem to be suffering that much." She hoped he wouldn't bring up the subject if he met Bert and Annette. She trusted them, but it could slip out that there had been an eighth guest. "I pampered myself while you were away. Did things for me. Exercised. Worked on my music and broke the back of a difficult song. You look as if you got in a lot of exercise with your right arm."

"Yeah, well you know how it is when your team loses."

"Better work it off." She prodded his gut.

"Fuck off and leave me alone."

He got up from the table, leaving her to finish eating, and clear up. She sighed. It couldn't go on like this. But she was trapped. She couldn't live here without a man at her side. And she couldn't ever live here with Jodie. She didn't even know if she was ready to make that commitment, even in secret. Though the idea was tempting. She thought about sex with her all the time and had been wet with a dull ache since they parted. She had woken up this morning having an orgasm, which had never happened to her before. She took out her phone and texted: * 'I miss your soft skin so much; I'm going crazy here. It's going to be a long two weeks.' After it went through, she deleted the conversation. Thorsten couldn't get into her phone, which had facial recognition, but she left nothing to chance.

It was now raining, and he lay slumped on the sofa, with his eyes closed.

"I've got a headache."

"Shall I get you some pain meds?" He grunted. "Thorsten, do you think you can get yourself together for tomorrow?" He was unshaven and looked a wreck. "You know we have a photo session here."

She was unhappy about the thought of it. She was scared a photo in a magazine would identify the house, but Andreas was insistent. It was for an upmarket publication, and they promised nothing would be shot that would give any indication of where the house was located. She was sceptical. In any case, she decided to restrict the number of rooms available to them. And she would refuse to let it go to print without her tacit approval.

"What do you think? I am still enough of a man to want to look good in the article."

She sat across from him. They looked at each other. "What are we going to do? This really isn't working anymore. For either of us."

"Do you have another guy?"

"No."

Thank god, the question was gender specific. She thought of her blissful two days with Jodie and felt guilty, which made her feel sorry for Thorsten. She had always tried to give him financial independence. She paid generously into his bank account. He had his own car and renewed it any time he felt the urge to try a new model. But that he was a kept man couldn't be denied, especially now that he had stopped getting work. She thought back. He hadn't had a job for a year.

His eyes were again closed. "Do you want a divorce?"

"I don't see how that's possible. You know as well as I do that I need your protection. I can't live alone, and I have no interest in looking for another man. You have your freedom. I never ask where you are when you disappear. I just ask you, or more to the point Andreas does, to be with me most of the time when I'm performing and to do photo sessions like tomorrow. At the risk of you shouting at me, I do wish you wouldn't let yourself go. It's getting difficult not to notice the weight."

He didn't shout, but he did get up, went into the kitchen and got himself a beer, which he took upstairs to his room. Juliette went down into her studio and put on her headphones, listening to the synthesiser tracks Bert had laid down for the new album. She sang along with them, thinking of Jodie when she had no trouble with *How could you leave me*. She groaned as she felt herself getting wet and left the studio to go for a swim. The filter jets gave her relief.

***

She allowed the photographer to work in the basement, and in all the ground floor rooms and then included her music room. Leaning over the piano made for good shots, even if she could hardly play it. She thought of Jodie's long fingers caressing the black and white keys. He wanted to shoot the outside of the house, but she refused. It would be too easy to recognise it from the lake, and in summer boats passed continuously in front of the garden.

Thorsten managed to make himself look presentable, but there was no denying the second bulge over his tightening jeans, in addition to the one in his crotch. She shuddered at the vulgarity. He would have to begin upsizing his clothes. They played the happy couple, though she avoided the expected kiss, and managed to get away with a hug. She wore a short denim skirt and a white vintage corsage, which showed her well-trained arms and more than a hint of the tops of her breasts and cleavage. She asked the photographer to take a photo on her smart phone, and she surreptitiously mailed it to Jodie.

She got a text back: * 'I've melted and am a puddle on the floor.' She knew she looked hot, but it was a measure of the state of their marriage that Thorsten appeared not to notice. He was too concerned with pulling in his gut.

The following day, he disappeared and was away for two nights. She was livid. Not about his absence, but for the missed opportunity to spend time with

Jodie. She cornered him on his return. "May I ask the same question of you? Do you have a new woman in your life?"

"No."

"Can we come to an arrangement? You let me know when you will be gone for more than twenty-four hours. Andreas needed us for an interview yesterday. It was rather embarrassing for me. Or do you want him on your back?"

He left her standing and went down to the basement, where she could hear him on the treadmill. She went up to her tower and called Jodie. "Can we talk?"

"I'll go into my room. Is something wrong? You said you wouldn't be able to call me."

"I can't wait another week to see you. I'm going to arrange a rehearsal for you, Sadie and Claudia. I've never done it before, but as these new songs are more difficult, Bert won't think it odd. He more than suspects about us anyway. We won't be alone, but at least we can be in the same room."

"Mmmm…agony, but delicious."

"Good, the day after tomorrow then." She arranged it with Bert, and he called the three backing singers. She had not intended to tell Andreas, but as luck would have it, he wanted another photo session at the exact same time.

"No problem. We can photograph you there. It's not a bad idea. A different location. Look sexy, please."

She grinned. She had intended to for Jodie, which Bert might have raised an eyebrow at, but now she had the best possible excuse. "Would you please call Bert and ask him to inform the girls? They should know too. In case they appear in a shot." He didn't much like being told what to do, and she heard him swallow back a retort.

The rehearsal was in the studio where they would record. It happened to be available. Bert had arranged for the record producer to be there too. They could start to work on the balance. Everything about her plan was turning out splendidly.

As Jodie had freaked out about her vintage corsage, she chose one similar, though in a deep red, with steam punk trimmings. Together with skinny black jeans and stilettos, and her hair pulled up in a chignon, she knew she looked great.

When she arrived at the studio, only Bert and Tom Braun, the producer were there.

"Wow, Juliette, who are you dressed for?" Tom raised an eyebrow. She was spared an answer by the arrival of Andreas and the photographer. Andreas nodded his approval of her outfit. Bert winked at her.

"Have you finished the Cooper-Nyman recording?"

"Yes. We had to be careful with Arabella though. But everything's fine."

Andreas looked puzzled. "What's wrong with Arabella Cooper?"

"Nothing." They both chorused. Claudia and Sadie walked in, looking smart. There was no sign of Jodie. Andreas looked at his watch.

"Typical. I think we need to have a word, Juliette. About the new backing singer."

Jodie flew through the door. It banged shut behind her. Everyone winced.

"Sorry, sorry. The tram." As everyone stared at her, Juliette could too. She wanted to take her in her arms and smother her with kisses. Her long pixie cut was dishevelled by the wind. She had on skinny white jeans and a tight black t-shirt decorated with a large sparkling butterfly, which left nothing to the imagination. Her nipples were erect, and Juliette had to smother a moan as she felt her thong getting very damp. She never would have guessed she was such a breast woman. Then she remembered her reaction to Marie's cleavage. *I want my woman to look like one. Curves and all. My woman*...she fought hard not to blush.

"You're late, Miss Sanchez. The photographer doesn't have all day."

"Actually, Andreas, I think we all appreciate that, but Jodie is only five minutes late, and anyway we are here to rehearse." She turned to the photographer. "It was made clear to you I hope, that this is a working session."

"Of course, Miss Simon, and I'm very happy about it. And not in any hurry either. Just ignore me and I'll try not to disturb you."

Juliette smiled at him. She couldn't resist a whispered *thank you.*

Andreas pursed his lips. "I'll be in the control room."

"Jodie, your hair's a bit of a mess." She leaned up and ran her fingers through it, fluffing it up. Jodie drew a deep breath, and Juliette saw her hips jerk.

"Now, girls, let's run through all the numbers, and see where we are going to have problems." Bert sat at the piano.

As it turned out, her ruse to get to see Jodie turned out to be a blessing in disguise. There were a great many problems which needed ironing out. It would have wasted expensive orchestra time if they waited until the sessions.

"We'll make this a definite date in future," said Bert when they finished. "It was a great session. Thanks everybody." Andreas and the photographer had left a couple of hours ago. They wandered out into the car park. The studio was on the outskirts of Munich on an industrial site.

"Jodie, you seemed to have tram problems getting here. Let me drive you home, or at least drop you off where it's easier to get the subway. Everyone else is mobile, I think." They nodded. Juliette led the way to an older dark green VW Golf convertible.

"Get in quickly before anyone else realises that I'm not going your way."

Bert drove towards them and lowered his window. "I see you have the old girl. I haven't seen her for ages."

"She needs a run sometimes. Don't be rude about my beloved." She turned to Jodie. "This is the car I bought with the proceeds of my first album. I can't bear to part with her."

"I could take Jodie if you want. You have to make rather a detour." His face was all innocence but there was a twinkle in his eye.

"Bert, please don't be evil." He laughed and drove off.

"Darling, the car doesn't have sat-nav. I think I know roughly but you will have to guide me."

"You really could just take me to the subway."

"Yeah, sure, after all the thought I put into this meeting, I'll do just that. I am driving this car so that I can at least take you to your door, and not be looked at twice. And somehow, I am going to kiss you. No idea how at the moment, but we'll find a way."

"Actually, I'm alone in my apartment, until late this evening."

"I'll try not to break the speed limit, but I can't promise."

***

When they arrived, Juliette put on an old baseball cap, and a trench coat. She was right. Nobody looked at the car or at them. The apartment was on the second floor of an old house. The neighbourhood was shabby, but the common parts of the building were clean and freshly painted. Jodie opened the door and called out but there was no reply. She turned the key and put on a chain lock.

"Where's your bedroom?"

"Wouldn't you like afternoon tea first?"

Juliette crashed their lips together. They both moaned. Juliette flung off her trench and reached for the clasps on her corsage.

"No, you don't. That article of clothing has been driving me crazy all day."

"I thought you might like it. I put it on just for you."

"And now I'm going to be the one to take it off."

Jodie pulled the curtains in her small but tidy room. The bed was only a queen, but as Juliette ached to be on top of her, it didn't matter. They slowed down and undressed each other. Juliette sighed as she traced her fingers down Jodie's neck and collarbone until she reached her full breasts.

"Everything is wonderful about being with a woman, but the thing that amazes me most, is the soft skin. And no body hair. Why have I wasted a third of my life?"

She pushed Jodie onto the bed and topped her. She pulled her arms above her head and held her hands while she licked and bit first one nipple and then the other. Jodie whimpered.

As she moved down and breathed across her navel, Jodie's hips bucked. She moved down and knelt between her legs.

"Put your legs on my shoulders. I want to see you come."

She knelt and dipped into Jodie's folds, watching her face. "Open your eyes." She continued stroking with her tongue, pressing in deep, until Jodie made little mewling noises. Her eyes widened even more. Juliette thrust two fingers into her as she sucked hard on her swollen clit. Jodie cried out and she pulsed over Juliette's fingers.

"Oh, Jodie, I don't think I will ever have enough of that feeling."

She brought her fingers out and licked her fingers, luxuriating in the sweet, salty taste. Their eyes never left each other.

Jodie lowered her legs around Juliette's waist. She clenched her thighs and flipped her over on to her stomach.

"Oof. You are so strong."

Jodie lay on Juliette's back and kissed her ears and then her neck. She nipped lightly, and she flinched.

"Don't worry, I won't mark you. Not this time anyway."

She licked down the backs of her arms, and then massaged her shoulder muscles tenderly.

"You don't have an inch of fat."

"I would do if I didn't exercise it all off. I wouldn't care, but the camera puts on pounds as we know."

Jodie rubbed her hard nipples across Juliette's back. It was very erotic, and she moaned.

"May I turn round; I want to kiss you."

"Later."

Jodie kissed her ass cheeks and parted them slightly. Gently, she entered her with two fingers.

"Ooh, that's good." She pushed back against Jodie's hand. Jodie increased the speed of her thrusts and added a third finger. She reached under Juliette and pinched a nipple hard.

"I'm going to come."

Jodie thrust, then curled her fingers and pushed in harder. Juliette smothered a scream in the pillow. Her walls clenched and unclenched, and she twitched again and again as she was shaken by intensive after waves.

Jodie came out and turned her over. They kissed tenderly. Juliette sniffed as a tear rolled down her face.

"I must stop crying. But I've never had an orgasm that wasn't clitoral."

"We'll have to practise more."

"Mmm, yes please. But for now, I'd better be going. We don't want to run any risks here. And it was an unhoped-for bonus. I really only had a kiss in mind." Reluctantly she stood and reached for her corsage. "Have you by any chance got something else I can put on instead of this?"

Jodie gave her an old soft sweatshirt, and she snuggled into it. She fixed her hair and makeup, which had smeared. She hoped her swollen lips would have time to get back to normal between here and home. She could feel where Jodie nipped her.

"Don't come down. I'm just going to scoot into the car. It's better if I'm alone."

She put on her cap and trench and carried her corsage in a bag Jodie gave her.

"Wait. The shoes are a problem. Here, I think we have more or less the same size. These are new."

She slipped into some sneakers, which were only a half size too big, and her stilettos joined her top, in the bag.

"Now you look as if you could actually live here. What about sunglasses?"

"That makes people look even more. I'll put them on when I drive."

There were more people about as it was a warm evening. But again, nobody paid her any attention. With a quick look up to Jodie standing at her window, and a blown kiss, she drove back to Starnberg.

Thorsten came in a few minutes after she unlocked the house and went into the kitchen. She had had time to put her car back in the garage but had not changed. He looked at her sweatshirt.

"What are you looking at? I've had this old thing for years. I needed to change after the photos, and it's so comfortable." She breathed in Jodie's scent. *If only he knew.*

***

Recording a new album was always tense. And it made it worse having a full orchestra in the studio, instead of a band. The time she could spend on each number was limited because of the costs. She had to concentrate hard and give all her energy to each number.

She was constantly aware of Jodie, who looked gorgeous every day, wearing her low-waisted jeans with a t-shirt or button down, both stretching across her breasts. The jeans were loose enough for Juliette to put her hand down the front, and she had to discipline herself to stop having those thoughts. They kept their distance. Jodie respected the duress she was under, and they had no more contact that the occasional fleeting finger pressure around a mug of tea or coffee, or a water bottle. It was enough to send pleasant shivers through her every time.

Andreas came in and out of the sessions. On the second to last day, he interrupted a conversation she was having with Bert.

"We need session photos tomorrow. Can Thorsten come in, please?" To have queried this would only make Andreas suspicious, as the loving husband was usually present whenever the cameras clicked.

"I hope he can make it."

"Why? Is he working again?" Juliette was not going to admit she hadn't seen him for nearly a week. He was sometimes at home, she had heard him moving about, but she was so tired after the sessions she had usually gone straight down to the basement to swim and have a light work out to release the tension, before collapsing into her bed.

"He has a project he is preparing. Yes." She would have to warn Thorsten about this.

"I'll call him."

"No, let me do it." She moved into the corridor and called him on his smartphone. Wherever he was, there was loud music in the background. "Thorsten, photos tomorrow at the session. Oh, and I might have given Andreas the impression that you have some kind of project. You know... work."

"Maybe I have."

"Well, that's alright then." *Am I curious? No, not really.*

"What time?"

"The session starts at eleven. Shall we drive in together?"

"No, I don't want to hang around all day. I'll be there at half twelve."

She went back to Andreas. "He can only do the morning."

Andreas shrugged. "That'll be enough. We need a couple of shots for album publicity. He's not a featured artist. I'll see you all then. Look pretty, you girls. Bert...we'll try to keep you out of the shots."

"Was that actually an Andreas Meyer attempt to be funny?" Bert snorted.

"Now that he's gone, I would like to try to get *How could you leave me* down today. I don't want a photographer disturbing me. It's too difficult."

"Does he know that it's your new single?"

"Not yet. I'm putting off the evil day until I know that I can actually do it justice. No point in having a row if I can't cut it. Can we have a short break, and then try it?" She saw Jodie move off towards the cloakrooms, and she wanted desperately to at least hug her for a moment. Jodie was alone when she went in, washing her hands.

"Hello, gorgeous." She double-checked all the stalls had open doors, and then she couldn't help herself. She pulled her in, and they kissed deeply, their tongues swirling around each other, their hips grinding together, until they heard Claudia and Sadie laughing loudly outside. Jodie leapt to the towel holder and rubbed her hands. Juliette ripped open her shoulder bag and took out her lip-gloss.

"Oh, sorry, Juliette." They were always respectful and wary of her moods.

"I think you girls have a disease. It's called *apologia*. You spend your lives saying sorry." They laughed and any tension there had been in the room broke. They hadn't noticed anything unusual anyway. And why should they? Thorsten had his uses, as did the thousands of *happy couple* photos in every weekly magazine.

Juliette slipped out, and Jodie stayed behind for a moment with Claudia and Sadie.

"She's been tense, but better than usual at recording sessions."

"I wouldn't know. It's my first time with her."

"It can be very different. She doesn't blame anybody else when things go wrong, but she's a perfectionist. It's much better with you than with Alex. You're so much more musical, and you help us both a lot."

Sadie joined in. "But we might be heading for trouble now. The next number is really difficult. There are bound to be tears before bedtime."

"I doubt it. She has mastered all the tricky bits."

"How do you know that?"

"We…heard her at our rehearsal. It…sounded pretty secure to me."

"Yeah, you're right. I'd forgotten. Deep breathe everybody." Jodie wiped a bead of sweat off her top lip. She must be more careful.

They recorded a complete take, and it sounded good. Juliette went with Bert into the control room to listen. The orchestra occupied themselves, as did all idle orchestras. Most of them played with smartphones or tablets. Some stared into space. The cellist played the solo out of *Tosca,* which he did before every session and in every break. The harpist took out his knitting.

Bert came back and rehearsed a few orchestra passages that didn't sound right to him. Jodie watched Juliette through the large quadruple soundproof glass window. She was pointing out things in her music to the record producer. She had a towel around her neck and Jodie appreciated yet again how stunningly beautiful she was. She felt hot as she thought of Juliette writhing underneath her, crying out her name as she climaxed. She fanned her face.

"You're a bit young for hot flushes, my dear." Sadie was watching her. "But I do agree. He is rather dishy." She breathed again. Sadie thought she was ogling Tom Braun the producer. He was a handsome man. They both looked on, as Juliette laughed and rubbed her long fingers up and down his arm.

"Just look at that. I had heard on the grapevine that all is not quite perfect in the De Luca household. If that's what's going on, you don't stand a chance with him."

"Who's telling tales?"

"You know this business. The good husband has been seen around in nightclubs rather a lot. On his own, or at least, not with her. Can you imagine the press if they split up?"

Juliette kissed the producer on the cheek. Jodie felt a pang of jealousy.

"As she is the butter on our bread, I think we should keep quiet, and not contribute to any rumours." Claudia glared at Sadie, who look chastened.

"Yes, boss."

"You too, Jodie."

"Me? I would never ever say anything to anybody about her sex life."

Juliette came back into the studio.

Bert tapped his baton. "Let's do sections. We can definitely put this to bed today."

Jodie squeezed her thighs at the thought. She caught Juliette's eye, who put her index finger deeply into her mouth, withdrawing it slowly across her lower lip before using it to turn a page in her music. Jodie stifled a moan.

***

* 'I could never have sung it as well without your help. Thank you.'

* 'The good news is that Sadie thinks both you and I have the hots for Tom Braun. The bad news is that I'm jealous if you have.'

Three emojis came back: laughing face, jealousy and two men holding hands.

* 'Can't wait to see you tomorrow. Photos remember.'

Juliette was early at the session. She wore designer jeans, and a bare shouldered t-shirt. Petra was waiting in the studio to make her up and put her hair into a chignon.

She was finished when the three backing singers arrived. Jodie looked at her with hooded eyes.

"Petra, give the girls a quick going over will you. I want them in some of the photos. They have a lot to sing on this album. Give Jodie a touch of kohl under her eyes."

"Arabella Cooper has a lot to answer for at the moment. It had gone out of fashion a bit after gothic faded, but she has brought the trend back."

"I know. On the right person, it's a great look. Better on brunettes though. It doesn't do much for me."

She went into the studio to prepare her music for the last three songs they were scheduled to record today. Then she went into the control room.

"Tom, have you done the rough edit of *How could you leave me*?"

"Just finished."

She put headphones on, closed her eyes and lost herself in the track. She was smiling as she took the phones off.

"Juliette, if I were you, I would put it out as a single."

"Good to hear. I want to. I'll have to fight Andreas on it." He looked at her surprised.

"I know. Is he out there making the money, or am I? He's fighting me on everything at the moment. I know he feels his influence is waning. I feel sorry for him. In fact, I feel sorry for two of the men in my life."

They both looked into the studio. Thorsten came in, sporting an unshaven look. She had knocked on his door before leaving, but there was no answer. She knew he was at home because his car was parked in the drive. A red BMW coupe. Only a man would buy a car like that. Its bonnet was considerably longer than the body. Had she caused him to have potency problems like Leon?

"Is he your type, Tom?"

"Honestly?"

"Honestly."

"He might have been once. Although no, not really. I prefer something more understated."

She nodded slightly and sighed. The backing singers came in. Jodie wore a halter neck top and slim black jeans, which made her long legs go on forever. Petra had done a great job on all three. The hint of kohl worked perfectly.

"If I was into girls, I would find it hard to keep my hands off Jodie."

"Thorsten can't either by the look of things." He had gone over to the backing singers and had wrapped an arm around Jodie. "Grrr. I better put a stop to it."

Tom laughed. "Jealous?"

"A little." If only he knew.

***

The album was fully edited. Juliette was in Munich, in Andreas's office.

"I don't like that number Bert wrote with Arabella Cooper."

"Why am I surprised?"

"It's totally different to your usual style. And I'm worried about the association with Cooper-Nyman."

"Not again, Andreas. We are living in the twenty-first century. You were completely wrong about that Bob Fosse dance number. The feedback was overwhelmingly positive."

"Yes, but we don't know if it will affect the sales of this new album. And it's in English."

"Aren't you glad it's not in Swedish then?"

"What?"

"Half the songs are in English. I thought that was the point. We are going to release the album in the States."

"I'm not sure about that anymore. I think we should concentrate on the domestic audience."

"What the fuck! Are you kidding me? We already have a deal with Pacific records over there. No way, Andreas, are we going to back out of that. And what's more, I am going to release *How could you leave me* as a single here and over there too."

"Over my dead body."

They glared at each other.

She didn't flinch. "If that's what you want. You can go anytime. I believe our contract states three months' notice…on either side." Her tone was icy. And she knew Andreas couldn't cope with her in full on diva mood. He always backed down. *I should do it more often.*

"I wash my hands of this decision. Now, perhaps we should get on with planning the New Year show."

He wouldn't walk out on her. There was too much money at stake for him. But if the single did backfire, his self-righteous sneering would be unbearable.

***

The album release was timed for the middle of January, to take full advantage of the publicity from the New Year show in which she would whet appetites for it by singing several numbers. But Juliette wanted the single out in mid-October. And that was just three weeks away. The session photographer spread dozens of photos out on her dining room table, and she sat with the label graphic designer, trying to choose one for the cover and another for the main publicity shot. The director of the video, due to be filmed the following week, was also in on the meeting. An atmospheric tie-in was a must.

"I want this one?"

"Really? It's great, but we'll have to cut out the backing singers. They look good, but it would be very unusual."

"Exactly why I want it. And I would like a rethink of the video. I know we talked about it being based around me alone in a boat on the lake, but I would much prefer to be in a studio singing the number, with Bert at the piano and the girls doing their bit. We don't need the orchestra. I can do sad-and-lonely in the studio and in that ugly industrial complex where the studio is located. I want the whole thing more grainy and darker rather than soft focus David Lynch stuff. And definitely in high grade black and white. No colour."

The director looked thoughtful. "You might be right. I have listened a lot to the track, and I'm going off the lake idea. I hope the studio is available."

He made a call. Juliette crossed her fingers. "You better check on the girls as well. They do work for other singers." She knew they were free that week, but it would look odd to admit it. The record company called back. "Green light all around. Let's go for it."

Andreas would freak again.

***

* 'Are you very busy today? Could you come over for a coffee? I hate to impose, but Marie is rather stationary at the moment.'

* 'Of course. In an hour? I wanted to bring you the demo of *How could you leave me* in any case. Just to check it's ok.'

The gate was open, and she ran up the steps. Arabella opened the door and led her into the living room where Marie was lying on the couch.

"Marie, are you ill?"

She shook her head. They both smiled happily. "Definitely not."

Arabella sat beside her and kissed her lightly on the lips.

"The transplant seems to have worked. It's been nearly a month, and I'm still pregnant. But the doctors are urging caution for another month. Hence, my prone position. Listen, we want to warn you about some building work over the next couple of months. It will be finished by Christmas. Promise."

"That's fantastic. I'm so happy for you both. And building noise is no problem. I'm away a lot during the daytime. What are you renovating?"

"Two things. The big office facing away from the lake will be halved to make a nursery, and the surprisingly large loft over the garage we are converting into a studio apartment. We are going to need a live-in nanny…we're expecting twins."

Marie reached up and kissed Arabella. "My wife is so clever." They moaned into each other's mouths. "Sorry. Our respective mothers are champing at the bit to help, but one lives in Stockholm and the other one in Cardiff, so granny care is not a long-term feasibility. Bella has a great deal of work coming up over the next few years. I am taking a full year off, but after that I'm going to have to get back to singing."

Arabella got up reluctantly from Marie's side. "Do you have the demo? I'm intrigued to hear it."

"Me too."

Arabella slotted it into a music centre built discreetly into the wall. The speakers were of a fantastic quality, and Juliette was relieved and happy to hear the result. Both Marie and Arabella applauded when it was over.

"That's great, Juliette. Totally different to ours. I love that Bert has brought the backing singers so much further forward. Talking of which, would it be very indiscreet to ask about Jodie."

Marie shook her head and put up a hand to stop Arabella.

"It's fine to ask. I love that I can talk to someone. It's great. She's great. It's agony to have to hide all the time and we don't see each other nearly enough, but I have never been happier. I regret the years I missed. I thought at first, I might be bisexual, but I don't think I am. I never felt remotely like this about a man. I think I'm gay. I wish I could tell the world, but I can't."

"I went through the same. Except I clung on to bisexuality for years, before I admitted to myself that I am lesbian. It was such a relief." Marie took Arabella's hand and kissed her long fingers. "I nearly destroyed this one in the process. Please be careful with Jodie. She is gorgeous and talented, and we think you make a wonderful couple."

Juliette felt herself tearing up.

"Bella, didn't you invite Juliette over for a coffee? I will suffer watching you both drinking it. I don't give a shit about alcohol but doing without coffee is hard. Camomile tea for me. Ugh."

"Thank you, Marie. Thank you both. Having you as neighbours is fantastically lucky."

***

"*Mein Puschelkopf.*" She murmured softly in Jodie's ear. They were alone in the make-up trailer. Petra had gone outside to fetch something from her car. Juliette was waiting to be lacquered. Jodie was next in line to be made up and sat in the chair facing the mirror.

"I want so much to kiss you, but I think Petra might notice when she gets back." Instead, she nibbled on her ear and stuck in her tongue, being careful not to smudge her own lipstick. Jodie shivered. There was a slight vibration as someone stepped on the trailer steps and opened the door. Juliette ruffled her hair.

"Give her hair extra body will you, Petra? She's a real *Puschelkopf.* We might as well emphasise it."

"Yeah. And kohl?"

"A fraction. Try putting it on all three girls. We are going for a bit of darkness in the film. Not on Bert though." Petra and Jodie giggled.

They would start filming the video in the studio as if it was a normal recording. After which they would go outside and shoot scenes of Juliette in the various dismal and decrepit old hangers and workshops surrounding the studio, alone, or with the three girls in the distance. The lyrics spoke of heartbreak and being abandoned. There would be a scene in the rain, in which Juliette's shirt would stick to her body, giving the sexiness the director insisted on. The local fire brigade agreed to provide the water. She shivered at the thought. It was going to be an unpleasant experience. The weather had turned autumnal.

To her surprise, considering he disappeared most days, Thorsten decided to come with her. He was fascinated by film and watched a great deal of Netflix when he was at home. His luck was in. As soon as they started the outdoor shoot, the assistant cameraman, responsible for moving the heavy power cable behind the tracking camera, slipped on the uneven ground and sprained his ankle badly. He was strapped up and sent to outpatients. He would not be back for two weeks or longer. Thorsten volunteered his help, and it was accepted. Juliette had not seen him so happy for months. She would talk to the director. As his looks were fading so rapidly, perhaps there was a future for him behind the camera, preferably frequently on location.

***

Apart from the few brief moments in the make-up trailer, Juliette had not been alone with Jodie. It was driving her crazy as she prepared for the rain scene.

The director came into the trailer. "We get one go at this. You don't have multiple costumes, and the water is too expensive. The budget only allows for one full tank. Are you absolutely clear about what is going to happen?"

"Yes. How long does a tank last?"

"About ten minutes."

"That's long enough to freeze to death. I hope you're not expecting me to film anything afterwards?"

"No, we'll do some shots of the building without you and the girls. I need Thorsten to help, but by the time you are dressed and warmed up, he should be finished."

She ground her teeth. Why did they come in together today? If he had driven himself, she could get away with Jodie.

"Petra, you're very quiet, and you look pale."

"I'm starting a migraine. I'm so glad this is just one shot. Then I can go home."

They went out onto the location set. The fire engine with tank was standing ready. Instead of a jet, it had several long bars attached to the hosepipe, which had small holes in them. The weather was overcast, which was perfect for a rain scene. And it was cold. Juliette shivered under her long trench coat. The girls stood watching. They were finished for the day but interested in the process. They wore coats and scarves against the northeast breeze.

Sadie grinned at her. "Rather you than me."

"*Schadenfreude* will get you nowhere." Juliette scowled at her only half amused, as Petra collapsed with a groan onto a nearby chair.

Juliette leant over her, rubbing her back. "She has a migraine. Can someone call a taxi?"

"No, I need my car, but I don't think I can drive. My vision...it's fuzzy and I'm dizzy."

Claudia stepped up. "I'll take her in my car, and Sadie can drive hers behind me. Jodie, do you think you could stay until the scene is shot? Juliette's going to need help getting out of those wet clothes when this is over."

"Sure. I can stay."

Petra groaned again. Her face was a grey colour. She spoke through clenched teeth. "Jodie, there's a blanket in the trailer. And I turned the heating up. Thanks so much for staying to help."

They moved off to the car park. Juliette couldn't supress a grin, as she whispered in Jodie's ear. "I hope she's better tomorrow. But…need I say more?"

They began filming. Eventually, the water from the tank slowed to a trickle.

"Cut! We have it. Well done everyone. Juliette, that was great, and so hot in that transparent shirt."

"You might be, but I'm fucking freezing." Her teeth were chattering. Jodie ran to her with a thick blanket, and with her arms around her, walked her back to the trailer.

"Need any help?"

"Sorry, Thorsten, I need you here with the camera. I'm sure Jodie can cope on her own."

They got into the trailer, and Juliette kicked the door shut.

"Lock it. Now come here and warm me up."

"Clothes off. It's positively dangerous."

Jodie lowered the blanket, and for a moment took in the sight of the cotton shirt clinging to Juliette's breasts. She was bra-less. Her nipples were peaked from the cold. She tweaked each one, then opened the buttons and slipped it off her arms, followed by the short skirt. She had bare legs. Jodie knelt in front of her and gripped the soaking thong in her teeth. She pulled it down her thighs before slipping it down her legs and over her feet.

"Jodie, I'm heating up already. Come up here." Jodie shook her head and stayed where she was. She slowly licked up the inside of her thighs.

"Have I dried you off too much? No, I don't think so." She pulled back Juliette's folds. They glistened in the trailer's low lighting. She gently pushed her legs wider, and slowly, her face turned up to Juliette, brought her tongue up the length of her slit.

"Mmmm. Does that taste good." Juliette let out a strangled moan and stuffed a fist in her mouth. "More?"

She nodded, and ran her fingers through Jodie's hair, pulling her gently back to her sex. She continued stroking the folds with her tongue, which were releasing more arousal. Juliette panted and ground her hips into Jodie, who moved up to her clit, circling and sucking it, until with a silent scream Juliette climaxed, her legs shaking with the intensity. She pulled Jodie up from her knees and kissed her passionately. Jodie pushed her hands through Juliette's still wet hair. "You must dry your hair. You'll get sick."

"No, I won't. This is central heating for lovers, and it's really warm in the trailer." She turned Jodie and pushed her against the door. "Now, let me see how wet you are."

She popped her jeans button and pulled down the zip. Then she pushed her hand down her briefs. Jodie moaned into her mouth.

"Competition, I see." Jodie bucked her hips against the hand giving her pleasure. Juliette tried to enter her, but the jeans were too tight. She yanked them down, pushed her legs apart and thrust into her again hard. Jodie flinched.

"I'll cut my nails, my love. You are much more considerate."

"It's ok. Harder please." She powered as fast and as hard as she could. Jodie drew in a breath and her legs began to shudder. With her thumb, Juliette rubbed hard on her clit, and Jodie's walls pulsed as she came. Juliette was getting hooked on the feeling. She stayed in her for as long as the contractions lasted, which was several long moments.

They leaned against each other until their breathing returned to normal.

"I'm addicted to this. I want to fuck you for a day and a night straight through…again…"

"I'm willing and able, but don't you think the filming might be finished soon, and your husband will come to see what you are doing and want to take you home."

"Back to earth with a crash. But you're right. How can you be so sensible and so gorgeously sexy at the same time?" She pulled Jodie's jeans up and closed the zipper and button. Then pushed her hands under her sweatshirt and massaged her breasts.

"I didn't get a chance to greet these two." Jodie pulled her hands away.

"Down, tiger. You are stark naked, and your hair is a terrible mess."

She helped Juliette dress in slacks and a warm cashmere sweater. She sat in front of the mirror and blew dry her hair, before hastily reapplying some basic make-up.

"You too should put yourself back together. You look rather well fucked. And we better get out of here and leave the door open for a bit. It smells of sex."

"You go outside. It's better if we don't leave together. I'll just do something to save your soaked costume, tidy up and turn the heating down, or else there will be a burning trailer, and as we know the water tank is empty."

"Sweetheart, I don't deserve you. You are so considerate." They kissed. Juliette shrugged into her trench coat and went outside. Thorsten was on his way to the trailer.

She jumped the steps and hurried over. She didn't want him to get too close.

"Are you ready to go home?"

"Yes. I'm dry now, but I was really wet when I got in the truck." She heard a low chuckle from the trailer. "Goodnight, Jodie, and thanks for everything."

"The pleasure was mine. Sleep well."

***

* 'I've written us a duet. How can I show it to you? We need a room with piano.'

* 'I'd love you to come here. But it's too risky. As it's for the show, I'll ask Bert if we can meet at his house.'

"Bert, can I meet Jodie at your house? She wants to show me, or rather us, a duet she has written for the New Year show."

"Sure. How about tomorrow, late afternoon?"

Jodie was already there when she arrived. She looked positively edible, in her black jeans and a tight V-necked sweater. Juliette held her and kissed her cheek, lingering slightly longer than necessary, breathing her scent in.

"You want me to leave you alone?"

"Bert. Stop please. You don't make it any easier. And I don't want to give you a reason to gossip, if anyone asks you anything. This is a working session for the New Year show. Jodie, I think you should start by playing the two songs we've decided on for your solos."

Bert looked more and more impressed as she sang and played. "Wow, I see what you mean. There is no reason for me to write something for her, or for her to sing someone else's songs. These are great."

Jodie blushed with pleasure and handed them both her handwritten music for the duet.

"Bert, I can't sight read well enough. Could you sing in my part, so I can first listen?"

At the end, Juliette sighed with pleasure. "Oh, Jodie, that is so good. It will be an honour to sing it with you. Come on, teach it to me."

They worked for an hour, until Juliette was note perfect. "Now, I'll just have to memorise it. I'll drive you home. Thanks, Bert."

She drove slowly, and parked under the chestnut tree again, which was fast losing its leaves.

"I so wish I could just take you out to dinner to a cosy little Italian restaurant, just like everybody else can. But you know, it's impossible. Even with a paper-bag over my head, I would be recognised."

Jodie laughed. "That I doubt, but it would make eating spaghetti rather difficult."

"It's dark now, and nobody is around. Let me kiss you at least."

It wasn't easy across the wide middle console of the Porsche, but they explored each other's mouths and bit each other's lips, and nibbled on ears and necks. Juliette left a mark on Jodie's collarbone; she couldn't help herself.

"Don't worry. It's getting colder. I have a lot of scarves. Talking of which, it's really cold sitting here. You can't risk laryngitis."

"Stop being so goddam sensible," she grumbled. "Just one more kiss."

Jodie climbed rather stiffly out of the car. "Ugh. A wet crotch and a cold wind are not very compatible."

"Good night, my love. Cross your fingers the single is going to be a success. It's out the day after tomorrow."

She drove off. Jodie waited until she was out of sight, before turning to walk the rest of the way home. She needed to attend to herself urgently. She suspected Juliette would want to do the same.

***

Juliette woke, remembered what day it was, and her stomach lurched. She was always nervous when a new album or single came out, and so much was riding on this one. It was a huge change of direction in her musical style.

Andreas would call her, she knew. She looked at her watch. It was eight thirty. No message yet. She got up and went for a long swim, followed by a workout and a hot shower, after which she lathered her body with oil. She made coffee and scrambled some eggs. Still nothing. She punched in his number.

"Andreas, what does your unusual silence mean? Is it the disaster you predicted?"

"Yes and no."

"Go on."

"There is a terrible review in the folk music paper. Truly awful."

Her heart sank. She felt almost faint. There was a roaring in her ears, and she had to sit down on the living room couch. Thorsten was reading a football magazine. He looked up.

"Is that all?"

"No…everything else is very positive."

"What does that mean?"

"Yeah. I suppose you would call them rave reviews." The blood rushed back up from her stomach to her head. She lay back on the coach, the cold sweat clammy on her face. She tried not to shiver.

"What about sales?"

"Streaming has gone through the roof. But of course, we don't know about the hard sales yet. They might not be good."

"But they might be."

"I suppose so."

She was furious but managed to keep her voice even. "Andreas, why did I have to drag this out of you this morning…afternoon? Are you really sure you want to go on working for me?"

Thorsten looked at her open mouthed.

"Juliette, I have been summoned to come to your house tomorrow when I will bring you everything in a nice, neat file. I am waiting for more feedback. I was just about to call you. There are two live talk show offers, and they obviously want to hear back immediately, as it's short notice."

"When, for fuck's sake?"

"Friday in Cologne, and Sunday in Hamburg."

"I suppose I have to sing?"

"Yes, no orchestra in Cologne, just piano, and a small orchestra in Hamburg."

"I need Bert and the backing singers. And put us all in the same hotel, will you please."

"That's expensive."

"Just do as I say," she snapped.

"You need a two bedroomed suite for yourself and Thorsten as usual?"

"No, Thorsten won't be coming. He has a football match to go to, and the invitation is only for me. Why should he hang around for three days doing nothing?"

Thorsten gave her a thumbs-up sign. "If Bert and the girls are in the same hotel, at least I can eat in the restaurant, instead of daily room service."

"That makes sense." His tone was grudging.

"I'll drive. I hate doing airports alone."

"Do you want a car and driver?"

"No. If I drive myself, I can take my time and travel when I want to."

"At least the others can take the train, and not fly."

"That's up to them. But it's probably more comfortable. First class please."

He blew out a breath but knew better than to argue.

"Andreas, haven't you forgotten something?"

"I don't think so."

"How about congratulations?"

She ended the call before she had to listen to him stuttering.

She called up the reviews, reading the bad one first. *What is Juliette Simon doing? This song has nothing to do with the folk music that made her famous. And why is she singing in English? She will lose a lot of her fans. We cannot recommend anyone to buy this recording, even if the song does have merit.*

She shrugged. It was bad but she had expected worse after Andreas's gleeful report. Curiosity might even engender a few sales. All the others were raves. *She is maturing as an artist, even if she is no longer the girl-next-door. The video is a knockout.* Bert was praised for his arrangements, and the backing singers were mentioned favourably in two reviews.

"You got away with it." There was no condemnation in Thorsten's tone. "Great, that the video is a hit." She smiled. *As if he had directed it himself.* She hadn't said anything to him yet, but the director promised to consider employing him for projects when he was short staffed. She probably never would say anything. It was important for him to feel he had got a job on his own abilities, and not because she called in a favour. He had been less surly since the filming and was working out again. He no longer suggested sex. He was probably getting it elsewhere. She didn't ask. How could she? He might point the finger back. She would lie if she had to, but she would rather not.

"That was ok about the weekend I hope?"

"Yeah, thanks a lot. I know we are in for another round of publicity when the album comes out after Christmas, but I am grateful if you can spare me as much as possible in the meantime."

"Thorsten, if you want out, you must tell me. We'll make it work somehow."

"Thanks. I will."

There was something going on. She felt a moment of panic. Then she saw a vision of Jodie's face and didn't care. It would be worth it, whatever the difficulties. For as long as everyone continued being discreet.

***

She scheduled another meeting with Andreas and Bert in Starnberg. She again refused to go into Munich for it. Andreas could get his arse out to where she was. She was not going to forgive him for his negative behaviour any time soon. Bert didn't mind either way. Parking at her house was considerably easier.

"So…I've made a list of what I want in the New Year show." Andreas opened his mouth to interrupt. "Andreas, I would be truly grateful if you could just let me go through the list without comment. It goes without saying I will give ample opportunity for your input when I finish."

Bert could barely supress a grin.

"We have three and a half hours to fill. That's nearly an hour longer than last year. The show will air from eight fifteen, directly after the main news through to eleven forty-five, after which the live countdown programmes in all three countries begin."

Her show was a Eurovision production and would air simultaneously in Germany, Austria and Switzerland.

"Last year, we taped the show over two days, with two days rehearsal. This year I want four days rehearsal…Andreas, please…the first two days only for the dancers and me. The cameras can come in on the second day. The third day will be for the backing singers and Bert. The guests and orchestra will only come in for the day before we tape, just the same as last year. So, I'm not increasing the costs dramatically. It does mean the sets will have to be ready two days earlier, and the lighting guys will work over nights, which they do anyway. It will actually help them when they see in advance what my numbers look like."

"How are the sets going to be ready on time?"

"They will be. The design team is coming to join us here this afternoon. I've already given them some of my ideas."

"All without telling me?"

"Andreas, you have been so negative recently about every goddam thing I do. Just think about it and ask yourself if I'm not justified. I'm beginning to wonder if I can trust you not to sabotage something you don't like. If you do, I'll get to hear about it."

He turned pale. *OK, then she wasn't wrong.* Bert looked uncomfortable, but it wasn't a pleasant conversation, so she didn't blame him.

"I want two big set numbers. Excerpts from musicals. *Evita* and *Elisabeth*. I would have liked something more modern for the second one, but I do agree that my public wouldn't appreciate something they don't know, so we are safe with these two. I don't need anyone other than Jodie and the dancers in Evita, but I need a big male musical star for Elisabeth. It shouldn't be too difficult. At least a dozen have played the role since the premiere."

"Jodie? The clumsy backing singer, Jodie… Sanchez, or whatever her name is."

"Andreas, she has a phenomenal voice."

"Thanks, Bert. She will sing *Another suitcase in another hall*, while I change my costume between *Buenos Aires* and *Argentina*. In *Elisabeth*, we will begin with *Der letzte Tanz,* sung by whoever we get for the Tod, then the duet *Wenn ich tanzen will*, followed by my solo *Ich gehör nur mir*, and we finish with the last duet *Der Schleier fällt*. The two musicals will cover at least a three-quarter hour span of the show time."

"If we can get the rights, it will be fine." Andreas tried to put another spoke in.

"Taken care of. Bert knows everyone concerned, and it is not a problem. The TV company has given the go-ahead for the budget. Now, onto my guests. Of course, we'll have at least half from the folk/soft pop scene. I have suggestions here, on this list. As you see, I'd like to give a spot to both my nearest rivals, Vivienne and Sabine."

"That's risky."

"I don't think so. It will go down well with the fans who like all three of us, and as you keep telling me, there are a lot of them."

"I also want two good rock bands and a male singer who is at the top of the charts right now. Cooper-Nyman will sing two songs from their new album, and Jodie Sanchez, as my young discovery, so to speak, will sing two of her own songs, and a duet with me. The dancers will have two numbers on their own, and five with me together. That's it, I think."

Bert brought his hands together and clapped. Andreas shrugged. "Some of it I agree with, some is rather dangerous. In any case, it will be a departure from last year."

"Exactly. If I do a carbon copy of last year, however successful it was, people will switch off. The fans won't, I know, but I need to catch the interest of the general public. That's where we will sell additional albums."

"Incidentally, we are going to have to take a rain check on issuing the album in the UK and USA."

"What? Why?"

"The single is going down well in both markets. You might just squeeze into the charts, which would be a great achievement for a first release. But they've changed their minds about the German songs. They say it will suppress demand."

Bert nodded. "I can understand that. An English language version will be much easier to market. I think we should do the same songs but with English texts. With luck, we would need only two studio days."

"And who is going to write the English lyrics?"

"Arabella is really fast; she is bilingual and she has a natural talent for rhyming."

"But she's so busy conducting."

"She has a few weeks off, to be with Marie. If we get everything to her quickly, we might be lucky. We need, what, seven texts. I know she is going to be working again at the beginning of November. Marie is out of the woods. Everything is fine."

"Thank god for that."

"Is Marie Nyman sick? I haven't seen them doing any promotion for their new album."

"She's pregnant," Juliette and Bert said together.

"I'm not going to ask how. I really don't want to know. It just gets worse. You know I told you to stay away from them."

"I'm sure she won't be showing when we tape in the middle of December. By the time the babies are born, the show will be long forgotten."

"Plural?"

"Twins."

"How do you know?"

"Andreas, don't be tiresome. See that hedge over there, and the house above it? We are neighbours. In more or less the same business, Bert is their arranger too, and besides all that, I am really happy and proud to say that we are friends."

"Me too." How she loved Bert. "I'll call Arabella." He spoke to her quickly. "She can come over in an hour or so. I can take her into the studio if you are busy with the designers."

"Perfect."

The gate buzzer interrupted them. She checked, and saw it was her design team, along with Petra and Jamie. She let out a long breath. Andreas had been such hard work. Now, they would have some fun.

***

Everyone left except Arabella. Marie came over to join them. Juliette made a quick minestrone soup and warmed a baguette in the oven.

"I'm getting so hungry. I'm going to blow up like a balloon."

"That would be your own fault for being so evil about Tasmin when she was pregnant."

"Explain. Who is Tasmin?"

"My ex-husband's new wife. A Hollywood starlet, the perfect arm dressing for action hero Nicholas Miller. Except she had a terrible pregnancy and there were no photo opportunities for months. I am going to look the same if I carry on eating so much."

Arabella hugged her gently. "I wouldn't care if you do, but you are not going to. Even I can't see anything yet."

"I hope it stays that way until the show recording. Six weeks to go."

"Jamie, my stylist is brilliant. He can dress you, so no one will know."

"I'll do my best, but this minestrone is so delicious. Can I have another helping?"

"It's only fresh vegetables and some stock. It won't do any damage to your delectable waistline."

Arabella raised an eyebrow. "Are you making up for lost time, Juliette?"

"No, just…um…what's the word…"

"Is Thorsten here?"

"Arabella, you didn't seriously ask me that question in this context."

"Just checking."

Marie leant over and poked her in the ribs. "Jealous, Bella? Serves you right." Arabella put her arms around her wife and kissed her head.

"Anyway, Juliette, I could have sworn the first time we met, you had eyes only for Bella."

"I was gawping at both of you."

"Thorsten was entirely out of his depth I remember. So where is he?"

"He's out somewhere. Whenever that happens, I sit here bitterly regretting the lost opportunity to see Jodie, but I never know far enough in advance. But tomorrow…"

Her eyes gleamed.

"Tell, if you want to."

"I have two talk shows to promote the single. Cologne tomorrow night and Hamburg on Sunday. Of course, I can't sing it without my backing group, so they will be there too. And I've insisted we all stay in the same hotel. We'll just have to be careful. But three whole days…and nights." She tried not to blush.

"I'm so happy for you," Marie spoke through a yawn. "I'm sorry. I get so sleepy. I love being pregnant, but it takes some getting used to. After so many years of non-stop work, it's like being in a different world."

"Come on, let's get you home. I'll stay up a bit and work on the lyrics."

"I feel so guilty making additional work for you."

"Juliette, please don't. I enjoy it. Because I have had time off, I've done all my preparation for the next few months. I really do have this little free slot in my calendar. I spend a lot of time in bed with this one of course, but there is a limit to how many hours I can watch her snoring her head off. If all goes well, I think I can be ready for the weekend. I start work in Munich on Monday anyway."

"Will you be alright on your own, Marie?"

"I won't be. My mother is arriving tomorrow."

"So now you know why I'm starting work on Monday."

Marie rolled her eyes. "Unfortunately, I can't blame my beloved wife. And she can't even turn off anymore because she has learnt quite a lot of Swedish. I'm so proud of her. She did it secretly."

"I had to. The twins are going to be bought up trilingual, and it would be awful if their second Mama didn't understand a word they are all jabbering about. Now there's a thought. You can speak to them in Italian."

Juliette felt herself tearing up. She was going to be included in this little family. So many things in her life were infinitely better than they had been a year ago.

***

The talk show was late night, but there was a rehearsal scheduled some hours before transmission began. Juliette wanted to take no risks. Cologne was a six-hundred-kilometre drive from Starnberg. She left at eight o'clock. Barring traffic problems, she should be there between two and three and could rest for a good three hours before having to get to the studio. She insisted on Petra accompanying her on the trip. She and the girls and Bert were taking a train, which would get them to the hotel around five. They would be collected by the television company and driven in a group to the studio.

She checked into her suite, which was smaller than usual. She didn't need the second bedroom, *no definitely not*. Not for what she hoped was going to happen. In fact, a single room with a narrow bed would have been enough. She had discovered just how much she liked Jodie underneath her. She unpacked. She had her two TV outfits with her. Usually, they were sent on with Jamie, but she wasn't going to wear real show clothes, and the logistics of getting them to Petra just wasn't worth the hassle, especially as she was underway in the Porsche. Petra would have to go over them with an iron in the dressing room.

She had brought a sandwich with her, so ate it and made herself a cup of tea in her room. She undressed and lay down and managed to sleep deeply for two hours. It was an unexpected treat and would come in useful later. *How much sleep would she get tonight?* She tensed her leg muscles and lifted her hips as she felt the now familiar arousal in her briefs. Her entire adult life she had suffered from dryness, except when she sometimes pleasured herself. Her hand went down to stroke her folds, but she stopped. *No.* She would save that for later. She took a long shower and blew dry her hair. Petra would dress it properly later. For now, she put on only light make-up.

She went down to the lobby. Her group were waiting, along with a minibus and a sleek black Mercedes. That she couldn't change. She kissed everyone lightly, making sure not to spend any longer with Jodie, although she did manage to breathe in her scent.

"Journey good?"

"Fine," said Bert. "And, you? It's a long drive."

"No problems. And I was early so I got in a good sleep. I need my energy tonight." Jodie bit her bottom lip.

"Yeah. It's the first time live with the song."

"Bert, did you have to remind me. I'm nervous enough. Come on. Let's go."

The studio was in its usual chaotic state before a live TV show. There were two interviewers and five other guests. A psychiatrist, an author, an actor, a woman who had been beaten for years by her husband, and a politician. They were all in the news at the moment or had something to promote. That is what these shows did. Juliette would be interviewed second to last and sing at the end of the show. It was inevitable as she had the pulling power to keep people watching, and it could continue until well after midnight. The show had an open end.

They rehearsed and went through all the necessary sound checks. There were still two hours to go before they went on air. It did not help her nerves. Petra was with her in her dressing room. She was the only one with a single. The other guests were together in the green room, and the girls were cramped together in what was no more than an airless broom cupboard. They took turns getting made up by the TV station's own staff. The camera had special needs. Petra, who had done a stint with a TV company was there exclusively for Juliette. She chatted about this and that and helped to soothe her nerves. She took her time dressing.

Ten minutes before on-airtime, they were called to the studio. Juliette wore an immaculately tailored black trouser suit, and stilettos. Her hair was in a chignon. She wandered over to the small side stage where Bert sat behind the concert grand piano and the three girls perched on high stools. Her microphone stand was positioned between them. Jodie looked at her and her eyes were dark and hooded. The girls were wearing their black slacks, and shirts with a red bow tie. Jodie's was fairly tight across her breasts, and as Juliette watched, her nipples hardened. She felt the dampness in her own thong. A fresh one she had changed into twenty minutes earlier. *Stop!* This was definitely not the time or place. As she returned to her seat, she was glad the experience had distracted her, and she was less nervous than she had been.

Then they were on-air, and each guest was introduced. Juliette naturally had more applause from the small studio audience than anyone else. The interviewers took turns speaking to each of them. She saw the red light of the camera was often on her face. She took care to react appropriately. She stopped smiling as she listened to the arrogant politician, who was defending himself and others against corruption charges.

"Excuse me, I've often wondered. Do all politicians have a criminal energy?" she interrupted. The audience applauded.

The question deflated his pomposity somewhat and he struggled to answer. When his interview ended, he scowled at Juliette.

It was her turn. "Your new single is very different." She nodded. "You sing about loneliness after having been abandoned by your partner. Is there anything autobiographical about the song?"

"No. no, there isn't. Remember, I didn't write the lyrics. Bert Schmidt wrote the music and Arabella Cooper the words. It was on Cooper-Nyman's last album, and they offered it to me to bring out as a single. I love the song and am thrilled."

"Is your profession lonely?"

She was very surprised at this rather personal line of questioning but had to continue answering. She was accustomed to much easier interviews, containing little content or depth. If this was the result of singing more serious music, she would have to get used to it.

"It depends on what you mean by lonely. I'm almost never alone. I have a team around me to help me and protect me, but it does mean I have almost always to eat room service alone when I'm on tour."

"Why?"

"Because it's not entirely pleasant when a dozen smart phones are trained on you, waiting for you to spill tomato sauce down your front. Which is what happens when I eat in a restaurant. The phones and the tomato sauce. I'm Italian. We take eating spaghetti very seriously." The audience laughed and applauded. The politician butted in.

"Isn't your husband usually with you? I don't see him this evening?"

"No, he has something better to do this weekend. Football. Dortmund are playing away in Munich tomorrow."

"So, you are on your own in Cologne?"

Evil shit. He knows quite well it would encourage stalkers.

"Of course not. Look. There's my dearest friend, arranger, and resident musical genius Bert Schmidt sitting at the piano, and my backing girls Claudia, Sadie and Jodie. We all stay in the same hotel."

The camera panned over them, and they waved. The interviewer took back the questions, effectively silencing the politician.

"You are at the top of your profession, with your second TV show coming up on New Year's Eve. Is there anywhere to go but down?"

"That's a rather brutal question, which I can't really answer. I am only up there for as long as my fans want to buy my recordings and watch my shows."

"Aren't you taking a risk with this new single which is so different?"

She sighed. "That's what some people tell me, but I can't stagnate as an artist. People won't want to watch and listen to repeats of old hits either. I have to move on and develop."

"Have you ever considered doing anything else?"

"I trained as a musical singer and dancer, and as an actress. I haven't exploited those talents yet. We are doing two musical segments in the New Year show. I'll have to see where the future takes me."

"Juliette Simon, thanks for now. We will be hearing from you after the next guest."

She breathed a sigh of relief as the camera moved to the woman opposite her. She looked over at Jodie, who surreptitiously gave her a thumbs-up. Bert was watching and echoed the gesture.

The next interview was very intense as well as moving. The woman was halting at first, before gaining confidence. She had been in an abusive relationship for fifteen years. She related how she was physically and psychologically tortured by her husband but didn't have the strength to leave.

"And now you have found happiness?"

"Yes," she said shyly.

"May the camera show your new partner?"

She looked into the audience where a woman sat, smartly dressed in a woollen dress. The woman nodded. The camera moved over for a close-up.

"I think everybody here wishes you both well. You deserve it."

The applause was loud and long, with bravos mixed in.

Juliette hadn't been expecting that. But the warmth of the audience's reaction was overwhelming. If only she could expect the same from her fan base. But she knew she couldn't. An enlightened public in a TV studio in Cologne had little to do with the real world. *Her* real world.

"After that interview, it's a relief that Juliette Simon's new single is not what we have come to expect from her. It is our great pleasure and honour that she will be singing it live for the first time with us tonight. Juliette, please."

To loud applause, she stood and walked over to her microphone. Jodie looked at her with such love in her eyes, that her nerves vanished. It went perfectly, and the audience leapt to its feet at the end.

They came off air.

"Thanks everyone. That was a great show. I'm looking forward to the ratings."

They were taken back to the hotel. Juliette was glad of the car. She had time to collect herself. It had been one of the most difficult evenings she had had for a long time. But it was over and now she had the prospect of being with Jodie for more than a few snatched minutes.

Sadie wanted to go to the bar. She shook her head.

"Not me, I'm tired after that, and the long drive."

Bert waved in sympathy. Jodie said she would go for a beer. That was sensible of her. Claudia and Sadie might be suspicious if she disappeared too.

"You are all going on the train tomorrow. I don't know what time I'll leave, but I would very much like us to all to have dinner together in the hotel restaurant in Hamburg. Would six o'clock suit everyone?" They nodded. "Sleep well, everybody."

"We will. It's such a luxury to have single rooms. Thank you, Juliette." Claudia spoke for them all.

She went into the suite, undressed and showered, feeling the tension leave her body. She blew dry her hair and took off her false gel nails. She now trimmed her own, so as not to hurt Jodie as she had done the last time they had sex. She slipped on a towelling robe. There was a soft knock on the door. She leapt up and opened it, looking out. The corridor was empty apart from Jodie, who was holding a small ice bucket.

"Quick. Come in. What are you doing with the ice bucket?"

"Just in case I met someone, I wanted a reason to be wandering around."

"My clever girl." She held her face and breathed in her scent. Shampoo and toothpaste. Jodie had showered as well.

"You were wonderful this evening. Those questions weren't easy. And the song was perfect."

"You helped me so much. The way your beautiful eyes looked at me. Come to bed. I want to drown in them."

Jodie lifted her sweatshirt over her head. She wore no bra. Juliette immediately cupped a breast and flicked a nipple.

"I nearly had to leave the studio when I saw these harden. I hope nobody else noticed."

"You see the effect you have on me."

"You think you're alone?"

She slipped down her jogging pants. She wore no briefs either.

"Oh, Jodie." Juliette pulled off her robe. They were both naked. They came together, moaning as skin found skin. Juliette pushed Jodie onto the bed and topped her. They kissed slowly at first, then faster and deeper. Jodie pushed her hips up to make contact with Juliette's sex. They were both slippery with arousal. She ground into her, supporting herself on her outstretched arms. She leant down and pulled on a nipple. Jodie drew her back to kiss her again, then ran her tongue around Juliette's mouth. She reached up and massaged both breasts. The nipples were painfully hard. Juliette ground down harder. Her hand fluttered over Jodie's stomach, causing it to clench, then she moved down and almost without touching her passed her hand over her clit. Jodie moaned.

"Don't kill me. The foreplay was all evening. I want you in me, please, Juliette."

Her hips strained up again, and Juliette gently eased two fingers into her.

"Yeees."

"Me too, she breathed." Jodie's hand found her folds and luxuriated in their slickness.

"Go in." She was entered. They both moved slowly, using their hips to help gain more penetration. Juliette speeded up her thrusting. She felt the familiar throbbing from deep inside.

"I can't hold back any longer." Jodie let out a wail and her contractions began just as she pressed Juliette's clit and sent her over the edge. They lay twitching together while their hearts and breathing slowed.

"That was fantastic. The first time we came together. And I hope not the last." She pulled the cover over them both, and they held each other tightly. Juliette was still quivering with the after waves.

"What have I been missing? You are so sexy. It gets better and better. That has never happened to me. I was always, or almost always, glad when it was over."

"There is a big difference."

Jodie slid down her body, her still erect nipples tracing a path over Juliette's stomach. She knelt between her legs and nibbled up and down her inner thighs.

"Jodie, I can't."

"Want to bet?"

She breathed on her folds, and then slowly licked up and down them.

"Mmmm. That tastes so good."

Juliette's hips moved up to meet her mouth.

"Oooh, you're right." She felt her orgasm already stirring and let out a deep groan. Juliette's tongue plunged into her and licked around her entrance. She gushed and held her breath. Then she felt her clit being circled and sucked, and it felt like the waves going out before a tsunami. As they crashed back in, she saw only white light behind her eyelids. She bucked into Jodie, who thrust three fingers into her to feel her throbbing. She opened her mouth, but no sound came out. She collapsed into the pillows.

Jodie crawled up to rest her head on her shoulder. She held her tightly, not able to talk for long minutes. She had no words to do justice to what she had experienced. After a while, she was conscious of Jodie breathing evenly. She adjusted the cover with one hand and kissed her head. What was she going to do? She couldn't live without this. Without this woman. After a while, she slept.

***

She woke out of a deep, dreamless sleep. It was still dark. Jodie was quietly getting dressed.

"Must you go?"

"Yes, I don't trust Sadie not to want to get to the breakfast buffet the minute it opens and drag me with her."

"Kiss me goodbye. I can't wait to see you again."

She left, closing the door softly. Juliette sighed and stretched. And slept again, until a knock on the door woke her with her breakfast. Thankfully, she had ordered enough, because she was rather hungry.

After dressing in her training outfit, she made her way to the well-equipped hotel fitness room. She hoped there would not be too many people there, and she was lucky. No more than half a dozen gawped when they recognised her, but soon turned away and left her to her exercise routine.

She got back to her suite, and after showering lay down again and shut her eyes for half an hour, revelling in the memory of the night's sensations. If Jodie were to walk through the door, she would be on her back in a second. She contemplated sending her a text, then realised she had most likely already left. Anyway, it would be a crazy thing to do. She packed and took the lift into the garage, loading the car before going back to reception to check out.

"Have my team left already?"

"Yes, they left for the station about an hour ago."

As she climbed into her car, she noticed a small piece of paper under the wiper. It was a full lipstick kiss. In the corners were a tiny J and an S, too small to be noticed by anyone if they had seen it. She carefully put it into her wallet.

The good four hundred kilometres took her nearly five hours because the traffic was bad, but she arrived before five o'clock, and could unpack at her leisure before going downstairs into the restaurant. They were all there, seated at a table in the far corner, but with a view out over the river Alster estuary. Bert stood.

"Here, sit looking out over the water with your back to the room. With luck…"

"I doubt it. Some have already seen me coming in." But the restaurant manager was very helpful, and he sat the other guests at a distance. Nobody could see her face. Bert sat on one side, and Claudia on the other. Jodie was next to Claudia, Sadie next to Bert, and Petra completed the circle, next to Sadie and Jodie. It's better this way, she thought after a moment of disappointment. I wouldn't be able to keep my hands off her, and someone would notice.

She enjoyed the meal. The rare occasions she ate out, she was invariably with Thorsten, and he positively relished the attention. Here she was surrounded by people who wanted to protect her. It was a good feeling. And the conversation was fun. Claudia and Sadie relaxed quite quickly. Sadie was a natural comedian, a devastating mimic, and she had them in stitches imitating people they knew and some they didn't. Tears were running down Juliette's face when she gave them her Andreas Meyer impersonation.

"Now, I know what he reminds me of, when he is disapproving, which is most of the time lately. His mouth purses up and looks like a chicken's arse." They all howled with laughter.

"I can never face him again. What am I going to do?" Juliette wailed. They were so loud that even the discreet diners were looking their way.

She turned. "I'm so sorry. We are disturbing you all. And you have been so kind. No flashing cameras at all. Stand up everyone." They did, and they stood holding each other around the waist. She managed to get Jodie next to her.

"If anyone wants a photo, please feel free." Most people jumped up and stood in front of them clicking frantically. She handed her own phone to the restaurant manager. "I would like one too please." She turned her head slightly to Jodie. Click. "Thanks. Now, we are going to enjoy our dessert."

"I'm so full," groaned Jodie who had returned to her chair.

"I'm amazed you could get anything down after this morning." Sadie waved her dessertspoon. "First, she wouldn't wake up and I had to pound on her door. Then she emerged, looking like she'd been working out all night, and when we got to the buffet, she was like a cloud of locusts, devouring everything on offer."

"I was hungry, but I have to admit it took hours to digest. Listen, you two, I am definitely not going to the buffet tomorrow morning. I'll order a light room service, and I'm going to sleep in, so please nobody hammer on my door, because I don't intend to answer it."

She's such a clever girl. Juliette pressed her legs together as she felt her excitement growing.

"But I love the idea of going for a walk along the Alster. Shall we meet at twelve in the lobby? Petra has already said yes. Juliette and Bert would you like to come with us?" Bert nodded.

Juliette hesitated, prepared to say no, her go-to reaction whenever it was suggested she go out among people.

"Yeah, why not. You are all there to protect me, and I'll dress down. Is everyone ready here?"

They all nodded, and there was no suggestion to go to the bar.

"I'm going to surf a thousand channels. I didn't know such hotel rooms existed. I've already photographed it from all angles and sent it to my folks."

"And I'm going to spend hours under the fantastic shower, spoiling myself with the beauty products."

Bert looked at Jodie and quirked his eyebrows.

"I'm going to fall onto a luxurious mattress and dozens of soft cushions and dream of someone very special."

Sadie laughed. "She really has a thing for Tom, the record producer." She looked at Juliette, "Shit, sorry I didn't mean to tread on any toes. She's only fantasising. She knows she doesn't stand a chance."

"That's fortunate," smirked Bert, "because Arabella has finished the lyrics. She's sent them to me. I think we can go back into the studio in ten days' time. He'll be there waiting."

"How wonderful!" Juliette clapped her hands. Her eyes were shining. She convinced Sadie and Claudia. Jodie hid a grin and tried not to look at Bert. Juliette Simon was a fine actress.

***

Juliette was standing next to the door as the soft knock came. She opened it, pulled Jodie in and slammed her against it. "So, you're going to be dreaming of Tom, are you? Grrrrr."

Jodie walked her back to the large bed. "Let's see how soft the mattress is. Mmmm, very soft, but not as soft as this skin on your neck." She nuzzled gently.

"Careful. Don't forget Petra's eagle eye."

"I promised I would mark you one day, but not tonight. I have other plans." They gently undressed each other, secure in the knowledge they had about twelve hours stretching in front of them.

"Let's shower."

They soaped each other, until Juliette took Jodie against the shower wall.

"I owed you that."

They rubbed each other dry. Juliette lifted the blow drier and quickly dried Jodie's hair. "My Puschelkopf. It's so easy for you."

"Let me." Jodie took the drier and gently rubbed her hair until it was dry. There was little point in styling it until tomorrow morning. Then she knelt on the soft bathmat, opened Juliette's legs and with the drier on low speed and warm air, blew across her sex.

"Oh, my god, that is so good." She gripped Jodie's hair, as the warm air was played back and forth, each time it reached her clit, she drew in a breath.

"It's a useless machine. You're still very wet and getting wetter." She put the drier to one side, pulled her folds apart and slid the tip of her tongue up and down. As she reached the swollen clit, Juliette whimpered. "Stay there, right there. I'm coming…"

She shuddered and held Jodie against her.

They fell into the bed. Jodie pulled her into a spoon position and held her tight. Juliette played with her fingers.

"Thank you for trimming your nails by the way."

"I'm so sorry I hurt you that time. It only takes me ten minutes to put on false ones, and actually it's much easier in day-to-day life, and more hygienic. And I don't have to worry about breaking one, which is a constant thought when I'm dancing."

After a while, they both slept. Juliette woke Jodie later by stroking the inside of her thighs, and they climaxed together. Later, Jodie gave her an orgasm so powerful it had her biting into her pillow to smother her scream.

This time, Juliette had set her alarm shortly before room service delivered breakfast. She threw on a robe and shut the door to the bedroom.

"A Sunday brunch as ordered, Madam." His eyes betrayed no surprise at the loaded trolley, but he did glance at the bedroom door. She gave him a hard stare, and a large tip. She wasn't worried. This hotel could not afford indiscretion, and anyway there was nothing to see.

"Sex definitely gives me an appetite. It's a good thing we are going out for a long walk."

After breakfast, they had another hour before Jodie had to sneak back to her room. She would be fully dressed and clutching a breakfast roll. As long as she was safely clear of Juliette's suite, she could say she was going outside to feed the swans. But they now had time for another round and were happily sated by the time Jodie cautiously left the room. Juliette tidied the bed and made it look as if only one person had slept in it. They would think she had drowned in the shower, the number of wet towels there were, but with luck, they wouldn't think anything at all when they cleaned her room. Other than that she liked to shower.

***

She dressed in simple skinny jeans and a floppy sweatshirt and tied her hair up in a scarf. Her leather jacket was rather too expensive, but she had nothing else with her. With unassuming sneakers on her feet, she waited a moment for the others to arrive. Nobody looked at her. Bliss.

It was crisply cold outside, and they walked fast to keep warm. Again, Juliette had fun. Some of her muscles ached, but it was a good pain. Jodie looked adorable in her old duffle coat, with a beanie on her head. She wanted desperately to link arms, but Bert got in first, so they walked together, trying to keep in step. They saw a coffee shop in the distance and ran to see who would get there first. Jodie, with her long legs, won easily.

She looked sheepish. "I did track at school."

"That's pretty obvious. What exactly?"

"Hurdles." Juliette stifled a moan at the thought of those spread legs flying over the obstacles. She could picture the tight shorts and her pudenda stretching the material.

They had fucked three hours ago, and she was already panting for the next bout. They drank a delicious hot coffee and walked back. She knew she had to be sensible and rest before the show. And it might be tempting fate for Jodie to be wandering around the corridors in daylight. They were all rosy cheeked and yawning from the cold air when they got back into the lobby.

"That was great. Thank you for the invitation. Now, I need my bed, and I think it would do everyone good. The rehearsal will be longer because we have an orchestra. See you all down here at six."

It was fortunate she set her alarm, because as soon as her head hit the freshly changed pillows, she fell into a deep sleep. She looked at herself in the mirror. Her eyes sparkled and she looked really well. She called Petra.

"I'm running late, I slept like a log, and I'm not even going to attempt to do anything with my hair. You'll have everything necessary with you?"

"No problem. I'm in the lobby with Jodie, but no one else is here yet. The cars can wait a moment."

The orchestra rehearsal took longer than even she expected. The conductor had no feel at all for the song. She was so grateful Bert was there. She hated the idea of having a diva fit, which would have been necessary. Bert took the man to one side and explained it wasn't Wagner, and they weren't in Bayreuth, and he shouldn't feel he had to impose his will on the singers as he would do there, if of course he was ever invited, which was unlikely. Some of the orchestra members heard and like a game of Chinese whispers, it circulated until they were having difficulties keeping straight faces. From then on, Bert surreptitiously conducted with his shoulders when his hands were playing, and the orchestra followed his lead, ignoring the man waving the overlong white stick.

Juliette went with Petra to be got ready. There was plenty of time, but her hair needed to be washed and styled, which Petra did with great care, telling some of her TV stories to keep her mind busy. Juliette had no opportunity to be nervous. She enjoyed Petra's chatter.

The Hamburg format with its single interviewer was different to the Cologne programme. She knew she would be asked the typical harmless type of question, and she dressed accordingly, in keeping with her customary image. She wore skin-tight black leather trousers, a black leather bustier and a black velvet bolero jacket. Her hair fell loosely onto her shoulders.

The effect on Jodie when she walked into the studio was electric. Luckily, the lighting was low level. Neither Claudia nor Sadie noticed. They were used to Juliette in this type of clothing. She saw Bert glance at Jodie and grin, but by now she knew that Bert guessed correctly what they had been doing at night, and it didn't bother her. He would tell Annette, but she trusted them both implicitly, and if she had to be cynically honest, Bert had too much to lose by being indiscreet.

There was a bigger audience than in Cologne, and some diehard fans managed to get tickets. They held banners with *we love Juliette*, and she thought she recognised a few faces. There were definitely girl couples, and boy couples. The applause at the end was frenetic, and she had unexpectedly to do a meet and greet to satisfy the waiting fans.

She whispered to Bert. "Take the girls back and have a drink in the bar. Petra can come with me in my car." She saw Jodie looking back reluctantly, but she waved her off with a wink.

A good half an hour later, the car drove them back to the hotel. She went into the hotel bar where the team sat around a small table in a dark corner.

"I fancy something I drink once every five years."

The barman came over, bringing a large dish of nuts. "A piña colada please."

"Me too." Sadie bounced in her seat. "It's my national drink after all. My family comes from Puerto Rico. It was created by the bartender in the Hilton Hotel there." So, they all ordered one, except for Bert who made a face and stayed with beer.

Juliette raised her glass, "Thank you all for making this a very pleasant weekend. I had fun and I hope you did, and I am confident we will have sold a lot of records."

Claudia reciprocated, "And thank you, Juliette, for inviting us to stay in these fantastic hotels."

Sadie raised hers, "And if you thought the breakfast buffet was good in Cologne, then you really missed out here, Jodie."

Juliette noticed Jodie's disappointed face. "You know I think I might join you tomorrow morning. I never usually go down to breakfast, but if you can shield me like you did yesterday, then I'm on for it. I have an eight-hundred-kilometre drive ahead of me, so attacking the buffet might be a good idea."

"Why don't you share the driving with Jodie? You do know she is a car freak and has been admiring your Porsche ever since she saw it in the studio parking lot." Bert winked. "I'd offer but I have a lot of work to do getting the music ready for the recording, and I can work well on the train. Would you trust yourself, Jodie?"

She looked at Juliette. "Yes, I think so, but do you really want someone else in the car? I know you like the peace and quiet driving alone."

"I do, yes, but I have to admit the thought of sharing that distance has its attractions. So, it's fine with me if you would like to."

She would find an opportunity to give Bert a big smacking kiss.

"Breakfast at eight thirty then? Good night, everyone."

***

"I thought you weren't coming."

"Sadie stood talking for hours outside my room."

"She doesn't suspect?"

"No way. She is fully convinced my tongue's hanging out for Tom. She was mortified to think she might have caused problems about it with you."

"Talking of your tongue…"

After the first round, they lay in each other's arms.

"I would love us to be joined, you know, down there."

"I don't own a strap on, but I can get one if that's what you want."

"No, I can have that with Thorsten, although thankfully, he seems to have given up on me at last."

Jodie slid down her, re-awaking her nipples as she went. "You are insatiable."

"And you're not? Let me slide a leg under your back."

"That's good." She felt their folds meeting. Jodie reached out and they took each other's hands and started rocking and grinding into each other. Their wetness mingled and Jodie groaned.

"This is a total turn on, but I don't think I can come. Will you fuck me, please?" Jodie disentangled herself and lay on top of her. They looked into each other's eyes, desire flaring in both.

"I need you inside." Jodie entered her and groaned as she felt the warm wetness.

"Lift your knee up under me."

Juliette felt the slipperiness as Jodie moved on her thigh.

"Look who's talking." Then there was no further need for words as they both felt the surge approaching. They exploded together. Juliette reached down and went into Jodie to feel her after waves.

"Oh, Juliette, that was good."

"Better than good." She sighed. "I suppose we should get some sleep. We have over eight hundred kilometres tomorrow, and as you offered, you are going to do your share."

"Just as long as I don't have to drive out of Hamburg. I'll take over as soon as we are on the autobahn, then I can get used to your very large SUV."

"Will you be alright with it?"

"Sure, I drove a truck in the States?"

Juliette moaned appreciatively. "My little dyke, how so?"

"I worked on a farm in my vacations. I had to get out of New York. It's probably my Spanish part. I love green and open space."

"There's so much I want to learn about you. Is Starnberg enough countryside for you?"

"Yes, but we both know that is not going to happen."

Juliette sighed. "No, I suppose it isn't…it's getting very difficult for me to be without you."

Jodie shrugged. "No point in thinking about it, is there?"

"I'm a dreamer, you're a realist."

"I can dream too, but I'd rather not torture myself."

"You find resilience in your songs, don't you?"

"Yes, I do."

***

Jodie left the room at dawn. Juliette dozed fitfully for another hour, then got up, showered and packed. She dressed casually as she had for the walk the day before, but without the headscarf. She put her hair up in a simple ponytail. There was a knock on the door. Petra and Bert stood waiting to escort her down to the breakfast room. She was touched.

There were a few photos, but the other guests left her pretty much alone when they realised that she was in a group. *I could get used to this.* She attacked the buffet as if she hadn't eaten for a month. There was so much to choose from.

When they couldn't fit in another mouthful, they all sat back and groaned.

"Please remind me not to stay in the same hotel with you all if we go out on tour. No amount of working out could get rid of this on a daily basis."

"That would be a shame." Bert looked disappointed.

"Yes, you're right. I feel really good with you guys. We'll manage somehow."

"Are you planning a tour?"

"I think there will be one next year. It's a question of venues, and how big they can be. Andreas is investigating, although he keeps making me doubt we can go for the really large ones. He's convinced I'm losing my public."

"Don't you think…?"

"Bert, I know what you are going to say. I will have to kick loose, but I admit, I'm scared to go it alone. He has been with me from the beginning. We are sort of wired together."

"You're leaving him so far behind he is already a distant dot on the horizon. He will only hold you back." There was much hilarity as Sadie contorted her face into her Andreas Meyer impersonation.

"I'll face the problem after the New Year show transmits." Her phone pinged. "Talk of the devil. Sadie, I hope for your sake, this corner doesn't have CCTV." It was a text: * *'How could you leave me* at number three in the charts. Congratulations.'

"We've reached number three."

"It'll be up to one by the end of the week." Bert grinned.

They said their goodbyes, with much hugging. Juliette drove out of the garage and continued behind the wheel for the first hundred kilometres, before they had to refuel.

"Can you do it? I don't feel like being photographed looking like this. Here's my card. My pin is 2299."

"You trust me with your pin?"

"I trust you with a lot more than my pin."

Jodie took over and drove around the parked trucks twice before she had the feel of the vehicle. She was a good driver, and Juliette relaxed enough to doze for an hour. She woke and smiled.

"As I said, trust. You look good driving. Hot as hell." She admired Jodie's strong pianist fingers on the wheel and her long legs in the well of the car.

She was sorry when after seven hours solid driving, they reached the now bare chestnut tree.

"Thank you for the best three days I can remember." She kissed her gently. There were people out walking, and the white Porsche was too noticeable. Jodie jumped out and grabbed her bag. She walked with long strides down the street. Juliette watched her and sighed. *Dare I admit what I know is true? Shall I tell her?*

***

There was very loud music coming from the basement as she let herself in. She called down.

"Any chance you can help me with my luggage?" There was no reply, and shouting was not good for her vocal cords. She made two trips and got everything inside. The lift did have its uses, even now, and she loaded her two heavy cases into it, wheeling them into her bedroom and dressing room. She unpacked, doing her best to tamp down her anger. She hated suitcases standing around. She made a pile of clothes to be dry-cleaned, then went over to the dresser to brush her hair. She lovingly picked up the little monkey and kissed it, before returning downstairs and going into the kitchen. She prepared a tuna salad, enough for two. The music had been turned off, so she called down.

"Thorsten, are you hungry?"

He came up, freshly showered and clean-shaven. He looked better than he had done for weeks.

"Hi, you're back."

"Um…I am. I'm not a fever dream. You look good."

"You do too. Did everything go well?"

"It did. I thought you might have watched."

"I was out…with some mates."

She shrugged. Up until now, he had always either been with her or watching from home.

"You want to talk about anything."

"No, not now."

He cut himself a large slice of bread to eat with his salad.

"Want some?"

"No, never again. I ate a buffet breakfast in the hotel this morning."

"You never do that."

"Bert and Petra and the girls were all staying in the same hotel. They were very protective. It was nice actually."

"That's good. So, you don't need me all the time?"

"I never did. I thought you liked all the attention?"

"I get a bit fed up standing three steps behind you, if you must know. The worst is being asked to photograph you together with some of those freaks who follow you around."

"You think I enjoy it? Just remember it pays for your car, and you're not quite cheap lifestyle."

She wanted to bite her tongue. She had never rubbed his face in it before.

"We'll have to do something about it then, won't we?" He hissed. "I'm going out."

"Thorsten, I'm sorry. I'm tired, and I needed help with my luggage, but you didn't hear me, and it pissed me off having to carry it all myself. It's an eight-hundred-kilometre drive from Hamburg, you know." She was speaking to his retreating back. She loaded the dishwasher and went up to her room. She was tired. Exhausted. Three nights with very little sleep now caught up with her. She took out her smart phone and found the photo from the restaurant. She made a copy, edited it, and cut out everyone except herself and Jodie. She enlarged it. The look in her eyes as she gazed at Jodie expressed only one thing. *Love.* She hoped nobody else had snapped the same moment. It was a giveaway.

***

Juliette sagged into the chair in her music room. She was so drained, she thought she would fall asleep, but that was not on the cards, and she forced herself to sit up straight. She had to learn the English texts before going back into the studio the following day. She did know them quite well, but the perfectionist Juliette required the words to be fully memorised if she was to be free to interpret spontaneously. She would have the music and lyrics in front of her, but it was only for emergencies.

The last ten work days had been twelve hours long, or longer. She was either in Munich at fittings, meetings or interviews, or team members for the New Year show came down to Starnberg. It was doubtful as to whether this was less strenuous, as she had to feed and water them. Anyone else would have got in caterers, but Juliette's Italian upbringing prohibited that. And actually, she could rustle up a simple pasta dish without a great deal of effort. The few minutes alone in the kitchen helped to ground her.

She was fascinated by the design technique chosen for the show. It was fiendishly expensive, but it saved on physically having to build scenery, and gave almost infinite possibilities to change the background setting. There was a massive back wall onto which a hundred LED monitor panels were mounted. They constantly changed the picture, giving a 3-D effect, which was thrilling to watch. The design team had to create or photograph the multitude of images to be used. Juliette wanted to see and approve everything.

She barely saw Thorsten. The director of her video called to offer him a week's work. She gave him Thorsten's number and asked him not to mention that she knew about it. He was behaving like a spoilt brat, but after the last run-in she didn't want to repeat her mistake about calling him a kept man, dependant on her even for carrying a film cable around. When it came to the divorce, and by now she knew it would, she wanted an amicable separation, with as little publicity as possible.

Much more of a problem was that she had not seen Jodie. They texted and telephoned, but Jodie was shy on the phone, so it wasn't entirely satisfactory. She wanted to see her, smell her and feel her silky skin.

The following day in the studio she would, even if they got no chance to be alone. With a renewed burst of energy, she concentrated on her texts.

She was early at the session and walked in eagerly, hoping Jodie might be there. She wasn't, but some of the orchestra members were tuning.

"Sorry about this, ladies and gentlemen. Having to do the numbers again, I mean."

"It's no problem," called a cellist. "We get paid for something we don't need to practise. Bring on this kind of work. Anytime." The string players tapped their bows on the music stands.

Jodie, Claudia and Sadie arrived.

"Are you three now inseparable?" She blurted it out without thinking and hoped nobody would notice the hint of jealousy in her voice.

"We've been working at my place. Jodie is a slave driver about the pronunciation." Sadie made a face.

"I never thought of that. She could have helped me too." Juliette could have kicked herself. She spoke almost accent free English, but nobody would have queried Jodie coaching her, and they could have spent time together.

"I thought Arabella was doing that. Not that you need any help."

"Another time." She gave her a meaningful glance.

"Sure."

They recorded the first song, corrected it, and laid down a complete version of the second one. The orchestra took a break. Juliette and Bert listened, and Bert went back into the studio to make a few changes to the orchestration.

Through the glass, Juliette watched Jodie. She wore dark brown leather jeans and a rose-pink sweatshirt. She fought back the urge to go into the studio, push her up against the wall and take her. She swallowed hard.

"I agree with you. I told you. If I was straight…"

"Tom!" She looked at him in horror. "Did Bert say something? I'll kill him. I trusted him."

"Bert has not said anything at all. But I have eyes. Juliette, how many of your albums have I worked on?"

"All of them."

"Exactly. I think I know you a little. And I've never seen you so happy or looking so well."

"But I'm exhausted."

"I can see that, but you exude something indefinable. As if you are at peace with yourself at last."

She snorted. "I'm anything but, I can assure you. I have no idea how I'm going to handle the situation. It's killing me having to keep her hidden. It's not fair on her either. We can hardly ever be together."

"Does Thorsten know?"

"No! I rarely see him. I'm sure he has someone else. But that doesn't mean I can be with her. You know what it would do to my career."

"At this moment in time, I agree. But if I'm not mistaken, you're gradually pulling away from the girl-next-door image. I watched the Cologne talk show."

"That's more than my husband did."

"You were forced into answering about acting, but I presume it's at the back of your mind."

"That sentence just slipped out without me thinking about it."

"But it's in your subconscious."

"I guess it is."

The orchestra started drifting in from the break.

"Juliette, I'm here if you ever need me. I can partner you, if Thorsten takes to the hills. I'm the kind of guy you go for, at least as far as looks are concerned. The rest I presume neither you nor I want anyway."

She leaned over and kissed him gently on the mouth. Sadie's face was a picture. A weight fell from her shoulders. Maybe, there was a way out after all.

***

* 'You looked good enough to eat. And that's exactly what I want to do to you.'

* 'What about that kiss with Tom? Sadie is trying to console me. My *heartbreak* is testing my acting abilities to the full.'

* 'Tom has guessed about us. But I trust him. I was saying thank you.'

* 'I suppose I have to believe you.'

She sent back a jealousy emoji.

* 'PS please wear the same outfit tomorrow.'

They finished the seven songs, and the orchestra clapped their approval.

"Jodie, do you have an hour? I would like to go through our duet together with Bert."

"No problem."

Everybody left except for Tom who stayed to watch and listen. He was impressed.

"You have something to say. It's an original sound. Do you want to make a demo? I would be happy to record it for you."

"That would be fantastic. But..."

"Don't even think about it. Tom and I will take care of that side. Please...don't argue. Now...I'm terribly hungry. As we are two men and two women, and the chances are nobody would find it a suspicious combination," she rolled her eyes, "do you think we could get something to eat together?"

"You got the taste for public eating in Hamburg, I see."

"There are six people who know about us, and you are two of them. I would love to take my…girlfriend…my lover…out to a restaurant, and it's only possible if you come with us."

Bert raised his eyebrows.

"Tom guessed, which I don't mind at all. It worries me a bit that he guessed so easily, but then as he rightly says; we have known each other for a long time. Any suggestions where we can go? Tom, you know the area best."

"There is a good Italian about three kilometres from here. Follow my car. It's possible to park as well."

As soon as they were driving, Juliette pushed her hand into Jodie's leather covered crotch. "For two whole days, I've been waiting to do that. You drive me insane in that outfit."

"Don't you need to keep both hands on the wheel?"

"No. My fingers need warming."

The restaurant was charming and as they were early it was almost empty. No one recognised her at first, and Juliette relaxed enough to hold hands with Jodie under the tablecloth.

They ordered, Juliette naturally in her mother tongue which prompted the owner to ask questions, which she dodged. The room filled gradually and eventually she was spotted. She knew photos were being taken. The owner came back with a large visitors' book for her to sign.

They left soon afterwards, and Jodie climbed into the Porsche. Instead of going in her direction, Juliette waited until Tom and Bert had driven off, then went back the way they had come, to the deserted parking lot of the studio. She drove into the furthest corner.

"Let's get in the back."

Juliette was wearing a skirt and boots, and she straddled Jodie, kissing her wildly, and pushing her hands under her sweatshirt, where she roughly unhooked her bra. She kneaded her breasts.

"I can't wait any longer," she breathed into her mouth. Her hands went down to pop the jeans button and pull down the zip. They were too tight. She balanced on her knees and Jodie lifted her hips and slid them down past her butt. Then she ground into her, while Jodie flicked her nipples under her tight shirt.

"I'm so wet. Please, Jodie."

Their hands clashed together as each pulled aside the other's thong and entered.

"Oh yes, you are." They both thrust hard, Juliette coordinated her hand movements as she bore down on Jodie's hand. All the time they kissed, their tongues dancing. It didn't take long. They came within seconds of each other, their pulsing in sync. Juliette collapsed against Jodie's shoulder.

"The windows have steamed up."

"Are you surprised?" Juliette giggled. "I'm regressing in time. I never did this is my teenage years. I'm a so-called super star and I'm fucking in the back of a car."

"At least, it's a Porsche."

They held on to each other convulsed in laughter.

"We had better make ourselves decent. This is about the most idiotic thing I've ever done in my life."

They climbed over the front seats, not wanting to get out of the car in case somebody was watching from the road. Luckily it was quiet, and they drove away without seeing a person or another car.

"Just drive me to a tram. I'm not sure how often the white car should be seen under that tree."

"I suppose you're right. I hate this secrecy."

"I know, but you saw the cameras this evening in the restaurant. That was such a lovely gesture, to take me out to dinner. And…and…you called me your girlfriend…and your lover."

"For the six people who know, that's what you are, and I'm so proud to be able to call you that."

"Here, you can stop here."

"Goodnight, my darling."

***

Thorsten was now regularly spending nights away from home, but she never knew when he might be back, so she dared not have Jodie over. Juliette buried herself in work, and when she wasn't, she exercised. She was fitter than she had ever been in her life. She looked at the muscles in her arms, and her abs. She had better stop. There was a danger she would start to look like a body builder, and she found that neither attractive, nor did it fit with her image.

The choreographer of her choice was hired for the show, and she fully intended to have her own input in the dance numbers, so they met and worked together in a studio. It was too early to bring in the dancers. The TV company would never pay for them a month ahead of the taping of a show, but she and Silvie had the routines more or less worked out by the end of November. They also staged the two musical segments themselves, without the input from a stage director. *Buenos Aires* from *Evita* would be the most taxing and would take all her strength to both sing and dance it live. She spoke to Bert. They decided she would lay down a vocal track during the rehearsal, so that segments could be dubbed in if she was too breathless from the vigorous dancing.

She also worked with him on the orchestrations of some of the dance music. She explained the sound she heard in her head, and he played it to her on the synthesizer and transcribed it into the orchestral parts.

She allowed Jamie to design her costumes. This was a risk. He was her stylist, not a professional designer, but she had always noticed his flair. Andreas was against it. He wanted her to work with the designers who had always done her clothes. She put her foot down and insisted. It was another nail in the coffin of their relationship. Sometimes at night, alone in her huge house, and sleepless, she despaired. Two of her most important relationships were capsizing. Did she have the strength to do without Andreas and Thorsten? She spoke to her mother, who calmed her down and promised to come up to stay over the Christmas period.

And she spoke to Jodie who understood, never tried to judge her or to make decisions for her but was a quiet bulwark of support. Juliette knew she was in love for the first time in her life, but she held her tongue. She didn't feel it was right for her to make a declaration to the woman she had to keep hidden.

She always looked at the photo of them together before she went to sleep and kissed the little monkey which lay on her night table, next to her pillow.

***

The venue for the taping of the New Year show was the giant conference arena in Munich. Normally, she was thrilled to be so close to home, but she wished it could have been somewhere further away where she might have been able to steal a night with Jodie in a hotel.

Five days before rehearsals were due to begin, she drove over to the centre with Andreas. The huge space teemed with carpenters, who were building the ramp into the arena, and constructing the lift on which she would make her first entrance. The floor was covered with long aluminium girders, on which hundreds of computer-controlled lights were being fixed, before being winched up to the ceiling. Giant screens were placed all around the arena. The words of the songs would be beamed onto them, as well as her introductory texts as she would be her own compere. This was a new idea; one she had thrown out casually at a TV meeting but which was taken up enthusiastically. She hoped the idea wouldn't backfire. She did have some experience. She had successfully compered some award ceremonies over the course of her career. After inspecting everything and talking to the lighting chief, she motioned to Andreas she was ready. She was more nervous leaving than when she arrived, knowing the responsibility rested to ninety per cent on her shoulders. As they walked out of the huge dock doors, all around her was chaos.

To her great surprise, the work was complete when she arrived on the set for the first rehearsal day with the dancers. She had worked hard with them for three days in a studio on the outskirts of Munich. She could already feel pain in her lower back, which was not a good sign. She called her manager.

"Andreas, I need a physiotherapist in the break. Could you send one here please?"

"Have you been overdoing it again?"

"Probably, but it can't be helped. You know my biggest competitor is myself. I have to top last year's show."

"I know, Juliette. Please be careful." This was something he could understand, and the solicitude in his voice was genuine. *He isn't all bad.*

She returned to the arena and stepped into the rosin box to make her shoes less slippery. It was a hazard during the filming. The surfaces were high gloss for the cameras. They wouldn't be able to use rosin, but their shoes would be specially treated. For now, they were making a mess of the gleaming surfaces leaving powder and scuff marks all over it, but it would be cleaned regularly all the way through the two days of filming. She rehearsed the numbers again and again. Martina, the physiotherapist, massaged her in the break, which helped. She checked her over thoroughly.

"No damage…yet…but be careful. I'll be here again at the end of the day. Next week, I've been booked to be here permanently. Until the shows are over."

She was grateful to Andreas for thinking ahead, and she relaxed a little.

The next morning, Thorsten offered to come with her and to drive. The cameras would be in position, and that's what interested him. She was quite glad not to have to fight her way through the morning rush hour alone. She relaxed into her heated seat, which she turned up to maximum to ease her back and went through the choreography in her head. As they stopped at a traffic light near the centre of the city and she saw Thorsten looking around and tapping his fingers on the steering wheel, she wondered if he was searching for someone. She was tempted to ask him where he was when he didn't come home at night, but then decided against it. There would have to be a confrontation, but she did not have the energy until the show was over.

Martina was waiting, so she had a half hour's massage before slowly easing into her standard warm up to prevent injury. The dance troupe were doing a so-called *bar* in one of the corridors, and she joined them to complete the warming up exercises.

They spent the day going through all the numbers. While the troupe worked on their two solo dances, she went back to her dressing room and texted Jodie:

* 'Tomorrow can't come soon enough. I can hardly wait to see you again.'
* 'Are you taking care of yourself? What do you want me to wear?'
* 'How about your leathers again. You know what they do to me.'
* 'Your wish is my command.'

Thorsten walked into her dressing room and saw her smiling at her smartphone. She turned it off and put it away.

"Are you sure you don't have another guy?"

"I'm quite sure, Thorsten. There is definitely no new man in my life. What about you? Do you have a new woman?"

"No, I don't." She looked at him. She was sure he wasn't lying. She wondered what he was doing and where he was spending so much time. *Is he gay too?* She coughed to hide the laugh, which threatened to erupt at the thought of Thorsten in the arms of a boy.

"Remember, we have the obligatory kiss at the end of the show." At least he looked better than he had last time, had lost quite a lot of weight, and his paunch was no longer visible.

"I've been rehearsing it."

What is that supposed to mean? But she was called back to the arena before she could ask, and then forgot about it.

Thorsten drove again the next morning. Bert and the backing singers were scheduled to rehearse. She was on tenterhooks, but with Thorsten hanging around, schooled herself not to show a reaction. It was difficult. Jodie had some new subtle highlights in her hair. Her leather jeans clung to her hips and legs and were taught across her crotch. The V-necked sweater fitted tightly over her breasts, showing a tantalising glimpse of cleavage. She wore heeled ankle boots, which made her taller. Juliette was wearing sneakers and she knew she would have to look up to her if they got close, which her body was crying out to do.

She walked over to Bert and kissed him on both cheeks, then to the girls and did the same. She inhaled Jodie's scent, which held a hint of lemon and coconut.

They walked over to their position and were fitted with their mikes.

Thorsten came over to her. "Jodie's like Eliza Doolittle. What a transformation. I mean she was always hot, but now she's steaming."

"Wait till you hear her sing."

"It's not her voice I'm interested in."

Juliette was tempted to hit him but clenched her fist instead. "So predictable, Thorsten."

"Any red-blooded guy would have the same reaction."

"She's not available."

"How so?"

Shit! "Sadie says she's madly in love with someone."

"Ah, well. Not that I could do anything anyway. Juliette Simon's backing singers are forbidden territory."

"Yes, they most definitely are."

The dancers had the morning and afternoon off, so it was only Juliette's musical numbers which were rehearsed. She was careful with her voice, and only sang quietly or marked, which meant she sang an octave lower than the key in which the song was written. But where she would stand and move to and from and where she made her entrances and exits, she rehearsed for the cameras. When it came to the duet with Jodie, she did sing with full voice, so that the sound technicians could balance the voices. Jodie's voice was much louder than her own. "Don't hold back, Jodie," came the voice from the control van outside. "We'll balance you over the mikes." Juliette leant across the grand piano, and they locked eyes as they sang. Bert, Sadie and Claudia applauded loudly. Jodie's colleagues were totally supportive and not in the least jealous. Neither of them had the talent for a solo career and neither was hungry for one.

Thorsten came over and whispered in Juliette's ear. "That was hot. If she was a man, you wouldn't be able to keep your hands off her."

"But she isn't," she snapped. *If only you knew where my fingers have been.*

They stopped for a dinner break and Juliette had another massage. The dancers came back for the evening session, along with the musical star who would perform the role of the Angel of Death in the musical *Elisabeth*. Claudia and Sadie left, as they were no longer needed. Jodie stayed to sing her number in *Evita*.

During the massage, there was a knock on her door. "Who is it?"

"It's me… Jodie."

"Come in, darl…" She bit her tongue.

"I just brought you a coffee and a sandwich. I didn't know if you have your own."

"Thanks. You're right. I didn't have time this morning. Sit and keep me company." She turned her head. Martina had covered her back with a sheet. "Don't mind Jodie."

Jodie eyed her back naked down to her hips and swallowed hard. Juliette winked and spread her legs a little under the sheet. Jodie turned her head, blushing, only to look into the make-up mirrors where her reflection could be seen. She turned back in confusion. Juliette supressed a giggle.

Martina looked at Jodie. "I was watching the rehearsal. I hope that was alright? You have a terrific voice."

"Thank you."

"Yes, she has. I predict a great career, which is why I invited her onto my show before she becomes too big a star."

Jodie snorted and blushed again. "Don't be ridiculous."

The physiotherapist finished and left the room. Juliette slipped into her dance clothes. Jodie's eyes darkened as she watched.

"Give me my sandwich. I realise I'm starving. And the coffee smells wonderful."

She moved to sit next to Jodie and nuzzled her neck. "You smell even better."

"Juliette, be careful. Anybody could come in. Thorsten…"

"Spoilsport." She moved back slightly and attacked her sandwich. The door opened and Thorsten came in.

"Jodie brought me something to eat."

He looked guilty. "Sorry, I could have done that. Do you need anything else?"

"No, it's enough, I'm fine."

"See you out there." Jodie left.

"I've been meaning to tell you. You know I had a week's work on a new music video?"

"You did tell me on one of the few occasions you were at home." The jibe slipped out, but thankfully he ignored it.

"They want to give me a six-month contract. To see how it goes. With a possible extension."

"Thorsten, that is great news." She was genuinely thrilled for him.

"Yeah, well, with the dancing not going so well, I think I can imagine going into film full time." *And you will have a steady job when we divorce.* She didn't say that.

"When will you start?"

"Top of the year."

"That's brilliant." She was called to the arena.

"I'm going to shadow one of the cameramen." He was excited. She kissed his cheek, and they left with their arms around each other's waists. Her guilty conscience just took a leap backwards.

The evening rehearsal was brutal. She sat back with a bottle of water and a towel around her sweating neck, to watch Jodie sing her simple song, which she did without any problems. She only had to sit on a suitcase for the number.

"You are so lucky," she called out, as she got back into position for *Buenos Aires.* Jodie grinned and gave her a thumbs-up sign and took a seat in the arena to watch.

They worked until nearly midnight.

"Jodie, are we going your way?" Thorsten asked as they left.

"I don't know."

"Come on, jump in. You shouldn't be on public transport this late."

It wasn't really out of their way from this location, Juliette knew full well.

"I'll programme the address." Jodie went white and put her hand up to her mouth, but Juliette looked relaxed. Thankfully, she had deleted the address the first time she drove her home and hadn't needed it since. Thorsten occasionally drove the Porsche.

A man in Jodie's road walking a dog looked curiously at the car, but Thorsten didn't react. It was not unusual.

Jodie leapt out and they drove home to Starnberg. Juliette crashed into her bed without bothering to shower. She knew tomorrow would be even worse.

***

In fact, it wasn't. Bert had already rehearsed alone with the orchestra and the conductor. As he had done the show the previous year, he knew Juliette and there were no musical hiccups. She had to cope with some egos among her guest artists but could relax during the times they sang their numbers.

When Marie Nyman and Arabella Cooper arrived, they were the centre of attention. Marie was glowing. Under her flowing shirt, nobody would guess about her condition. The way she and Arabella looked at each other made Juliette envious. She led them onto the stage and when they saw Jodie, they embraced her fiercely. Thorsten looked on surprised and when Juliette jumped down from the stage, he wandered over to her. "How do the dykes know Jodie so well?"

"Will you please stop calling them that? You won't get sympathy from anybody if you're overheard. They are adored. Just look at people watching them."

Everyone in the arena had big smiles on their faces.

"Ok, but how do they know Jodie."

"Through Bert." She prayed Thorsten would not check with Bert before she could warn him.

Marie asked for a high bar stool, which she perched on while singing. She sang the old Springfield number *All I see is you*, with luscious orchestral accompaniment and a big sound from the backing singers.

Still standing next to Thorsten, Juliette sighed. "How does she make that sound so easy? Those high phrases at the end are a killer."

Marie called out to her. "As you have stolen our song, we have to do a new one, again written by Bert and Arabella. It's a duet called *Forever*."

Some people watching had tears in their eyes at the end of the beautiful ballad, in which they clearly expressed their love for one another.

Arabella waved over to her. "Ok, Juliette, let's do your duet with Marie. I'll just play this time." There was no mistaking the natural authority of a successful conductor. Some members of the orchestra watched her open-mouthed. The bass player came over to join them, and Marie and Juliette sang *Mockingbird*.

"For the taping, everyone must be onstage at the end, but you can go now if you want to."

"Has Jodie done her songs yet?"

"She's up next, because we have the grand piano in position. You won't follow each other in the show itself, but it saves manpower if we rehearse them together. Jodie's numbers are taping on the first day. Yours on the second."

"We want to stay and hear her now."

Jodie came over, looking nervous. Juliette squeezed her arm.

"I'll be fine tomorrow. It's just now, for the first time with the orchestra."

She sat down, was a little tentative at first, but then found her courage, and her confidence.

"Wow!" could be heard around the arena. Claudia and Sadie yowled their enthusiasm. They looked like two mother hens, proud of their chick.

When all the acts had rehearsed, only the two musical segments were left. Juliette had a break and a massage. As she lay on her sofa for a moment trying to relax, Thorsten came in.

"Mind if I take a taxi and go?"

"Of course not."

"See you tomorrow then. I'll probably be late coming in, if at all. You don't need me until Friday anyway. In fact, I'll skip tomorrow altogether if that's alright? You can drive yourself in, I presume."

"Of course. You'll miss the fans when I arrive."

"It'll be quite enough on Friday."

She lay pondering after he had gone. She was too exhausted to even think about sex, but wouldn't it be wonderful just to wake up with Jodie instead of alone in her cold bed. She was nervous and needed to be comforted. She picked up her phone. * 'Please come home with me tonight. Would you?'

Jodie was waiting by the Porsche.

"Are you sure?"

"Darling, I am too exhausted for sex, but I just want to curl up with you. Thorsten told me he won't be home. And quite frankly…no, I don't mean that. It would not be a good idea if he knew. He's not to be trusted to keep his mouth shut. Let's just go home now."

"Let me drive."

"Would you. Bliss. I'm zonked."

The house was in darkness when they arrived. Jodie helped her up to her room and undressed her. She led her into the shower and soaped her clean.

"Mmm, I want to, but I'm too tired."

"Shhhh, let me dry you." She helped her into an outsize flannel pyjama top and took a sweatshirt for herself. She hugged her and manoeuvred them into a spoon position, and Juliette fell asleep immediately.

She woke briefly as the dawn began to lighten the curtains and snuggled deeper into Jodie. Yes, exactly. She needed this so much. Then she slept again. The alarm shrilled at eight.

"That was the best sleep ever. Today is the day. Well, the first of two days. Kiss me, then I'll make you breakfast."

"Morning breath?"

"You always smell sweet. Come here." They kissed softly, then faster, until Juliette moved away. "Too dangerous. I'm not worried about my energy level, but I am worried about my back. I hope it's going to hold up. Let's get going so that I can have a massage before it all starts."

It was Jodie who scrambled some eggs and made toast for them both. "You had better take one of my sweatshirts. If you go back in the same clothes, it might look odd." She found a large enough one. Jodie looked good enough to eat. She felt the familiar surge and wriggled her hips.

"Enough of thoughts like that. We must go."

"Just drop me near the U Bahn, up by the Centre. I'll take it for the last few stops."

"Good idea. I hadn't really thought that part through."

She arrived at the Conference Centre alone. As expected, there were fans waiting, but not too many as it was just after ten thirty, and the taping wouldn't begin until three o'clock. She signed and posed. Some of the other guests began to arrive, and they were included in the fan worship. Jodie slipped past unnoticed, brushing against her as she went in.

The physiotherapist was waiting. Juliette groaned as Martina pushed deeply into her aching muscles. "You must take at least a week off after this."

"Don't worry. I intend to. My mother will be coming to take care of me. I'll be a zombie until Christmas."

She did her warmup exercises and joined the dancers for the *bar*. The massage had helped a lot. She wandered into the arena to soak in the atmosphere and tried out the lift again. Then she went back to her dressing room. Jamie brought in all the costumes she would change into during the course of the show. There were five per day, not including the musical costumes. Petra was waiting. She would do her make-up and hair, but there was a wig specialist for the *Evita* wig, as well as for the huge and heavy *Sissi* wig for *Elisabeth*.

There was no time now to be nervous. Over the relay system, she heard the audience arriving in the arena. There would be about five thousand. Most of them were seated in the tiers on three sides above the stage, but a few hundred stood in the well of the arena. It was these who were picked up by the cameras, and they accordingly dressed flamboyantly and carried banners and balloons. They paid a lot of money for the privilege of standing for upwards of eight hours. Her back twinged at the thought.

It was time. She waited under the stage. The sound technician checked her ear monitors and her battery pack for the third time and handed her the golden microphone.

There were monitors under the stage, and she could see the orchestra and next to them the backing singers. They wore sparkly black halter-tops and elegantly cut black slacks. Jodie's highlights shimmered under the lights. She suddenly stiffened as if she knew she was being watched, and staring straight into a camera whose red light was probably blinking, she gave a little thumbs-up sign. Juliette smiled. Then she got her signal and crossed herself. Some catholic habits never died. She balanced herself on the lift as it went up, none too smoothly, and she was greeted by an overwhelming wall of sound.

Everything went according to plan for the next three hours, including the inevitable factored in hiccups. Irritatingly, most of the guests wanted to repeat their numbers, but it at least gave her time to change her costumes in comparative peace. Two of the dance numbers were repeated when dancers slipped on the glossy floor, and in one number, half the fireballs didn't work, which looked particularly silly, made the dancers laugh, and caused a half hour delay while they were fixed.

There was an hour break so that the five thousand fans could be fed and watered. The old hands brought their own provisions to avoid standing in a queue for fifty-five minutes.

The second half began with Vivienne, one of her rivals. She had decided on a more traditional folksy song and wore a sexy variation of a dirndl. Juliette was interested as to how it would go over with the public as Andreas was always telling her that was what they wanted from her. She changed into a costume, which hinted at the dirndl cut and showed a great deal of cleavage, and sang a duet with Viv. It was also a rather folksier number, a return to her roots. As she suspected, the applause was the most muted up until that point in the show. It wasn't embarrassing, and there were pockets of cheering from the tiers, but she thought of the satisfaction her conversation with Andreas in the New Year would give her. *Yeah! She was right.*

Another guest followed and she changed into her tux outfit, complete with bow tie, but with only a white waistcoat and no shirt. Her hair was loose on her shoulders. Jamie patted her butt.

"Hot," he breathed.

She sang a big ballad with her backing singers. At the end, she went over and finished the song standing next to them. When the applause ended, she took Jodie by the hand, and walked with her to where the grand piano stood waiting.

"Ladies and gentlemen, I very much wanted to introduce a new talent this year in my show. Well, to my great surprise, I didn't have to look far. This young lady joined my backing group earlier in the year. We got off to a bumpy start. She nearly broke my neck when I fell over her, and then fused the sound system, but I listened to her voice as she sang, and I heard something very special. And not only has she a voice, but she also writes her own songs and accompanies herself. Please welcome, Jodie Sanchez. I think you will be as blown away as I am."

Jodie sat down, moved the microphone nearer, and began. A ripple went through the crowd. The applause was massive after the first song and deafening after the second.

Juliette came back on. She had been watching off camera.

"Did I promise too much?"

"No," they roared.

"And the good news is you will hear her again later, and the even better news is that Jodie has written a duet for us to sing together."

As she had done during the rehearsal, Juliette leant across the piano, and they sang looking into each other's eyes. There was a long moment of silence at the end, and then tumultuous applause. A number of the audience were moved to tears. Juliette fought not to join them. She took several deep breaths.

Jodie went back to her place with Sadie and Claudia. A rock band took over, and Juliette went to her dressing room to prepare for *Elisabeth*. Her first costume was a diaphanous robe, and her hair was loose on her shoulders. This time she did the announcement off camera and the musical star jumped onstage for his number with the dancers. She then joined him for their two duets, one of which would be cut in at the end. There had to be a pause for her to change into the *Sissi* costume, made famous by Romy Schneider in the films of that name. The wig weighed a ton and was pinned securely. She groaned. "Add my neck to the parts of my body that'll never be the same."

Petra took her arm and supported the weight of the wig until she reached her entrance. She walked on for the last number of the day and sang the lengthy *Ich gehör nur mir.* She sang it perfectly, for which she was more than grateful. She could feel the weariness creeping up, despite the adrenalin coursing through her.

When she got back into the dressing room, she could barely move. Petra and the wig specialist removed all the hair, and she cautiously rubbed her neck muscles. She could feel a tension headache announcing its presence.

Andreas came in.

"Everything went very smoothly I thought. A most successful first day. Well done. Where's Thorsten?"

"He's coming tomorrow."

Bert came to congratulate her and saw immediately how exhausted she was.

"Andreas don't make her do meet and greet, or you might have to do the show yourself tomorrow. Bring the car down the ramp."

"But Thorsten's not here."

"I'll get Jodie. She can drive the car. You have the Porsche, I imagine. She can take you home."

"What? Jodie? Why?"

"Andreas, please just help Juliette now. Give me your keys. I'll call you from the ramp when the car is there. OK?"

She nodded. "Andreas, I need to get changed. Do you mind?"

He left and Petra and Jamie helped her get ready. Her phone pinged. * 'We are ready and waiting.'

Jamie helped her down to the loading bay. Jodie waited with the car.

"This is really selfish, Bert. Jodie should be meeting her fans. There will be masses waiting for her."

"There will be plenty of other opportunities for that. I don't think Jodie has a problem."

"Of course not."

"Thanks so much."

Juliette nearly fell asleep on the way down to Starnberg. Only her aching back kept her awake. At least, the headache receded. Lights were on in the house.

"Typical."

"Thorsten, I'm home. Jodie had to drive me. My back is killing me. She'll sleep over tonight and drive me back tomorrow morning. You can drive yourself later in the day, can't you?"

"Sure, of course, hi, Jodie. Did it go well?"

"Very." She deliberately didn't mention Jodie's triumph. "I'll take Jodie up to her room, then I'm going to crash. The goddam lift will have paid for itself tonight."

They went up to the second floor in the lift, and into one of the guest rooms.

"I'm sorry. You know where I would much rather you slept, but he is in the room next to mine. We can't risk it."

"Nothing is as important as that you get a good night's sleep and wake up feeling better tomorrow morning."

"I know. I'm going to take a strong muscle relaxant, and some pain meds. Please make sure I'm awake by eight thirty. We have to go in early again. I will need at least an hour and a half massage. Kiss me." Jodie supported her back.

"My darling, you were wonderful. You do know that, don't you?"

"Thanks for making it possible. But it doesn't matter at the moment. You do."

Juliette took the stairs down to her bedroom wincing. A very hot shower helped a little, and the painkillers kicked in fast. She slept a dreamless sleep and overslept. Jodie woke her with a steaming cup of coffee. "Any better?"

She stretched gingerly. "Yes, not too bad, I think. Is Thorsten up?"

"I don't think so. I'll be in the kitchen."

The coffee and another hot shower made her feel a lot better. She fixed her hair and make-up and went downstairs. She heard voices in the kitchen. Thorsten was sitting on a bar stool watching Jodie frying eggs and bacon.

"We should keep her around."

"Fat chance. After her success yesterday, Claudia and Sadie will be looking for a new colleague." She felt a jolt of unhappiness as she realised this was probably going to be true. In her mind, she had been thinking of Jodie being with her on tour, but she doubted if it would happen.

"That's great."

They ate breakfast, and it was Jodie who stacked the dishwasher. *Thorsten really is a useless lump.*

"We must go."

"The only advantage to this back of mine is that today you can drive me directly to the centre. The ramp again please. I'll do the meet and greet tonight, I promise."

"Can I then take the car quickly to my apartment? I really need a change of clothes."

"You look just gorgeous the way you are, but of course. Come back soon."

Jodie drove the car back to the allocated parking space, after changing and packing another outfit just in case. She had to go to the artist's entrance to get in, and some of the crowd recognised her, and started clapping. She spent over half an hour with signing and selfies, which was a new experience and rather pleasant. She wasn't in a rush as she had only the backing numbers and the *Evita* solo, which was easy for her to sing, and would be taped at the end of the show.

Juliette was on the massage table for a long time.

Martina pursed her lips. "How many dance numbers do you have today?"

"Luckily, only two and then *Buenos Aires* right at the end. We did most of them yesterday."

"You will be alright. Just. But it will be a close thing."

"I hope everyone stays on their feet today. The two repeats were the killer yesterday."

"I'll give you another treatment in the dinner break. And I'll be here right up until the end. I'm sorry about last night. I should have been there to help you with your neck. Nobody told me about the wig, and I thought it was safe to leave, after the last dance routine."

About half the audience was the same, but there were many new faces especially around the walkway in the arena. Juliette's first costume was a denim outfit. A short skirt, waistcoat and high boots. She stood on the lift with the sound technicians fussing around her, trying to zone in. She was tired, but when she saw Jodie in the monitor, her adrenalin kicked in. She felt her energy come back as the lift went up and she was again met with the wall of sound. She sang an old hit, then another, and introduced the next two artists. Then it was her other rival Sabine's turn. She had selected a less folksy number than Vivienne had, and even danced a very simple choreography with the dancers. Very simple. She couldn't compete with Juliette on that front. Her applause was generous. They sang a duet, and a band came on to perform two numbers with full lighting and smoke effects, while Juliette changed into a simple outfit of white jeans and a wide blouse, taken in at the waist. It was Jamie's idea to match her with Marie Nyman. But first she quietened the public down for *How could you leave me.* It had been at number one in the charts for over a month, and most of the standees were mouthing the words along with her.

"That number was written by my favourite composer and long-time musical companion Bert Schmidt." Bert stood up from behind his piano and was greeted with enthusiasm.

"Unlikely, as it might seem, the lyrics were written by one of the most up and coming classical conductors of our times. It gives me great pleasure to introduce my friends and near neighbours, Arabella Cooper and the one and only great operatic soprano, Marie Nyman."

They took up their positions on the stage, Marie half sitting on her bar stool. Jamie had designed her a short, tight leather skirt and a flowing silk blouse. She wore stilettos and her long, elegant legs took any attention away from the upper body. Arabella stayed true to her gothic style, although with her increasing fame as a conductor, she was toning down the kohl around her eyes. She had on skinny black designer jeans and a silver waistcoat with arm bangles. Elegant stilettos completed the outfit. Her layered jet-black hair and stunning blue eyes made it difficult not to look at her face. She had film star looks.

Marie sang *All I see is you*, again nailing the difficult end to perfection. They sang *Forever* in a totally different style, softly and gazing into each other's eyes. There was utter silence from the five thousand in the audience.

Juliette wiped a small tear away as she joined them. She was a little lost for words. Arabella noticed it and leaned into her microphone.

"And now for something completely different, people. You know that Cooper-Nyman can rock, don't you?"

"Yeees," the audience shouted back. The bass player joined them, and Juliette and Marie launched into *Mocking Bird*. Juliette sang the melody while Marie improvised around her. The applause was never ending. The audience was jumping and screaming.

Juliette had to go straight into a dance number, which went without mishap, and it was time for the break. She had a thorough massage. Her back was holding up, but she called the TV director to come to her.

"It's going great, Juliette. Only a quarter left."

"Yes, I know. Sorry about the summons. Look, I'm happy, but worried about my back and *Buenos Aires*. I want to change the order. You can switch it back during editing. Let me do *Don't cry for me Argentina* with costume and wig first. Then I'll change while Jodie sings her solo and come back for the dance number. Then I only have an easy costume, but no wig change before the last number and the sign off. And please keep the tape running during *Buenos Aires* in case I run out of breath." They had recorded it during the rehearsals. The vocals alone, without her running around dancing the strenuous routine.

"Ok, it'll take some organising at such short notice, but the audience will just have to be patient and wait for you between numbers. The LED walls make it possible. They were a great idea."

Thorsten arrived before the end of the break. He had taken care with his appearance and looked well rested and handsome. Juliette, who felt completely hollowed out resisted an eye roll.

"Everything good?" *As if you care*. She left it better unsaid.

The last quarter began with the German chart topper, followed by the last folk singer, with whom she sang another duet. Then she had her last up-tempo number to sing and dance together with the troupe. She slipped slightly on the last turn, and her dance partner's lift at the end was agony, but she managed to not show it on her face, although she was sweating profusely.

At the end of the applause, she made a joke of it with the audience.

"Phew…that hurt." She looked up into the air. "You're not going to make me do that again, are you?" The audience laughed.

"No, we have it covered. Let's just have the dancers do the number alone, and we can edit," said the disembodied voice of the TV director.

She tried not to limp as she went off for the change into Eva Peron's costume and wig. She caught Jodie's eye. She looked worried, but Juliette smiled at her bravely.

Martina sprayed her back with an anaesthetic cold spray, which numbed the pain.

"I don't like using this on you."

"I know, but it's an emergency, and I assure you, after this, I'm resting completely."

After her transformation into the Eva Peron white dress and matching wig, she was again helped to the bottom of the lift. The introduction to *Don't cry for me Argentina* began and the lift went up. She had only to stand and sing. The

LED wall had a spectacular montage of the balcony on which Eva Peron made her famous speech. She was winched down again at the end and changed quickly into a simple dress. Her hair was restyled and fell around her shoulders. She could hear Jodie singing beautifully. Sabine had kindly volunteered to join Claudia and Sadie during the *Evita* section to balance the sound required. To Juliette's surprise, Jodie asked for a repeat. It wasn't necessary, but Juliette knew she was doing it to give her more time to recover.

Taking a deep breath, she took her position with the dancers for *Buenos Aires*. In her ear monitors, she heard the countdown for the tape. She had only to synchronise. As long as she did it well, the audience wouldn't know. And there would be few close ups. The dance sequence was too wild. The orchestra and backing singers played along, with their microphones turned off.

She put all her energy into the dance and thought it was going to be alright, until right at the end she felt a searing pain in her left knee. The injured one. She managed the last few steps and she and the dancers threw their arms in the air. For a moment, she thought she was going to black out, then she felt Thorsten's strong arms around her, and he leaned in to kiss her. She had never been so glad to see him. The audience went crazy, and he helped her off the stage.

She collapsed into her dressing room chair.

"I can't move. But I have to finish. More cold spray, and the strongest, fastest working pain medication you have please. My knee has gone as well."

Jamie and Petra changed her as gently as possible into her last costume, an elegant short black dress with high boots. Tears streamed down her face as they pulled up the boot on her left leg.

In the arena, the director was talking to the public, and introducing each guest act to take their final applause. It gave her valuable minutes. She heard the loudest roars for Jodie, Arabella and Marie, and she smiled and dried her tears. Petra fixed her face and put her hair up into a simple chignon. The cold spray had made her so numb it was difficult to walk, but with each step she became more confident and was barely limping when she got back to the stage. She started to feel a little disembodied as the strong painkiller began to work. She summoned the last of her energy, burst through her pain barrier and walked on for her number, one of her most famous hits, and fortunately a ballad. Her voice at least was holding up well. At the end, she joined the line-up of stars, standing in the middle between Jodie and Arabella. Their strong arms held her up. She squeezed Jodie's waist. Golden glitter came down on them and hundreds of white balloons fell from the arena ceiling onto the public below. She held up her hand to quieten them.

"Happy New Year, everyone. May the next one fulfil all your dreams, hopes and wishes." She forced herself not to look at Jodie. "Goodnight!"

The dancers came out with trays of champagne and everyone on stage lifted their glasses as the gold glitter continued to rain down. *It's over!*

Thorsten came onstage again, and he and Jodie helped her back to her dressing room.

Andreas was waiting.

"You still have to meet and greet. We'll restrict it to an hour. The tables are set up. You can sit."

She looked at him with hatred. "And then? My knee has gone. I can't possibly drive."

"Thorsten is here."

"I drove in myself. I have my own car. I didn't anticipate this happening."

"But you have to leave together. It's not possible for you to drive off in separate cars."

"I told you, Andreas, I can't drive anyway."

"If Thorsten doesn't mind, I can drive his car back, while he drives the Porsche."

"Jodie, you are a life saver."

Thorsten and Jodie exchanged keys.

"Now, get out everybody, I have to change."

She thanked Martina and promised to keep her informed about her recovery progress. She kissed Petra and Jamie and limped out of the door. Thorsten was waiting to help her to the large foyer where it looked as if half the audience were waiting. She slipped into a chair and started signing as quickly as possible.

"No photos please tonight." Andreas stopped them. At least, he could do that for her.

Some of the other guests were also signing. She couldn't see Arabella and Marie, but that was fully understandable considering Marie's condition. She saw that Jodie had a large group around her, and she smiled.

Andreas did a good job of making sure the fans left as soon as they had their autograph, and gradually the crowd thinned.

"Another ten minutes and you will get them all. We won't have to send anyone away." She was in a daze and her hand ached from signing, although the pain medication probably helped that as well. *Be thankful for small mercies.*

Jodie and Thorsten disappeared. Andreas helped her up and she had to lean against him. Her knee was swelling rapidly.

"You'll have to take the weight on my left side." They moved slowly towards the entrance. There were still dozens of fans waiting to see her leave. Thorsten came to meet her and lifted her up to carry her to the car. She played up the scene and put her arms around his neck, her head nestled against his shoulder. The fans screamed. He put her gently into the passenger seat. There was no sign of Jodie for which she was grateful. The embrace would have hurt her, even if it was just acting.

"I hadn't planned on being home tonight. I have a job tomorrow morning early and I want to stay with a mate tonight."

"You can go as soon as we get home."

"Will you be alright alone?"

"I'll ask Jodie to stay over again until my mother arrives tomorrow afternoon."

"If that's alright."

"I'm sure she won't mind. Her bed upstairs is still made up."

The rest of the drive went by in silence. Jodie was waiting next to Thorsten's BMW.

"Thorsten wants to disappear again. Could you stay with me until my mother arrives?"

"Of course, I can." She took her bag out of Thorsten's car.

"You'll have to carry me again, at least as far as the lift. I can't put any weight on my knee."

They got her into her bedroom, and she sat on the edge of the bed.

"Shall I help you undress before I go?"

"No need. Jodie can help me." She bent her head to hide the smallest of smiles.

"I hope you feel better in the morning."

"Bye."

He left, looking a little bit conscience stricken. They waited until he clumped down the stairs.

"Come here." Juliette pulled her down and kissed her, her tongue exploring Jodie's mouth gently. "Why aren't I the least bit upset that my husband is cheating on me? I suppose this answers my question." She kissed her again, and pushed her hands under Jodie's sweater, stroking her breast, and bringing the nipple to life.

"Juliette, the pain killer is going to wear off and you will be in agony. I think it would be a good idea to get you showered and lying down before it happens. You can have another pill to sleep, but I don't think you can risk another with that strength."

"Right as always. You have such an old head on your young shoulders."

"I'm not sure that's a compliment, but I'll take it as one." She laughed. "Let me help you."

The designer sweatshirt and bra were the easy part. Juliette shivered slightly and wrapped her arms around her chest.

"The cold will make it worse. Can you lie back on the bed, and I'll slip the jeans over your legs."

"Please be my guest. I can't feel much in my left leg, except that my knee must look like a grapefruit." It did. As Jodie slipped her thong down, she saw Juliette's folds were glistening with arousal. She swallowed hard.

"Yes, I know. I'm still very much alive." Jodie took off her own clothes, and Juliette squirmed. Very slowly and gently, she was helped into the bathroom, onto the toilet, and under the hot shower. "Hold onto the armature." Jodie soaped her carefully and washed all the gunge out of her hair, then quickly soaped and rinsed herself. She turned off the shower and towelled Juliette dry, then helped her out of the shower so that she could support herself on the washbasin. She dried her hair, quickly blew dry her own, and walked her back onto the bed. She pulled a big shirt over her head, and another one over herself. Then she drew back the covers and helped her to lie down with her head on the pillow. "What do you think? Can I risk it? Staying here I mean."

"You are not going anywhere. Lie down immediately."

She pulled the covers up over both of them and pushed herself into Juliette's back.

"You wake me if you need another painkiller."

"You are the best painkiller anybody could wish for."

They slept. At four o'clock, Juliette woke, her back and knee throbbing. She tried to stifle a groan, but Jodie was awake instantly.

"I won't be a second." She fetched the pill and some water, and Juliette swallowed them.

She softly massaged her back, and the warmth helped. "Come back and spoon, and let's try to sleep again." Gradually the pill took effect, and they slept.

In the morning, she woke, again in pain, but it was not quite so brutal.

"It'll all be ok. I just need to rest now and let the muscles and tendons heal."

"What time does your mother get here?"

"Sometime this afternoon."

She picked up her phone. "Ciao Mama. Are you already on your way? …Good, then drive carefully please. I've got some muscle problems after the show, so I can't move much for a few days…There's someone with me until you arrive…No, Thorsten's working…See you in about six hours…Ci vediamo dopo." She ended the call.

"You can go if you have something to do. I'm sorry I can't drive you. Wait…I know. Why don't you take my old car? She's in need of a run again. Yes, it's a perfect idea."

"Maybe, but I'm not leaving you until your mother arrives. I'll help you into the bathroom now, and then I'll make some breakfast." They both used the toilet, the intimacy not a problem for either of them. When Juliette was back in her bed but sitting up with her back against a bank of cushions, Jodie went downstairs and scrambled eggs and made toast, coffee, muesli and fruit salad. She loaded a tray and took everything back up, using the lift.

"Oooh. And I'm really hungry." She had been answering calls, and sending texts, assuring Andreas and Bert, Petra and Jamie, and Janina, her secretary, the TV director and several others that she was alright and being looked after, though she only told Bert it was Jodie with her. The phone pinged again. "Look. How sweet. It's Marie asking if I need anything." She answered that Jodie was with her until her mother arrived.

"Now, I'm really full. I think I can sleep again."

"I'll just go down to the supermarket. The fridge is almost empty."

"I know. I was going to go shopping with my mother. She loves German markets. Just get some pasta and vegetables and stuff. Take my card again. Here."

"That's not necessary."

"I insist. You know the pin." She yawned and snuggled down into the bed.

"Don't be long."

Jodie took the elderly VW to get used to driving it. It was in perfect condition and a lot easier to park than the Porsche. Juliette was still asleep when she got back in. She sat in a chair and watched her. Could she love her more than she did at this moment? She didn't think so.

Juliette woke, and needed the bathroom again, and another painkiller. Jodie massaged her back gently, stripped, and got back into bed.

"I want you so much. Please straddle my face." Jodie hesitated. "Please." She did as she was told. Juliette nibbled up her thighs, and she was soon gushing, and whimpering. She could feel Juliette's hips moving, and carefully supporting her own weight on her knees and thighs she leant backwards and slid her fingers up the soaking folds. Juliette bucked and pressed her face into Jodie's sex, licking her, and sucking on her clit. They entered each other simultaneously and it did not take long before Juliette breathed. "I'm coming, darling." They both thrust deeply, Jodie pressured Juliette's clit with her thumb, and she sucked on Jodie's. They exploded, riding out each other's contractions until they were still. Jodie climbed off her carefully and kissed her gently. Juliette held her face and looked into the beautiful dark brown eyes.

"I love you. And I know I have never loved anybody before. Only you."

"I love you too." They kissed again. Juliette sighed. "You'll have to get dressed. I don't think I can tell my mother just yet, although she won't cry many tears about Thorsten. My parents never liked him. Help me again. I need to wash you off my face, and I think we should open the windows wide."

Jodie packed her things together and took them downstairs. The gate buzzer sounded, and she let Anna-Maria Simon in, going out to meet her and to help her unload her car. They got everything into the lift, and Jodie continued up to the second floor, while Anna-Maria stopped off at the first floor and went into Juliette's room.

"I'm fine, Mama, please don't worry. I need to lie down today and tomorrow, but then I can get up. My knee is swollen, but it's now stabilised, and definitely not getting worse."

Jodie came back into the room. "I've put your things into the middle room, the largest, Signora Simon."

"This is Jodie Sanchez, one of my backing singers, and…my best friend."

Anna-Maria who was a smaller version of her daughter, with the same colour eyes and hair, looked her up and down keenly.

"Call me Anna-Maria please. I've no doubt we will see more of each other. Thank you for looking after my daughter."

"Thank you…Anna-Maria. I'll be off now. I hope you have everything you need in the kitchen for a couple of days until Juliette can shop again."

"Come here." She leaned over the bed, and Juliette brushed her lips with her own, a feather light touch but it went straight to her core. She suppressed a moan. "See you soon, and thanks for everything."

Jodie left the room.

"Do you always kiss your women friends on the lips?"

"Oh, you know how it is in the theatrical world, and I couldn't have done without her over the last three days. Now, tell me about your trip? Was there snow over the Brenner Pass?"

***

Juliette missed Jodie but enjoyed catching up with her mother after so many months of not seeing her. She tried hard not to mention Jodie in every sentence.

Anna-Maria cooked in the luxurious kitchen, and carried a light pasta dish up to the bedroom. They ate together, and the older woman retired to her bedroom for the night. Juliette took another pain killer and waited for it to work. She phoned Jodie and they spoke until she couldn't stop yawning.

"Good night, my darling. Dream about me."

"I will."

By the evening of the following day, Juliette's back was sore, but more from lying down for seventy hours than from muscular damage. She got up carefully and slipped on her baggiest jogging pants and Jodie's sweatshirt. Using the lift, she made her way down to the kitchen where her mother was again cooking.

"You shouldn't be up."

"I have to. You know I can't lie around. All the other muscles, which aren't hurt, are starting to scream at me. I'll lie on the couch with my knee up." She balanced on the breakfast bar. "Mmm, it smells good."

"You miss your mamma's cooking?"

"My darling mamma did teach me some of her tricks, so I don't go entirely hungry, but I am an amateur compared to my mamma."

They ate in the living room. Juliette held the bowl on her chest and lay against the cushions. Her knee throbbed slightly but there was a definite improvement.

"I've held off asking because I thought you would tell me yourself. Where is Thorsten?"

Juliette sighed. "It's over, Mamma. I'm sure he has someone else."

"And you're not tearing his eyes out, or kicking him in the balls?"

She laughed. "Like this? I don't think I could, and anyway I have no desire to. I don't love him at all, and most days, I don't even like him. And I certainly don't hate him. I'm indifferent."

"What are you going to do?"

"Divorce, of course. Let him go to whoever it is. But quietly, without anyone knowing. The publicity would be disastrous. I'm waiting for him to make the first move which will give me an advantage in the proceedings. I'm not stupid. We signed all the papers when we got married, but I know from friends what a good divorce lawyer can achieve. I want to keep my hard-earned money, not share it with Thorsten, who hasn't earned more than a few pennies of his own for over a year."

Anna-Maria was quiet. "Your father and I never liked him."

"I know. I was stupid. I liked his looks, and his name, and the press more or less forced us into it. And, Andreas, of course."

"I don't like Andreas either," she said heatedly.

"I know, Mamma, but he has done very good things for me over the years. I would not be where I am now without Andreas."

Anna-Maria snorted. There was a long pause. Juliette could hear a boat on the lake.

"Juliette, are you in love with someone else?" She met her mother's gaze for as long as she could, before having to look down.

"Yes," she whispered. The atmosphere in the room was thick enough to cut with a breadknife.

"It's Jodie, isn't it?" Juliette practically dropped the bowl she was still clutching, and her back spasmed as she caught it.

"Oww! Mamma, how did you know?"

"Your father suspected a long time ago. You always came back from your Liceo raving about a teacher or another girl. You never had any interest in boys. We thought you might grow out of it, but then we watched you with Leon, and then with Thorsten. Even if you didn't realise it, you were just using them as camouflage to further your career."

"But I had no idea. I never even thought about it. Until…until I met my next-door neighbours. And then…Jodie."

"I saw how you looked at her. You have never before looked at anyone like that. Juliette," she took her daughter's hand, "it's fine with me, and it will be fine with your father. More than fine. He wants to be the only man in your life." She chuckled.

"But the church? It's a mortal sin."

"The church! You think in Italy we don't know about the Curia and their live-in boyfriends. And as for the Popes. You remember the red Prada shoes? *Popessa* we called him."

"I just don't know what to say. I love you both so much."

"Just be happy."

"I want to be. But I can't come out of the closet and admit it. It would be the end of my career. Nowhere in the world does the public for my kind of music accept…accept…homosexuality. There, I've said it. Mamma…I'm gay. But I can't tell anyone."

"I can't help you there. It's your decision. Your father and I, and I'll tell him tonight, won't say a word to anyone until the day you allow us to."

They heard the door opening. Juliette supressed the urge to panic and whispered, "And Thorsten must not know. He's a real homophobe."

He came in, looking the worse for wear.

"That smells good."

Anna-Maria looked at him scathingly. "I'll get you some. Do you want to eat in the kitchen?"

***

* 'We know you have your parents with you, but we are entertaining on Christmas Day, the twenty-fifth. Suzanne and Beth are staying with us. We are going to invite Jodie. Your parents are very welcome. Ours are here too. Can you ditch Thorsten?'

"Thorsten, I'm invited over to Arabella and Marie on the twenty-fifth. You don't want to come too, I imagine?"

"No, thanks very much. What a horrible thought. And you should be careful. It might be catching."

Anna-Maria, who was reading a newspaper, looked at him with her mouth open, but snapped it closed without saying anything.

"I'd like to visit my mate anyway. I might stay for a few days. You don't mind, do you? We'll be together on Christmas Eve, if that's enough?"

"Stay away as long as you like." She kept her voice even.

***

Giuseppe Simon arrived on the twenty-third on the train from Verona. She drove with her mother to the main station in Munich. She stayed outside while her mother went in to collect him. She would like to have gone onto the platform with her, but it wasn't worth getting mobbed for. She didn't want to put her parents in any danger.

The train was uncharacteristically punctual. Her beloved father pulled a heavy case behind him as they approached the car. She got out of the Porsche to help and was recognised. Before her parents were even seated, there was a small crowd. She dealt with it gracefully and accelerated away from the station forecourt.

"Poverina. My darling daughter. I've missed you so much."

"Me too, Papa. But we're going to have a wonderful Christmas."

"The best news, Giuseppe, is that Thorsten will be away after Christmas Eve," Anna-Maria's tone was acidic.

"Mamma!"

"And you will meet Jodie on Christmas Day. She's a lovely girl, quite beautiful to look at, and humble and polite as well."

Her father squeezed her shoulder. "We want you to be happy, cara."

Juliette felt her eyes mist over. She sniffed. "You'll make me crash the car. I love you both so much."

Thorsten occupied himself for hours in the gym the following day. Giuseppe joined him in the basement for a while and enjoyed the heated pool. Juliette and her mother spent most of the day in the kitchen. Anna-Maria felt it her mission to cook vast quantities and varieties of food, which were then frozen. Juliette let her. She loved cooking with her mother, quarrelling occasionally about the use of a particular herb or spice. They chatted together in the Veneto dialect, which meant they could talk freely. Thorsten, even if he could be bothered to listen, wouldn't understand a single word. Not that he had learnt more than a few phrases, despite being married to an Italian. They called Jodie *Gianetta,* just in case. Juliette told her everything about how they met, how talented Jodie was, how she was expecting a huge response to her appearance on the New Year show, even if Jodie was more circumspect, and how she was sure it meant that she would leave the backing group and not be able to tour with her the following year.

They ate at eight, beginning with a delicate calamari pasta, followed by four perfectly cooked salmon trout which her father had fished out of Lake Garda and brought with him. Giuseppe and Thorsten drank a bottle of wine, the lion's share inevitably landing in Thorsten's glass. Juliette didn't want to drink, as it was her last day on painkillers. Anna-Maria only ever sipped on a tiny glass.

As they sat around the open fire in the living room, eyes glazed after eating too much, Thorsten heaved himself to his feet.

"I'll be off then."

"I thought you said you were going tomorrow."

"Yeah, well, I'm sure you are all going to midnight mass. I don't want to sit here on my own."

Juliette's stomach roiled with anger. "Give her my regards, whoever she is."

He stopped in the doorway but didn't turn round. They heard him upstairs in his room, before he came down and shut the main door firmly.

Her mother took her hand. Her father came to the sofa and put his arm around her.

"I will be the happiest man if I don't ever have to see him again."

"You won't." She reached for her phone and texted Jodie: * 'Please stay the night tomorrow after Marie and Arabella's invitation.'

* 'But what about your parents? They are still with you, aren't they?'

* 'They know about us. My mother guessed. They are fine with it. I was saving up to tell you when we meet tomorrow. I love you so much.'

* 'Me too, you too.'

They sat around the fire, nibbling on homemade cookies and sipping Chateau Rieussec, a wildly expensive dessert wine, until it was time to go to midnight mass. Juliette would not have gone on her own, but she knew the pleasure it gave her parents. She dressed in a simple black skirt and sweater, with an old duffle coat on top, and a woollen beanie. She thought of Jodie wearing a similar outfit in Hamburg when they walked down the Alster esplanade together and felt close to her. The church was candlelit, and she hoped she wouldn't be recognised. She wasn't, except for a brief encounter when they walked in. She saw Wiebke Brandt, the Cooper-Nyman's housekeeper, standing in the aisle with a very pretty teenager. The girl's eyes widened, and she blushed attractively. Wiebke put her finger to her lips, and they sat down, leaving Juliette and her parents in peace.

***

They slept late. Juliette not very well. It was her first night without pain medication. *It's a good thing I'm breaking the habit now.* The dreamless sleep she had been enjoying could become addictive, and she knew of too many artists who had gone down that road, never to find a way back.

The invitation was for late lunch, so breakfast in the Simon household that morning was coffee and a small bowl of fruit salad, after which Juliette stepped gingerly into the pool, and swam thirty lengths. It felt so good to exercise again. She didn't have the courage to start working out, but swimming was ideal.

The gate buzzed at one o'clock. Juliette let Jodie in and waited for her to park the car.

They kissed. "I needed that. How has my old car been running?"

"She's lovely to drive, but I'm glad I could bring her back."

"Why? I thought you could go on driving her."

"I worry about my neighbourhood. I don't like leaving her on the street. Better not to. What if she got scratched, or even stolen. I would never forgive myself. She is the love of your life."

No. You are. "Come in and bring your stuff. Take it upstairs and then meet my father."

"Which room?"

"Crazy! Mine of course."

"If you're sure."

"Darling, my parents are more than fine with it, and I'm quite sure they know I'm fucking you senseless."

***

"Papa, this is Jodie. My father, Giuseppe."

"Sei bellissima." He took her hand and kissed it. There was only warmth in his eyes.

"Invero lo è," Anna-Maria kissed her on both cheeks.

Jodie blushed. She spoke no Italian, but Spanish helped her to understand what they said. They reverted to English, which all the Simons spoke very well. Conversation in the neighbouring house would most likely be a mixture of English and German.

They walked over just after two o'clock. A delicious smell enveloped them as Marie opened the front door. She made no attempt to hide her condition and her bump was now evident. Anna-Maria and Juliette handed over the gifts they were carrying. "Vitello tonnato for tomorrow, and two pandoro," the star shaped so-called-golden-breads which Anna-Maria had baked two hours previously and which were still warm.

"Oh, they smell good. I think I've died and gone to heaven." She called over her shoulder. "Bella, can you come here a moment?"

Arabella came out of the kitchen and wiped her hands on a cloth she carried.

"This is my wife, Arabella Cooper. Here, darling, lunch for tomorrow, and something wonderful to eat with coffee later."

Giuseppe and Anna-Maria stared at Arabella.

Marie laughed. "She often gets that reaction. She is beautiful, isn't she?" They nodded. Arabella put her arm tenderly around Marie's waist and stroked her bump. "I'm carrying her children." The Simons looked puzzled.

"They were conceived in Arabella's womb. Come and meet their father." Jodie and Juliette looked at each other and shrugged.

"Fredrik, Mr and Mrs Simon, and their daughter Juliette, and Jodie is her…colleague?"

"Girlfriend," corrected Juliette.

Giuseppe was staring at the tall blonde man with his mouth open. "Fredrik Rasmusson?"

Juliette laughed. "My father Giuseppe is a tennis fanatic. I think you have just made his year, if not his decade."

"My friend, Mats."

"Mats Borg," breathed Giuseppe.

"And here is…" Marie gestured to Suzanne.

"Suzanne Weigl," exclaimed Anna-Maria. Now, it was her turn to stare.

"I'm not sure my parents will ever get over the shock of seeing their crushes together in one room."

"Let's not forget the in-laws." Marie and Arabella's parents were introduced. They were obviously the best of friends.

"There is just one more person for you to meet, but she's busy in the kitchen."

On cue, Beth came in laden with a tray full of slim champagne glasses. Arabella followed with two bottles of Moet. Suzanne moved over to help with the heavy tray.

"This is my wife, Beth," she said proudly, putting a strand of her snow-white hair behind her ear.

"What beautiful people," said Giuseppe before he realised he had spoken. He looked embarrassed, despite everyone laughing kindly.

They sat down in the book-lined dining room to eat. The table was extended to its full length, and it was a bit of a squeeze, but they managed. Juliette and Jodie sat next to each other, with her parents opposite them. Fredrik was next to Giuseppe, Suzanne next to Anna-Maria. Juliette pressed her thigh against Jodie's and occasionally took her hand, once lifting it to kiss it.

Beth and Arabella had cooked two large turkeys with all the necessary fillings and vegetables. They were tender and succulent, and were followed by sorbet and cheese, and as dessert a small portion of white chocolate mousse. Afterwards everyone more or less staggered into the living room and fell into the large sofas or chairs scattered around the huge room.

"Shall I wait awhile with coffee and the pandoro?" The group nodded, too full to speak.

Jodie had been preoccupied for the last couple of minutes. "Could I ask a really personal question?" She looked at Marie, who inclined her head invitingly. "Fredrik is the twin's father? Did I understand correctly?"

"You did. Fredrik is the donor. He is my oldest school friend. We wanted the children to have a Swedish father, because of course they are no blood relation to me in the strictest sense. We were looking for a donor, and Arabella said why were we looking through catalogues when we already knew a beautiful tall blonde Swede."

"And I was flattered and thrilled. I am unlikely to have children of my own." He looked at Mats fondly.

"And will you tell the children?"

Marie answered. "We don't know yet. Fredrik will be their godfather, and we will decide as time goes on. They will grow up speaking Swedish."

Slowly, the group split into smaller conversational units. Giuseppe, Fredrik and Mats talked tennis. Anna-Maria sat in a huddle with the mothers-in-law, Simone and Ulrike. Jodie helped Beth with the clearing up. Arabella, Marie, Juliette and Suzanne talked music. The fathers-in-law Anders and Gareth went for a walk. They had spent time with each other during the summer and shared a love of angling. Giuseppe was torn. He did too, but the lure of tennis talk was too attractive.

"Where does everyone sleep?" Juliette wanted to know. Jodie came back and joined her on a wide sofa.

"Beth and Suzanne in the guest room next to ours, but only until the day after tomorrow."

"I have *Fledermaus* performances in the state opera over New Year."

Arabella kept her voice low. "Good thing they are going. We might get some sleep."

Suzanne looked embarrassed. "You can talk. I distinctly remember the long summer nights." Juliette remembered hearing them too. That was when her whole life began to change.

"Yes, well anyway. My parents stay in the downstairs guest room, where they can't hear anything going on upstairs, and Bella's parents are in the new apartment over the garage. They say it's very comfortable. It will be for the nanny, when we get one. Oh, and Fredrik and Mats are in a hotel in Starnberg. They are here on a skiing holiday, and to watch biathlon."

Beth and Arabella brought in coffee, tea and the pandoro. Everyone ate a piece. Anna-Maria was delighted.

Juliette could see people were tiring. The in-laws were definitely in need of a nap, as where her own parents. She looked at Jodie. *Me too.*

They left, as did Fredrik and Mats, and after the cold air outside made them yawn, Juliette let everyone into the house. "I think we all need to lie down for a couple of hours. We can watch my rival's TV show later, if anyone is interested. I don't think we want to eat much."

***

Juliette pulled off Jodie's high riding boots, which she was wearing over slim jeans.

"Now, let's do a bit of riding ourselves. We don't need a horse."

"I thought you were tired?"

"The night is for sleeping. But we must be quiet." She pulled Jodie's roll neck sweater over her head. "I haven't paid these two beauties nearly enough attention lately." She unhooked her bra and Jodie's breasts tumbled out. She circled them, with her tongue, until the nipples stood up hard.

Jodie was breathing heavily. "What about your knee?"

"I'm underneath today. You can indulge in your fantasies and top me." Jodie undressed her, taking care as she pulled the pantyhose down over the left knee, which was still a little swollen. Then she pushed Juliette backwards and climbed on top of her.

"What have we here? A superstar pillow princess." Juliette squirmed under her. Jodie reached down and gently ran her middle finger up her fold. She brought the finger to her mouth and sucked it lasciviously. Juliette smothered a groan with her hand.

"Mmmm. That tastes good. Oven ready I think."

***

They all watched at least part of the TV show. Then they went back to bed.

"I have just a little thing for you."

"Me too." Jodie went to her bag and took out a rather bulky parcel. Juliette reached into her night table and took out a small package.

"You first."

"No, you."

"Alright, together."

Juliette unpacked a beautiful antique wooden music stand. "Oh wow."

"I noticed you didn't have one in your music room, and I thought it might come in useful."

"My darling, you are a great present giver."

"Oh, Juliette, this is so gorgeous." It was a heavy gold charm bracelet with just one charm hanging from it. Two letter J's entwined.

"You, or I, can add to the charms. As we both have the same initial nobody will ask awkward questions, but we both know what it means."

They made love, slowly and joyfully, and eventually fell asleep, entwined in each other's arms.

It was still dark when the phone rang. It woke them out of deep sleep.

"Shit, I forgot to turn it off, but who the fuck is calling at five o'clock in the morning on a holiday?"

"Better answer it."

Juliette groped sleepily for her smart phone. "Hello, who is that?"

"Juliette, Ms Simon…this is Gerda."

"I don't know a Gerda. I think you must have the wrong number."

"Gerda. I was with Thorsten, before you…you know…stole him from me."

It all came flooding back. She had no idea he was with anyone when they started being together. He only told her afterwards, and even then, made it sound as if he and Gerda were distant history. She found out the truth from some fellow dancers, but by then they were married.

"Gerda, you must believe me, I never knew. I thought he was single."

"If you say so. Anyway, Thorsten and I…we were in a car crash, and he's badly hurt."

"Where is he?"

"Klinik Rechts der Isar." It was the largest hospital in Munich.

"I'm on my way."

"Wait…Juliette, I'm afraid there are reporters waiting."

"Why?"

"Someone in the emergency room must have tipped them off."

"Is he still there?"

"No, he's in intensive care. But they know that too."

"They can't get to him, I hope."

"No, but they will be waiting when you arrive."

"Fuck! Ok, but I am on my way in any case."

She explained everything to Jodie, who had more or less understood while listening.

"I'm coming with you."

"Darling, I wish, but it's too dangerous with all the press waiting. I need you to stay with my parents and explain when they wake up. I'll keep in touch as soon as I get there and tell you everything."

She dressed hastily but had to stop to style her hair and make herself up.

"Fucking press." She called Andreas and explained what had happened.

"I'm on my way in from Starnberg. I need you to get there before me to keep them back when I arrive. Can you do that?"

She didn't doubt him. That was his job, and he was good at it. Fortunately, he lived only a stone's throw away from the clinic.

There was very little traffic and she arrived in under an hour. There was plenty of available parking, and she pulled into a slot just out of sight of the main entrance. Taking a deep breath, she approached the crowd of journalists and photographers. The flashing began immediately. She tried to push through them doing her best to keep a slight but concerned smile on her face. Andreas shoved them out of the way roughly and guided her through the doors. Two doorkeepers kept the press from following.

"Where is he? Andreas, do you know?"

"Yes, follow me."

A doctor met them in ICU. "Mrs De Luca?" Nobody ever called her that, but it was an uncomfortable truth. For the time being.

"How badly is he hurt?"

"Much less than we feared an hour ago. He has a broken arm and jaw and concussion. We were worried about his head, but the scan shows that there is no permanent damage. We will keep him here overnight, but he can go into a normal room tomorrow, and if no complications arise, you can take him home in two or three days."

She shook her head but didn't speak.

"I'll leave you now. His companion in the car is with him. At the end of the corridor, on the right." His tone was even. *He knows though.* Coming towards them were two police officers. They looked at her but didn't stop.

"I'm afraid alcohol was part of the equation."

"I see."

She walked towards the room with Andreas following a step behind her. She looked through the glass. Gerda was holding his hand, and she was enormously pregnant. Juliette reeled. Andreas caught her.

"I'm so sorry, Juliette."

"Andreas, I couldn't give a shit. In fact, it's going to be a blessing in the divorce proceedings, but I don't know how we are going to avoid the most terrible publicity. And that he was drink driving is not going to help."

"Divorce? I thought you were both happy."

"Actually, I am, but it has nothing to do with Thorsten. You believed what you wanted to. Now, you are going to have to earn your money. Andreas, listen to me. I'm serious. His appearance at the end of the New Year show has to go."

"But it's long edited, and ready to roll."

"I am quite aware of that. I don't care what it costs, just make sure it's cut. I'll have to deal with all the other fall-out, but that is just too humiliating. Now, let's speak to him."

They walked into the room. Gerda didn't move or let go of his hand. Thorsten tried to extract it, but he was too weak. Juliette took a chair and sat at the other side of the bed. Andreas stood behind her.

"Congratulations, Thorsten. When is it due?" Gerda shrunk back at her tone. She obviously had not expected Juliette to be so cool or so forthright.

"Six weeks."

"You are a little rat. Why didn't you tell me before? We could have had everything done and you out of my life months ago. We could have smudged some dates, and nobody would have been any the wiser." She looked at Gerda. "Have the press seen you in this condition?"

She nodded. "One did."

"Photographs?"

"No."

"You cannot allow yourself to be photographed."

"Why shouldn't I? I don't care about your reputation." Juliette heard the hate in her voice. It took all her strength not to flinch.

"I understand that. But if you make this any worse than it is, I will ensure that Thorsten doesn't get a penny of the divorce settlement, and let me tell you Gerda, Thorsten will not be very pleased with you." She knew it was an idle threat but was counting on the bluff working. He was too stupid to know otherwise, and Gerda had no idea what was in the marriage settlement.

Thorsten's eyes, like slits under his heavily bandaged face, widened. "Don't worry Juliette, we will do everything we can to keep this under wraps." His voice was muffled and slurred.

"I'll have the divorce papers served as soon as there is an office open somewhere." She stood up. "Andreas, I need to speak to you outside, but then you will stay and make sure Gerda gets out of the hospital unseen. Ditto Thorsten when he is released. If either of you talk to the press, there will be no money.

Capito? Oh, and please give Andreas your new address. Your possessions will be delivered as soon as you are out of hospital."

They left the room and went into a thankfully empty waiting area.

Juliette was shaking. "I'm going to have to tell the truth to them now, outside. It will only be worse if they find out later. Please come with me but let me talk. And then go back and make sure the happy couple are both muzzled."

She went into a cloakroom and fixed her appearance. She wanted to call Jodie but decided to wait. She was entirely focused and wanted to get it out of the way. She walked purposefully to the entrance and took a deep breath.

Smiling she faced the barrage of cameras and recording appliances.

"Ladies and gentlemen, I am deeply flattered to know you care enough about me to come out at dawn on a public holiday." There were a few chuckles.

"Thorsten de Luca has been in a car accident. He is hurt, but he will mend, and is expected to leave the hospital tomorrow." She hoped they would stop hanging around after that. Andreas would ensure that they thought he had checked out.

"Will you collect him yourself?"

"No, I won't be doing that. We have been unofficially separated for many months. We remain friends, but the pressures of our profession have become too great, and we will be divorcing within the year."

"But you are permanently interviewed and photographed together."

"Yes, I'm sorry about that and it's entirely my fault. I lacked the courage to disappoint many of my fans, who have viewed my marriage as a part of my persona. It isn't though, and I will have to disappoint them, and hope they understand and can still support the contribution my music makes in their lives."

"Are other people involved?"

"I'm not prepared to discuss that."

"We understand your husband was drunk."

"I can't answer that because I wasn't there. Perhaps he had imbibed a little too much Christmas cheer." Again, there were a few laughs. "Thank you for taking such an interest. I really must get back to my family who are staying with me for Christmas."

She walked with Andreas to her car and drove away fast. She didn't want to be followed. She knew it was now only a matter of time before they would be parked outside the gates in Starnberg. She called Jodie on the speaker phone.

"Darling. It really couldn't be much worse than it is. He's not badly hurt and will be out of hospital in a couple of days, but his girlfriend is eight months pregnant. I've talked to the press and told them we've been separated for months, which is essentially the truth, but I don't want pictures of her to get into the papers. It makes me look too stupid. Which I do anyway, but I want damage limitation. Somehow, we have to get his stuff out of the house today. The paparazzi are going to get to Starnberg within the next couple of days. They will be watching and waiting for everything and everybody coming in and out. I don't want pictures of a removal van. Sweetheart, what a mess."

"Juliette, I hear you. I'm going to order a transporter right now, in my name. I don't know how much stuff he has, but I have access to a quite large cellar in my building. We can dump everything in there for the time being."

"Jodie, darling. I'll see you soon."

The four of them attacked Thorsten's room and cleared everything out, putting it in large plastic bags for lack of moving boxes.

"It looks as if he has moved stuff out already. Now, it's just a few things from the gym. There are no books for sure." She laughed humourlessly "He hasn't really made much of an impression on my life, has he?"

Giuseppe and Jodie collected the transporter from a hire firm near the station. "What a good thing this is near a skiing area at the height of the season, otherwise they wouldn't be open today."

They loaded it. Juliette took Jodie into her arms. "This is not what I imagined today would be like. We'll take a rain check on what we were doing please. I'm so sorry. I'll call you tonight."

Anna-Maria and Giuseppe came out of the house with a large bag of food. Jodie hugged them both.

Giuseppe held on to her. "Thank you so much for being in my daughter's life. You make her so happy." He had tears in his eyes. She drove off. A little more than an hour later, Juliette saw on the monitor that a car was parked outside the outer gate. The paparazzi had arrived.

***

Juliette called Marie and explained what was happening. She had been so strong up until now but when she heard Marie's sympathetic voice, the tears ran down the side of her nose, and the lump in her throat was agony. "I can't believe it. We had such a wonderful day yesterday. Jodie was going to stay for a few days. My parents love her. My life has never been so good, and now this. And it's going to affect you too. They will be camped out there until they get something to satisfy their piranha appetites. I hope they leave you alone. How can I apologise?"

"Oh, my darling. I'm so sorry. Please don't worry about us. All our guests coming and going will give them something to photograph. Suzanne and Beth have already left, so they won't be bothered."

"Yes, but you haven't announced your pregnancy yet."

"We have been pre-emptive. Bella and I gave an interview last week, which will come out in the New Year. So what, if they get a few pictures of my bulge? I'm not ashamed to be having children. I won't go out much anyway. Bella will get furious with them when she goes to work, which she will from tomorrow onwards. She'll give them a tongue-lashing. But what will you do, when your parents go back?"

"They are going to stay on until the middle of January, in the hopes it will have died down by then. We reckon the worst will be this week, before and after the show. Marie, I want Jodie to come and live with me, but it's impossible until they go away, and even then…"

"I went through the same thing. I told you about it. Don't wait too long. You will have to face it at some time in your life, unless of course you are not convinced of your sexuality."

"Of course, I am. And now that my parents know, and have apparently always known, long before I did, I am totally at peace. But I'm too much of a coward to face my professional world."

"So was I."

"What changed?"

"Like you my husband, in name only incidentally, left me for another woman. But that wasn't the real reason. I existed without the love of my life for a year. And it was not more than an existence. I definitely would not call it living. Gradually I came to see that nothing else mattered, and I found my courage. I am aware there is still smirking behind my back, and sometimes I catch innuendoes, particularly from macho men, but I know that the motivation for those sniggers is either jealousy or their own hidden sexual preferences. But I was met with overwhelming support, and it hasn't hurt my career in the least. I threw away a year of my life. Wasted, completely wasted. So…"

"I'll try. But the folk music world is not the opera world. They are not forgiving."

"Then leave that world behind you. You are already halfway there."

"I know. I just need a little more time."

"Be careful. Jodie is young and incredibly beautiful, although she is too humble to realise it herself. And she is immensely talented. And that talent is going to be picked up on…and not only her talent."

"I know."

***

Juliette forced herself to watch the New Year show, dreading the end. Her parents enthused for the entire three hours. She knew it was good. She knew she was good. Cooper-Nyman and Jodie were fantastic. Even on TV, it was possible to hear the level of the applause being so much greater for them than for the other artists. She watched herself singing the duet. She saw the love in her eyes when she looked at Jodie. Would other people notice too? She saw the pain when she slipped, and the agony she was in during the last number, but her parents said nobody else would, and she believed them. There was an elegant edit at the end of *Buenos Aires*, an away shot to the orchestra where Thorsten had come onto the stage, and helped her off. She sent a text to Andreas, thanking him.

At midnight, her family toasted one other, then went to bed, and she called Jodie. They talked into the night. She didn't want to read the press. Andreas would tell her. Which he did over the next few days. The reviews were a confused and confusing mess. The overwhelmingly positive echo went under in the so-called scandal of her separation from Thorsten. The drink driving charge was made public. In some populist papers, she got the blame for driving her poor husband to alcohol. Andreas pressured Gerda not to visit him and managed to get him out of the hospital unseen. For the moment, her pregnancy was not public knowledge.

Juliette was furious when she was forced to pay the rent on a house on the outskirts of Rosenheim, where Thorsten and Gerda were hiding out under Andreas Meyer's name until the baby was born. The press had almost immediately found out her identity and where she lived. It was not difficult. At the time of their marriage, Gerda sold her story about the poor abandoned girlfriend to a cheap magazine. Now, the same paper was doing a sob story about Thorsten going back to his true love.

***

As expected, Jodie got fantastic press for her appearance, and almost immediately received two invitations to appear on TV magazine programmes. This thrilled Juliette at the same time as it terrified her. She had Marie's warning constantly at the back of her mind.

"I miss you so much," Jodie said quietly during their next call.

"I know. What can I do? There are cars parked outside day and night. As soon as I leave, I'm followed. It is beginning to frighten my parents."

"Perhaps, I can sneak in at night?"

"You would never get past the gates. There is even a boat on the lake that seems to sail back and forth all day long. I see the sun reflected from what I presume are binoculars and long-distance camera lenses. I am so glad I had special glass put into the windows. They can't see into my bedroom or my music room, and downstairs we keep the curtains drawn. I've contacted the police, but they say they can't do anything, unless any of them actually set foot on my property."

"Can I at least visit Marie and Arabella?"

"Even that is too dangerous. You will be recognised from my show. I'm sorry, darling. The way I looked at you during our duet is such a goddam giveaway. If anyone were to watch it again, and you were photographed coming through the security gate they would notice. And the fans do watch the programme over and over again. And they blog. Shit, shit, shit!"

***

Foremost in her mind was the action she had to take as soon as offices opened again for business, and that was to visit a divorce lawyer. She drove into Munich and was followed. Which is why the meeting was held in Andreas's office. The young lawyer from the most prestigious firm in Munich waited for her, having arrived a good hour before she did.

"My name is Lucas Schneider from the firm *von Reichenbach und Fischer*. I apologise on behalf of Frau von Reichenbach that she isn't taking your case personally, but she has too many pending. She has read through the brief and sees no particular difficulties. She recommends me to you to deal with matter."

"Fine. Yes, I think things were tied up properly at the time of my marriage. I am willing to pay the settlement due to my husband, but as the wronged party, I would like to keep those payments to the minimum."

"That is quite understandable, and I will do my best to make sure that happens."

The meeting went on for two hours. She said goodbye to Lucas Schneider, and he slipped out of the rear entrance of the building. She and Andreas sat down to discuss some details about the planned autumn tour.

"What about the album release in the UK and USA?"

"The UK will be releasing at the end of March. The USA is holding it back until the summer. You know how it is out there?"

"Not really, no, but I trust that they have their reasons. What about promotion in the UK?"

"Yes, definitely. You will have to go over."

"It can't be soon enough. I doubt if they are interested in my marital status, especially to an unknown dancer like Thorsten."

"No, you would have to be in a relationship with a star known to them. Talking of stars known and unknown, do you want me to take over the management for Jodie Sanchez?"

She felt her heart thud uncomfortably in her chest. But Andreas didn't look as if he knew something.

"She has an agent as far as I know. One in the States who has a German partnership in Berlin. Anyway, Andreas, why the interest? It's not your kind of music. You make my life hell for trying to sing numbers nowhere near as daring as Jodie's."

"She's going to be big, and I'd like to get in on the ground floor."

"Too late, my friend. Just please help me a little more constructively with my attempt to change my image a few millimetres. Admit it. The new show was a huge hit. My single is still at number one, and the album release next week will almost certainly hit the top spot within three weeks."

"It would get there even quicker if you did a few talk shows."

"We agreed that it's not a good idea. I would be asked the same questions over and over. We want it all to die down, not flare up even more. It's not fun having the paparazzi outside day and night. My parents are leaving at the weekend. I need twenty-four-hour security after that." He picked up his desk phone. "Don't worry. Janina has it all arranged."

"Nobody new on the horizon? Another he-man?"

"Most definitely not another he-man."

She went down to the garage under the offices, which served three adjoining businesses. She drove to the furthest exit and cautiously edged her car out into the road. She saw a paparazzi car waiting at the other entrance. She drove away from the centre, stopping in the corner of a large supermarket car park.

"Jodie, I'm in Munich. I don't think I'm being followed at the moment. Can I come to you?"

"I'm not alone. But you know that park near my apartment? Can we meet there?"

"Yes. I'll park near the chestnut. Go into the middle of the park, and I'll come to you. Try to look as unrecognisable as you can."

Juliette had her eye on the rear mirror the whole way, but she noticed nothing suspicious.

She saw Jodie cross into the park and walk over to some trees in the middle. She rammed her beanie over her hair and put on her long leather coat. Stupid. It was wildly expensive looking. She just hadn't thought this through. They met under the trees.

"My love, my darling. It's so wonderful just to see you. I know we can face time, but you know I hate it, and anyway I'm told it's not a secure method of communication."

"It's not a substitute anyway. I want to see you as you are, the most gorgeous woman, who I love and adore, and not a flat distorted image. So, I prefer just to hear your voice. Juliette, you look tired and stressed."

"I am. I hate to think of my parents leaving."

"You will be safe, won't you?"

"I'll have security from tomorrow. Don't worry."

"I so wish…"

"It wouldn't work anyway. You have your TV things coming up. Your face will be even better known. You can't possibly come and go through the gate. By the way, Andreas was angling to represent you."

"Not if he was the last manager on earth. And I do have those people in Berlin."

"I told him. Darling, I had better go. The longer I stand here, the greater the risk." She looked around. Nobody was watching them. "Kiss me." They hugged each other desperately, frantically exploring each other's mouths. "I want to take you against that tree."

"And I want to be taken against that tree. One day soon, I hope."

"I promise. Can you leave out of the other side of the park, just in case?" They parted. Juliette walked back to her car, keeping her head down as low as possible. She thought she saw a flash as she got into her car but could see only a man playing with some children and a dog. She drove home.

***

Her parents left, having extended their stay for yet another week. Still, the paparazzi waited. She felt more alone than she had ever done in her life. Her security guard pairs came and went in eight-hour shifts. She insisted on one of each sex. She often invited them inside. It was bitterly cold for them in their cars. They occupied the dining room, keeping a constant eye on the gate and the garden. She spent a great deal of time in the gym, and gradually worked up full strength in her back and knee.

Arabella called and invited her over. She slunk over to their house, keeping in the shadow of the hedge. *Perhaps we could cut through the hedge and build a gate.* Juliette wondered if she was going a little crazy.

"I nearly ran over one of the shits this morning. And it wouldn't have been an accident."

Marie grinned at her. She was expanding by the day.

"Are you alright, Marie?"

"Blissful. Well, they are beginning to make me a bit uncomfortable. And they kick all night, but I wouldn't change it for the world. Having said that, Arabella is going to carry the next one."

"Don't try to provoke me, even in jest. We are not going through that process again."

"I was teasing, darling. The twins will be quite enough. I wanted them before I reach forty, and we will achieve that, and then I'm going back to singing. I have a good ten years ahead, fifteen at the most. A female opera singer's life is short."

"I have no intention of doing this in even ten years' time, I can assure you."

"What do you want to do?"

"Act. But it might not work out. No one will take me seriously."

"Bella will have to support us both. Or Jodie."

Juliette sighed. "We had to resort to a ten-minute meeting in the middle of a park."

Marie shifted on the sofa, letting out a soft groan as she tried to get comfortable.

"What you must have gone through on the show with your back problems. I can only begin to empathise. Bella, are you thinking what I'm thinking?"

"I assume so, yes. Listen, we have a tiny apartment near the Gärtnerplatz theatre. You could meet there. I'll give you a set of keys, and I'll get Marie's set to Jodie. That won't be difficult for me."

"Don't you need it yourself?"

"I'm away for ten days."

"What about Marie when you're away? You won't be alone, will you? I can come over regularly, or stay with you, or you stay with me."

"My mother is coming from Cardiff for three weeks. The mothers are doing three week shifts until the due birth date, then they'll both be here."

Arabella rolled her eyes.

"We'll be grateful they are."

"I know. But I'll need my keys back then…at the latest."

She winked. Marie threw a cushion at her.

***

Jodie made the first of her TV appearances. The studio audience loved her. Her short interview was harmless. *Yes, she was a backing singer for Juliette Simon, who had given her the opportunity of a lifetime on the New Year show… And would she continue to work as a backing singer?… For the foreseeable future, yes. Her group backed other singers as well… Juliette Simon was having a creative pause at the moment, and they didn't meet.*

Juliette swirled the dregs in her wine glass and laughed bitterly. "How true."

But if everything went according to plan, they would see each other the following day.

She took her old car out of the garage and accelerated out of the gate. She was out of sight before the paparazzi realised it was her driving it, and nobody was fast enough to follow her. She jumped a set of lights in Starnberg to be sure.

On the outskirts of Munich, she parked in a garage, and changed into an old coat and hat, which completely covered her hair. She wore no make-up. She took a taxi to the Gärtnerplatz. The driver didn't give her a second glance. She wandered down the road, taking care to avoid doing anything to make people notice her, let herself into the little courtyard and hurried up the two flights of stairs to Arabella's apartment. The key wouldn't work at first, and her panic mounted, but then it did. She almost fell into the little living room, which was charmingly decorated. She removed her snow-covered boots. There were fresh flowers on the table, and bottles of red and white wine, with a note. *More white in the fridge, and water. Enjoy.* On the bed were clean towels. She hastily drew the curtains although she doubted anyone could see in. She heard a key in the lock, and Jodie came in cautiously. She kicked off her boots.

Juliette held to her promise, and pushed her against the wall, grinding herself against her centre.

"I can't believe it. And we have all night."

"Then, let's hit the bed."

"I insist on it."

Juliette undressed her slowly, intermittently kissing her lips, and nibbling on her ears. She cupped both her breasts and squeezed them together, letting her own saliva run down the deep cleavage, then sucking it up. That made Jodie squirm.

Juliette slapped her lightly. "Keep still. Patience will be rewarded." She caressed the soft skin on her stomach, which made her own hips buck.

"Mmmm, do you bathe once a week in donkey milk?"

"No, but I Botox my navel."

"Don't make me laugh, I'm serious here. Sit on the edge of the bed."

Juliette knelt in front of her and pushed open her legs slowly. Jodie's sex gleamed. She had to swallow hard. She nipped up her inner thigh and breathed on her folds.

"Juliette, please don't torture me. It's been too long." She leant back on her arms and offered herself. Then she felt a strong tongue stroke up her folds and let out a long groan. She strained her hips up to meet Juliette who circled her clit and sucked it.

"I can't hold back. Go in, please." She entered her with two fingers, which she kept still. Jodie ground her hips against her hand and began to undulate. Her breath was coming in short spurts. Juliette dug her tongue into her clit and sucked the swollen knob. Jodie cried out and her walls pulsed. She fell back against the bed. Juliette climbed on top of her and kissed her deeply. They lay still.

"You are still dressed and it's absolutely not fair."

"Then undress me."

She did, spending a great deal of time on Juliette's collarbone and then her breasts, nibbling and sucking until her nipples were painfully hard. It was a pain she could live with.

She was aching and slippery. She had been even before Jodie arrived. She began to writhe, but Jodie ignored her.

"You tortured me, so…"

"Sadist."

"Now that's not a bad idea." She was flipped and lay on her stomach, her face pressed against the pillow.

"Oh yes, I like that." She lifted her arse to show her appreciation and felt a sharp slap on her buttock. She felt her wetness pool even more.

"Again?"

"Again." The other buttock got it this time, then two more slaps. Her skin was tingling. She grunted. Then a hand stroked her folds and rubbed her clit. She jerked. Jodie entered her. The position helped her fingers to go in deep, and she already felt the wave starting. Jodie lay across her back, and she could feel the hard nipples pressing down on her. Jodie's soft skin soothed Juliette's stinging butt, as she started thrusting hard. Juliette held her breath as the wave engulfed her. Jodie's fingers curled deep inside her, and the tidal wave crashed, the after waves making her twitch uncontrollably.

They lay wrapped in each other's arms, not speaking, until they both closed their eyes and slept for a while.

They woke and lay peacefully watching the darkness descend behind the curtains.

"What am I going to do? The paparazzi are still at the gate. I feel so trapped. The only good thing is that Thorsten's baby is born. Early, but not soon enough. Andreas made sure he didn't go into the private clinic I paid for. I'm sure he was grateful not to be at the birth. I certainly wouldn't want him there. Her mother was with her. They obviously can't go back to her apartment in Munich. Andreas is looking for something new, near her mother. She lives somewhere further north. Nuremberg, I think. Which is a lot better than in Munich. They will move up there and hopefully won't be found. If she keeps her mouth shut, that is. She made it clear through Andreas that I have to give her more money than that disgusting magazine would pay her for an exclusive. After the divorce, I don't care anymore. They are on their own. I won't be blackmailed, whatever the cost. All the trash magazines have come down more in my favour than his. The drink driving charge helped me there. But enough about me. Tell me something positive…please, darling."

"I don't know how positive it is. My American agent wants to arrange a campus tour."

Juliette felt cold. "That's fantastic, darling. Some of those universities have huge concert halls. And it is exactly your target audience."

"I know, but I don't want to leave Europe. I want to stay with you, and continue to back you, and tour with you."

Juliette turned to look at her. "You must not sacrifice your career for me. I'll still be here when you get back. If you want to come back, that is. My album will be released in the States sometime soon. I will probably be over promoting it, if it manages to get into the charts. We can perhaps be together."

"I don't know. I haven't decided. I need more time."

"Of course, you do." Juliette prayed she would make the right decision.

"I'm hungry. Is there anything edible in the fridge?"

"Trust Arabella. Yes, there's gnocchi and parmesan and what looks like a freshly cooked tomato sauce."

"Perfect. Let's eat it."

There were two bathrobes hanging behind the door. "I'm sure they won't mind." They put them on and prepared and ate the food, drinking a good half of a bottle of excellent Montepulciano.

Then they went back to bed and made gentle slow love. In the morning, they made love again, then showered and dressed. Juliette left first, while Jodie tidied the apartment. They agreed not to change the sheets because they wanted to use the apartment again the following week.

When she got back to Starnberg, there were even more cars parked in front of the gates, but she opened them with her fob, and drove through. They didn't dare follow her, as they knew she would call the police immediately. She spent the rest of the day in the gym, swimming, and looking through song suggestions Bert sent her. In spite of all her problems, it was entirely satisfactory not having Thorsten in her house and the thought of meeting Jodie the following week shone like a beacon.

***

"All hell is breaking loose." Andreas woke her the next morning. "Who is it?"

"What are you talking about?"

"I've sent you the link. Read it and call me back."

With trembling fingers, she opened the link to Germany's most disreputable daily paper, the *Blick Zeitung*.

Juliette Simon didn't come home last night. Who is her new lover? There was a picture of her getting into the Porsche in her expensive coat, and another blurry shot of her kissing Jodie under the tree in the park. She felt faint. She pulled the picture up as large as it would go. She was easy to identify because of the coat, but Jodie's face was not clear enough. She could have been a man, especially as she was taller. *What was Juliette Simon doing in the park in a decidedly insalubrious area of Munich?* And so, the speculation continued. Practically every male guest on the New Year show was named as a possible lover, and many others as well. But no women.

It would only be a matter of time before they linked the park to where Jodie had her apartment. It was only five hundred metres away. Trembling, her teeth chattering, she called Andreas.

"Who is he?"

"In this case, I'm not going to tell you, Andreas."

"This is not going to go away."

"Give me time. I'll think of something. For now, no comment to anyone, and I'm not leaving the house."

She sent the link to Jodie and called her. "I don't know what to do. Nobody will recognise you until they make the connection to where you live. Then they'll know."

"They'll never do that. The apartment isn't in my name."

"They are capable of anything. If you leave your apartment, can you go in the other direction, and not pass the park? My guess is they will be staking it out."

The following day, there was a photo of a man with two children. Yes, he had seen the white Porsche several times in the area, usually parked under that chestnut tree. No, he hadn't seen anyone getting in or out. Her secretary called her car dealer, and she sold the Porsche and ordered a slightly smaller Audi hybrid. A black one. The Porsche was collected, but she held off on the delivery of the Audi. Not while there were so many photographers still at the gate.

Jodie called. "I think we should meet again in Munich." They were both now paranoid about hacking and had stopped sending text messages. "Can you get away tomorrow?"

"I'll ask Bert if he can help. Tomorrow evening then."

Bert and Annette arrived the next afternoon in his SUV. They were photographed, and Bert held up a bunch of music so that they could see what he was doing. They waited for three hours until dusk. She left lights on and told the security guard to move around the house as if she was there. She lay flat on the floor of Bert's car with a blanket over her, and they left. The paparazzi did not take too much notice, and they were not followed. The Schmidts dropped her off near the apartment and she let herself in. Jodie was already there, and she jumped up to take Juliette into her arms.

"You look awful."

"I feel it. Let's lie down, and talk. I'm not sure I can manage anything else, but I need to be close to you." They undressed and got under the covers. It was warm, but Juliette was shivering. "I can't eat. That's why I'm so cold."

"Juliette, you are going to have to come out. They won't leave you alone. I'm here for you, and I'll stand beside you, and we'll get through it together."

"I can't, I can't." The tears were rolling down her cheeks.

"Then there is only one solution. I'll have to go. I'll accept the American tour."

"You can't leave me. I can't live without you."

"Maybe…maybe it's only for a while. You said it yourself. Someone is going to spot me, and then it will come out anyway, and without you being able to control it. I have to leave the country."

Juliette clung to her desperately and rubbed her hands all over her body. She thrust her tongue into her mouth, and climbed on top of her, her hips grinding into Jodie's sex. Jodie flipped her. They were frantic for each other. She bit Juliette's neck hard, knowing she would mark her. She cried out. Jodie didn't care. She entered her hard, and Juliette did the same to her. They thrashed around on the bed, panting and moaning until they both climaxed. They lay clutching each other, the tears streaming down their faces.

"I'm going to go now. They want me in Berkeley next week."

"So soon."

"Yes."

"Will I ever see you again?" she whispered.

"Juliette, I don't know. I can't continue skulking around like this. But I love you, and I always will."

"I love you too. Forever."

Jodie shrugged. "That's a long time...for both of us."

Juliette sobbed. Jodie dressed. They clung to each other again, and then she left. Juliette curled up in a ball and sobbed herself into an exhausted sleep.

Almost catatonic the next morning, she tidied the flat and stripped the bedding, putting it into the washing basket. She tried unsuccessfully to do something about her swollen eyes and winced when she touched the bite on her neck. Then she called Bert who collected her. She wore sunglasses so that he couldn't see her eyes. She sat in silence in the rear seat, a scarf wrapped tightly around her neck, until shortly before they reached her home, when she lay down again and covered herself with a blanket. The paparazzi looked into the car keenly, until Bert waved them off angrily, and opened the gate with her fob. He got out and searched the sky for drones. They didn't dare fly onto her property, but a drone with a good camera could see into the drive from the road. It was a new danger. Only when he ascertained the sky was clear, did he help her out of the car, and they hurried inside.

"You had better eat something. You are going to make yourself really ill."

He made toast, which she managed to choke down. The coffee also revived her, and she looked at him.

"Bert, she's going to the States. I can't blame her. I just don't have the courage. But I love her so much."

He pursed his lips but said nothing.

"Life must go on, mustn't it?" Her eyes filled with tears again, but she willed herself to stop. "Since you're here, let's look at the songs you sent me for the new album."

They went up to the music room. She put her music onto Jodie's music stand and caressed it lovingly. Bert began to play.

***

She tracked Jodie's flight on her laptop and spent hours watching as it slowly inched its way across the Atlantic and then across mainland America until it approached San Francisco. She watched nervously until *Plane Landed* came up on the screen and even then, didn't close the lid, waiting for *Baggage in Hall* to flash. She imagined her, coming out into the bright sunlight and being collected and driven to a hotel somewhere near the campus. She wanted to text but didn't. She was the one who had messed up, not Jodie, and she had to let her enjoy what was now about to happen in her life and her career. She was out of it now.

The bruise on her neck was fading, but she clung on to it, pressing her fingernail hard into the wound, hoping it would leave a permanent mark.

She knew Arabella was back, and she phoned and invited them over for the evening.

"I always seem to be sitting in your gorgeous house. You've only been here once."

"Juliette, you look rough." Arabella was nothing if not honest. "And you've lost kilos which you don't even have on you to lose."

"I can't eat much, and I'm exercising a lot. It's the only way I can shut my brain down."

"I did that too, when this one left me. But it didn't make me look any better. So, I stopped."

"What did you do instead?"

"I worked, and if you don't mind me saying…us saying, I think you should get out there again."

"I can't bear the thought of the questions. I don't know what to answer, without lying through my teeth."

"Is there any solution to getting them off your back?"

"Only another relationship. And I can't do that. I want only Jodie. And I've sent her away." She almost choked with the effort not to cry. Her throat ached as she tried to swallow.

"Is there nobody who can help you? A friend you can shack up with. At least get away from here for a while."

"I don't have a lot of friends."

"Fredrik helped when Nick left me. He was a shoulder to cry on, not I hasten to add because of Nick leaving me, but because of my pride. Those sorrowful, mock sympathetic looks were a nightmare. Fredrik was someone beautiful to be photographed with."

Arabella snorted. "Don't remind me of that. I nearly jumped off a high building. You texted me from the States that you couldn't wait to see me again, and three weeks later I had to look at pictures of you hanging on Fredrik's arm looking gooey up at him. How was I to know that I'm butcher than he is?"

"No, you're not, darling. You're about the same."

Juliette laughed in spite of herself. "There might be someone I can ask. He once offered his help if I needed it. I'll have to think about it. He might not agree of course." She stood up. "Enough now. I've made fresh pasta. Come into the kitchen and talk to me while I cook it."

She ate with some appetite for the first time since Jodie's departure. They sat and talked, drinking only water to keep Marie company. She now looked as if she was carrying triplets and moved with difficulty.

"I'm getting very impatient."

"You can't yet. I have a production in Frankfurt, and I can't get back very often. They will have to wait."

"When are they due?"

"March the 17th," they chorused.

"My premiere is on the fifteenth, and after that, if necessary, someone else can conduct a few performances."

After they left, Juliette poured herself a glass of wine and sat brooding in front of the fire. She picked up the phone, put it down again, then held it firmly and called a number.

"Tom…"

***

Tom arrived at the gate, making sure he was photographed as he got out of his car and pressed Juliette's door buzzer. There was a lot of coverage the following day, and even more two days later after they ate a candlelight dinner together at an expensive restaurant in Munich. He collected her and drove her home, then left.

A week later, he stayed overnight, and she gave her first interview.

"We are just taking it very slowly."

"Is he the man in that photograph?"

"No comment," she said looking coy.

For the first time, there were a few less cars at the gate. The news was hot, but there was only so much they could write about her having an affair with her record producer. It must have been disappointing that he wasn't one of the stars they had coupled her with for weeks. Tom was even better looking than Thorsten, because his masculinity was not as overpowering.

An amenable Andreas called her. "I approve. He's favourite son-in-law material for the lady fans. And big brother for the younger ones."

"And the gays?"

There was silence. Andreas coughed.

"He's not, is he?"

"Andreas, you are so naïve. You are incapable of recognising a gay person, are you? Of either sex."

"In our world, I have never needed to."

"You would be very surprised. I have to go. Someone keeps calling my mobile."

It was Arabella. "Juliette, thank goodness. It's Marie. It's started. I'm in Frankfurt, on my way to the airport. The ambulance is on its way." She heard the siren outside. "Her mother will go with her, but I need you to take mine to the clinic. Could you?"

"Of course."

"Thank you." She cut the call.

Juliette grabbed a coat, hurled herself out of the house and ran next door. Marie was being loaded into the ambulance, looking pale and sweaty. "Which clinic?" The driver gawped at her and held out a piece of paper. She scribbled her name. "Where are you taking her?" He looked down at the paper, not believing his eyes. "For fucks sake!"

"The clinic in Starnberg."

She took hold of Simone Cooper and they ran back to her driveway, where she backed her old VW out of the garage. The new Audi would finally be delivered tomorrow. They were able to follow the ambulance once they had forced their way through the paparazzi. She lowered her window. "The police will be on to this, if you don't let us through." They shrank back.

"Phone Arabella, and let her know it's the Starnberg Clinic."

Simone did so. "Yes, I'm on my way to the clinic with Juliette… Everything's alright. Stop panicking. They're only ten days early. It's nothing to worry about…You're boarding in half an hour. That means you should get here at the latest in three hours. I'll let you know what's happening when we get to the hospital."

Simone and Ulrike scrubbed up when they arrived, and after half an hour were allowed into the delivery room. They said goodbye to Juliette, but she told them she would stay. She left a message on Arabella's phone to say the mothers were with Marie, and she should call her about her progress. She was staying in the clinic and would relay messages.

She was not alone in the waiting room, and it was becoming uncomfortable as people stared and whispered. A kind sister saw what was happening and took her into a small private room.

"Thank you so much. You'll let me know all developments. I'm in touch with...her...wife."

"Of course." The nurse smiled warmly. *No censure there.*

She called Tom and told him. If word got out where she was, it would be natural that he knew too.

"Do you want me to join you?"

"Tom, you are so sweet, but no thanks. It's definitely an all-woman thing here. But if everything goes well, we have our next restaurant date tomorrow, and you will stay the night, won't you?" She said in a sultry voice.

He laughed. "I'll be bringing someone with me down the line. You know, for a threesome."

"Ugh, no thanks. But do feel free any time to bring a friend." She had given him the guest room on the second floor with its own kitchenette so that he would be independent. She alternatively paced and tried to read a magazine. An article about her rival Sabine held her attention for a while. She was managed by her best friend from school. Juliette looked closely at the photos of the two women. *Am I putting two and two together and making five?* The sister came in with a cup of coffee.

"It won't be long now."

"Arabella won't make it then?"

"When will she get here?"

"In about thirty or forty minutes."

"I think Miss Nyman is holding on for as long as she can. But nature will take its course."

Juliette went out into the corridor and walked up and down, willing Arabella to arrive in time.

Twenty minutes later, she came flying down the hall.

"Where is she?"

"Stop. You must scrub up first."

The sister helped her and at last she could go into the delivery room. Ten minutes later, Simone came out, holding Ulrike firmly by the arm. "They should be alone for the birth."

"But I'm her mother."

"And I'm actually their birth granny. But I know when I'm not wanted."

They waited in the small room, until the sister came back in, a smile on her face. "A lovely little girl. Now, we have to wait awhile."

"How big is she? What colour hair?"

"I don't know, they haven't weighed her yet, but she's a nice medium weight by the looks of it. And very blonde."

Both mothers squealed in delight. Half an hour later, the little boy was born. The sister came in to tell them. "Strange. He has jet-black hair. It's unusual for twins to be so different."

"There's a reason, but we won't go into it," smiled Simone.

"You can all go in soon, if you want to. Miss Simon, you have to scrub up."

When they went in quietly, Marie was lying back looking exhausted but as beautiful as ever. She was holding the baby girl. "Meet, Clara Ulrike Simone Cooper-Nyman. It's a bit of a mouthful."

"And this is Anders Fredrik Gareth Cooper-Nyman. Also, a mouthful." Both babies were asleep, and both were beautiful.

"Kids, meet your grandmothers, and one of your godmothers."

The tears coursed down Juliette's face.

***

Arabella remained in the clinic. Juliette drove two exhausted but happy grandmothers home. She was thrilled to be a godmother, but as she walked into her own dark and empty home, she was hit with a wave of the deepest melancholy. She poured herself a glass of wine but tipped half of it away before going to bed. She pulled Jodie's old sweatshirt over her head and curled into a ball in bed. She had heard nothing from her since she left for San Francisco. She knew she was in the middle of a very strenuous tour, and the time difference made communication difficult, but she had so wished for a text, until she kept reminding herself, they had decided not to for fear of hackers.

Fuck it. She pulled her phone under the covers and texted: * 'Hi. Hope you are a fabulous success. I'm sure you are. I have two beautiful godchildren, both healthy. Both mothers doing well. The situation here much as before. A few less at the gate. Take care of yourself. Juliette.'

She grimaced when she sent it. How could she be even less personal? Why couldn't she say she cried herself to sleep most nights? Why couldn't she say she now had to hand wash her sweatshirt because it was disintegrating? Why didn't she tell her about Tom? She didn't really know. Except that she did. Jodie had offered to be there for her and to share the fall-out. She had offered to stay in Europe just to be in her backing group and sacrifice her own career. Jodie had offered her everything, and she had in the end forced her to leave to protect her, Juliette's, reputation. She didn't deserve her. She waited for a reply for the next three days, with ever diminishing hope. Then she sent a PS: * 'Can you send me another sweatshirt? The old one has fallen apart, and I can't sleep in anything else.'

It was so needy. Was Jodie lying by a pool or sitting in a bar, laughing at her?

***

There were still a few paparazzi at the gates. Arabella and Marie came home with the babies, which gave them something new to photograph. Juliette went out with Tom to restaurants, and an award ceremony.

"I'll have to move in for a while to get rid of them completely."

"Just until the end of the month, when I fly to London. They won't care over there."

The cars left eventually, and Juliette flew to London to promote her album. Bert went too, but they picked up backing singers locally for the TV shows she did. She wished Petra was with her as she needed some expert help to make herself look less tired and worn, especially in close-up. She was thin, and it worried Bert.

"You are not far from looking anorexic. Your head is now out of proportion to your body. This can't go on, Juliette. Or you will get really sick."

"But I am eating again."

"Like a sparrow. We are going out now for fish and chips. And you are going to eat more for the rest of this week, and you are going to be two kilos heavier when we get on that plane to go back."

He was as good as his word. She wasn't easily recognised in London, and they could eat freely in restaurants. She did enjoy sampling the huge variety of ethnic menus, and, not having to look over her shoulder all the time to see who was watching her eat made her stress levels fall considerably. She began to look better. But she still cried herself to sleep most nights.

And when she got back to her house, she was lonelier than ever. Tom realised she was not doing well, and he came to stay with her most nights. They became close friends. It was nice to sit with him in front of the fire, drinking a bottle of wine. He also insisted that she ate, and either he cooked, or she did. She put on weight, which she could then exercise off without losing it again, and she slowly regained the physical fitness she had always had.

Gradually, she left the front pages of the magazines, and was relegated to the middle or the end, the usual position before the Thorsten scandal.

Her working life returned to normal, and she began to plan her big concert tour. The meetings took place in Andreas's office, until he started to cramp her vision again, and as punishment, she transferred them to the dining table in Starnberg. Her idea was to use the same LED video-wall. It enabled so many special effects, without having to build heavy scenery. Unfortunately, it was prohibitively expensive. Her designer was worried about moving it between concerts, as it was extremely delicate and weighed several tons.

They looked for a compromise and settled for two much smaller walls with far fewer monitors. They could be placed either side of the orchestra, and there would even be room in the budget for a third replacement wall in case either of the others developed problems. In the largest venues, two cameras would follow her during the concert, projecting her image onto large screens for the fans furthest away. To them, she would look like a distant dot.

Again, she insisted on Jamie for the design of her costumes.

There would be no supporting acts from the folk world. She intended to have a band and a young pop singer just making his name. They had to fill in while she changed clothes. The concert hall and arenas would sell on her name, and hers alone, and booking was already looking promising. Some of the concerts were sold out.

There would be a six-week block from the middle of September through to the end of October, after which she would return home to prepare the next New Year show, then continue with a second block from the end of January through to a final week in the Olympia Halle in Munich at the end of March. It was a potentially punishing schedule, but she welcomed it.

She called Claudia. "Hi, I hope Andreas has been in contact to engage you for, well, sort of most of next year?" They both laughed.

"Yes, Sadie and I are thrilled and so grateful."

"What about your third singer?"

"We have someone good. Marianne. She's classically trained. We realised after Jodie that we needed someone more musical than us. It helps us all."

"What about her languages?"

"No problem. She sings English, French and Italian."

"Sounds perfect. I look forward to working with her. Um…have you heard from Jodie?"

"Yes, but she has more contact with Sadie, than with me. Sadie comforts her after…you know."

Her stomach lurched "After what?"

"After…you know…Tom moved in with you."

She wanted to laugh, but bit it back, again relieved that she didn't indulge in facetime.

"Yes, sorry about that. But I did know him first. How is she doing otherwise? Still touring?"

"I think that's finished. But I know she is making an album. She has a contract with a record company."

"That's fantastic."

"And she's writing songs for Laurie Porter. You know, the out-and-proud, Laurie Porter."

"I see." She suddenly wanted the conversation to end. "I'm very happy for her, and so happy we will be working together again soon, even without her. You made a great trio."

"Yeah, perhaps we can have the occasional fun night in a hotel like we did in Cologne and Hamburg."

She had to get off the line before she lost it. "I'm sure we will."

Laurie Porter was a beautiful young actress and singer who caused headlines the previous year when she came out. It hadn't hurt her career. She had since topped the US charts twice. But she sang light rock, not folk music. Against her better judgement, she pulled up Porter's website. Under actual news, was a picture of Jodie and Laurie sitting on a piano bench smiling at each other. The caption read: *New musical partnership.* Juliette was overcome with nausea and had to rush to the bathroom. No wonder she hadn't heard from her.

***

"Miss Simon, this is Lucas Schneider. I'm afraid we have hit a problem in the proceedings, and Magdalena von Reichenbach wonders if you could come to her office within the next couple of days."

"I can come into Munich the day after tomorrow."

"Let me check." He put her on hold. "Yes, would three o'clock be possible?"

It was like getting an appointment with royalty. Juliette was used to the reverse situation. She swallowed her pride. "Yes."

She was made to wait for ten minutes when she arrived at the elegant suite of offices. She thought about leaving, but then the door to an inner office opened, and she caught her breath. Magdalena von Reichenbach was simply stunning. She had short dark grey hair combed off her face. Her skin was dark gold, her eyes a piercing blue, her eyebrows perfectly arched, her nose classical, and her lips full. She was an inch shorter than Juliette but appeared taller in her very high Prada stilettos. She wore a black pencil skirt suit, perfectly cut, and a cream-coloured silk shirt, the two top buttons undone, showing a tantalising hint of cleavage. She was probably in her early forties. She was only the second woman for whom Juliette felt an instant attraction. And it went straight to her core.

"Miss Simon, I am very sorry. It is unforgiveable to keep you waiting." Her skin was soft, but the handshake was firm. She wore her nails long and polished. *That answers that question anyway.*

"Please come in and sit down." She was led into the large office dominated by a commanding desk laden with neat piles of paper. The lawyer gestured to a furniture group opposite the desk. Juliette sat on the sofa, the lawyer on a chair opposite. Her tight skirt rode up a couple of inches. Juliette looked away quickly but not before von Reichenbach noticed where her eyes had been. Her lips curled a fraction.

"As Lucas indicated, we have a problem. We have been working on the premise that you are the injured party, which makes a considerable difference to the financial settlement, but Mr De Luca's lawyer has submitted a counter claim. To the effect that you were also engaged in a relationship before your separation. Lucas Schneider tells me the story has appeared in several magazines, which might or might not make it true."

Juliette felt a trickle of sweat between her breasts. "My relationship with Tom Braun began after Thorsten and I broke up. Of course, I have known him for years. He has always been my record producer."

"Could Mr De Luca find witnesses to disprove this?"

"Unfortunately, yes." She thought of Sadie. "One of my backing singers was convinced we were having an affair last summer. But it is nonsense. I played up the situation as a joke."

"A rather dangerous joke, considering your marital situation at the time, and the damage it could have caused in the press."

"Yes, but Tom is…"

"Yes?"

"What a mess. I can't talk about all this."

"Miss Simon, I can't represent you in this case unless I have all the facts. It doesn't necessarily mean that your secrets will be revealed in court, but I must know…everything. What you tell me won't go any further than these four walls. Not even Mr Schneider will know because I have now personally taken on your case."

Juliette sat looking at her hands for a long moment. The lawyer kept perfectly still.

"Tom Braun is gay. He is a dear friend, and he has been helping me since Thorsten left. If I don't have a man at my side, my life is made a misery by the press. I had them camping outside my gates for nearly three months, and twenty-four-hour security was necessary to protect me. It was unbearable."

"And that has now stopped? As a result of your new liaison?"

Juliette supressed a bitter laugh. "More or less."

"So, there is no truth in the accusation that you were romantically involved before your separation?"

Juliette again looked down at her hands.

"Miss Simon, I have to know everything."

"It's over."

"And who is this…person?"

"I can't tell you. If it ever came out, my career is over."

Magdalena von Reichenbach looked at her for several moments. The air in the room was heavy. Then she said, gently, "Who is she?"

Juliette looked at her, her eyes wide.

"My private life is nobody's business either. There, you now know my secret too."

"She was one of my backing singers."

"Jodie Sanchez."

"How could you know?"

"I watched your New Year show, or at least part of it. I caught her act, and your duet."

"Was it that obvious?"

"No, you shouldn't worry. Your smokescreen with the men in your life is convincing. But a few people might have wondered. People…like us."

"So, what am I going to do? I lost her because of my career. I can't now let it be ruined by Thorsten fucking De Luca, or his girlfriend Gerda, who I suspect is the driving force behind this. Thorsten hasn't the guts, or the brain."

"The timing is essential. I can conceal in a court of law, but I can't lie. Can you reconstruct the timing?"

Juliette took out her smart phone. Her calendar showed all her work-related details. "We kissed…and I panicked…towards the end of July. Nothing else happened between us until the middle of August. Thorsten's child was born at the end of January."

"You know this for certain? It means the child was conceived in May."

"It was a few days premature, but no later than the end of May. Yes."

"When did you first meet, Ms Sanchez?"

"The middle of June, during a TV show. I noticed her vocal ability, but nothing else about her except how clumsy she was. Actually, I was tempted to sack her, but relented because of the quality of her voice."

"And it can be proved that you hadn't met her before?"

"Yes. The backing group engaged her just prior to this date, because her predecessor left suddenly to return to Australia. I'm not sure, but I think she had recently arrived from New York. In any case, I was on holiday for nearly a month and had no contact with my backing group until that TV show on…June 19th."

"I am hoping Ms Sanchez will not be mentioned at all in this divorce case. I see no need as long as I am convinced your husband had resumed his relationship before you met her. We can be thankful for the birth of the child."

She snorted. "I wasn't but I am now."

"I will do my best to protect Mr Braun. If we are lucky with the judge, details of his sexuality will just be between the two of us. If the case ever gets that far. Thank you for coming in to see me, Miss Simon. Perhaps we can have dinner at some point. May I call you?" She held Juliette's hand for longer than was usual in a client relationship.

"Yes, we can do that."

Her first instinct was not to. Magdalena von Reichenbach was hot as hell, but Jodie was the only woman who she thought of for hours of the day and night. She would make some excuse. After all, she had an enormous amount of work to do. It would be easy.

***

Bert brought her a new song he had written with Arabella. It was hauntingly beautiful, rising to an enormous orchestral climax at the end. A really big number, he told her proudly. Entitled *Heartbreak*.

"Arabella wrote the text for you and Jodie, so it's very personal, not that your fans would know. I don't think there is any danger."

"Except that I will break down every time I have to sing it."

"You're a talented actress. Be objective. It will be a number one, I can guarantee. I don't think I have ever felt so strongly about a song I've written."

"Bert, you're right, and I don't mean to sound ungrateful. I am honoured to sing it. And you know what they say. Time heals."

"And does it?"

"I haven't noticed yet. Claudia was kind enough to point out, not intentionally of course, that Jodie now has a new relationship. With Laurie Porter of all people. Can you imagine? She has exchanged a provincial German star for a Hollywood one."

"Are you sure about this?"

"If you look at Porter's website and see the photo of them, you will be."

"I have to admit I'm surprised. That's not like the Jodie I know. She was deeply in love with you…and you with her."

"Bert, I sent her away. I refused to acknowledge that love. I made it look like an affair. I didn't have the guts to fight for her."

"You did her a favour for her own career. For the rest, we'll see."

"I don't think we will. She hasn't contacted me once, even though I did reach out after the twins were born."

"I can understand that. She thinks you want her out of the way, and out of her life. She's trying to make it easier for you."

She sighed. "I'm sure you're right. But I don't want her out of my life."

"But you want her to hide if she's part of it."

"What can I do? I can't risk it. Look at my divorce. Thorsten, or the miserable Gerda, is trying to fleece me for huge sums of money. They think I was with Tom before he started up with her again. Ridiculous as we both know. But if they find out about Jodie, I don't know what will happen."

"When is the divorce due to be final?"

"It should have been next month, but now it's going to go on for at least another month because of the intervention. At least, the head of the firm is taking on the case."

"Who is working for you?"

"Magdalena von Reichenbach."

"The very best I see. She's married to the boss of an oil firm, though rumour has it she swings both ways." He winked.

"How do you know?"

"They sponsored a programme for young composers I was involved with. She's a hot cookie."

"Yes, I suppose she is."

***

"Miss Simon, Madam von Reichenbach is on the line. Can you take her call?"

"Yes."

"Miss Simon, I think I have good news. I have persuaded Mr De Luca's lawyer that he doesn't stand a chance, and that the attempt could further prejudice the judge against him. They are going to drop the motion, and I think we can finalise without you having to appear in court at all. By the end of June at the latest."

"That's a huge weight off my mind. How can I thank you?" She regretted it as soon as she said it.

"By having dinner with me, this week if possible." There was a slight pause. "Though there is nothing odd about a client having dinner with his or her lawyer, I imagine you prefer to be discreet, unless you are using public appearances for promotion purposes."

Juliette had to laugh at her accurate analysis. "Spot on, and I get terrible indigestion anyway. Every bite I take gets photographed."

"I thought so. I will arrange a caterer to bring in something nice to eat, to my apartment. I don't have time myself to cook."

"Will we be alone?"

"I think that would suit us both, don't you? I will text you through my address. I look forward to it."

Juliette sighed. There was no mistaking the flirtatious tone in her voice. She didn't really want to go. Then she thought about Laurie Porter. *Fuck it*!

***

Juliette drove her new Audi SUV into the underground garage of one of the most exclusive apartment buildings in Munich. She was buzzed up to the penthouse and von Reichenbach opened it. She wore a dark blue pencil skirt, and a white starched dress shirt. The obligatory stilettos gave her height over Juliette who had dressed in comfortable ankle boots, and a light black woollen pants suit with silk top.

Magdalena unashamedly looked her up and down. "Please call me Magdalena…Juliette? Might I?"

She nodded.

"Shall we eat now or later? Juliette, I'm not going to pretend here. I want you, very much indeed. I think that's why you're here too, but if I have completely misunderstood, then by all means, we'll eat dinner, and forget all about it. But if we are going to end up in bed, I personally prefer to have sex on an empty stomach and enjoy a nice meal afterwards."

Juliette hesitated. *Why am I here?* Yes, she had known what was going to happen, and she did want to have sex with Magdalena who really was wildly attractive. Her damp throng testified to that. She bit her lip. "Lead the way."

Magdalena took her by the hand, none too gently, and led her to a spacious bedroom with a king size bed, and a door leading into an ensuite bathroom. Apart from the obligatory elegant and expensive furniture, the room was bare. There was nothing except a lamp on each night table. Juliette raised her eyebrows.

"A guest room. Even I'm not so crass as to take you into the marital bed. May I undress you?" She didn't wait for an answer but slipped Juliette's jacket off her shoulders. Then she turned her around to face a large mirror on the wall, and from behind her she pulled her top over her head.

"Mmmm." She locked their eyes together in the mirror, and snapped her bra clasp, both hands coming around her back to cup her breasts. She flicked her nipples until they hardened. Juliette moved her hips backwards to make contact. Magdalena stroked down her abdominal muscles.

"I know you show these on TV a lot, but they are much much sexier in the flesh." Her eyes were hooded. Juliette was fascinated and couldn't look away. It was like being hypnotised by a serpent. Magdalena's hands moved downwards and opened her zip. She pushed a hand down the inside of her thong, and Juliette gasped.

"Good, you're ready for me." She pulled her slacks and thong down her legs going on to her knees to help Juliette step out of them until she stood completely naked, feeling aroused but exposed. Only then did Magdalena stand and pull her round face to face. The kiss was not gentle, but it was expert and Juliette responded. She was pushed backwards towards the bed, until Magdalena sat her on the edge and knelt in front of her. She pushed her legs open and stared at her sex for a moment. It was a turn on to see this fabulous looking woman kneeling for her, and Juliette took the initiative and pulled her hair towards her.

"You want me to eat you?"

"Yes, I do."

"You are my client, and your wish is my command." Her tongue moved deeply into Juliette, who gasped, and pulled her in more. She waited a while before moving up to her clit, by which time Juliette was on the brink, and when she first rubbed her with a finger and then sucked her, her orgasm was fast and furious. It was over quickly, and she fell back with a groan, suddenly wishing she was anywhere but here. Melancholy threatened to overwhelm her, but she had invited this, and she must at least return the favour.

"May I?" She reached out towards the still fully dressed woman. Admittedly, she looked hot in those clothes, but Juliette felt ridiculous being naked in front of her.

"You may indeed, but I need a little help. Why don't you get under the covers, you must be cold. I'll be a minute." She went into the bathroom. Juliette thought about dressing and leaving, but the woman was going to get her divorce through, and that was the most important thing at the moment. She lay under the covers and felt a little better. It was now dark in the room. The bathroom door opened. Juliette took in Magdalena's silhouette. She was naked and wearing a strap-on. She almost groaned. She could have that with a man.

"As I said, I need this, and I hope you will enjoy it too."

She climbed under the covers. Juliette knew what she loved best about a woman's body and stroked her soft skin, hoping to rekindle her desire. Her breasts were full, though not as full as Jodie's and the years were beginning to take their toll, but the nipples responded immediately to Juliette's touch, and she leaned across and sucked on each one in turn.

"Yes…that's good. Those lips which caress the golden microphone are doing a great job."

If it hadn't been clear to Juliette before, it was now. She was a notch on the bedpost, a star to be fucked. As if Magdalena could read her thoughts, she moved on top of her. She could feel the shaft of the dildo lying across her stomach.

"I want to fuck you." She slid the shaft into position at Juliette's entrance. "Are you wet enough?"

Juliette nodded. The experience was not unerotic, she felt a pool between her legs, and was still lubricated from her orgasm. Magdalena pushed in with a moan as if the dildo was her own flesh. It didn't hurt, but Juliette knew it would do nothing for her. Only Jodie could give her a vaginal orgasm. Why did she have to think of Jodie at this moment? She was deeply ashamed of what she was doing. She squirmed in embarrassment, until she remembered the internet photo and imagined Jodie on top of Laurie Porter. Or vice versa. She bucked her hips and pushed back against Magdalena.

"Oh yes, please do that." Magdalena pushed herself up and balanced on her outstretched arms. She began to thrust harder and deeper. The base of the shaft was presumably digging into her clit, because she began to pant and moan. Juliette reached down with her hand and rubbed her own clit as hard as she could.

"Yes, yes, I'm coming, I'm coming." Juliette wasn't but she faked it. Magdalena fell over her, breathing hard, her face glistening with sweat.

"Dear god, Juliette, that was something." They lay for a while, not saying anything, until Magdalena's breathing slowed.

"I'm getting old. I don't have the stamina I used to have, otherwise you would be here all night."

Juliette made a sound, which could be taken as acquiescent, or not.

"I invited you to dinner, and I would be a terrible host if I didn't honour the invitation. Shall we get dressed and go into the dining room?"

It wasn't pleasant putting her clothes back on, especially the thong. She lined it with tissue paper to absorb some of the damp, and fixed herself up in the bathroom, until it no longer looked as if she had been in bed having sex. Magdalena had left her the bathroom and disappeared into another room. When Juliette was ready, she heard noises, and found her in the kitchen. She had changed into beautifully cut slacks and another starched shirt. She was a gorgeous sexy woman, and Juliette knew why she was here. She stopped feeling guilty. They ate a lobster salad, followed by roast beef. The food was wonderful, and the one small glass of wine she drank was exquisite. Thankfully, Magdalena was a great conversationalist, which wasn't surprising, but a relief that she didn't want to talk about sex. Juliette would have liked to ask her about her marriage and if her husband knew about her proclivities, not out of voyeurism, simply to compare her own experiences with Leon and Thorsten, but the opportunity didn't arise, and she didn't force it.

She left well before midnight and turned to Magdalena at the door.

"Thank you for tonight."

"It was my pleasure." It was obvious they both knew the experience would not be repeated.

Juliette lay in bed with thoughts whirling through her head. It had been a ridiculous episode, but it answered a question she had long asked herself, knew the answer to, but lacked the proof. Jodie was not the only woman capable of turning her on. She was definitely not bisexual. She was a lesbian.

She turned to the little monkey, which sat on her night table. She picked him up and kissed him. She looked at the photo of Jodie, taken in the restaurant in Hamburg, which she had printed, and which lay in a drawer. It was dog-eared from constant handling. She took out the paper kiss from her wallet and smoothed it gently. She shrugged off the guilt hovering at the back of her mind. It was sex on the rebound. That was all.

***

A parcel arrived from New York. Inside were two sweatshirts, one with a baseball logo, the other American football. They were worn and she put her nose into them. They smelled of Jodie. She groaned. There was a card. *You can wear me at night. I wear you twenty-four hours a day. I can't forget.*

Juliette was puzzled. What did she mean by twenty-four hours, and what did the cryptic *I can't forget* mean? She couldn't forget what Juliette had done to her, or she couldn't forget her? There was no way of knowing. She tortured herself and looked at the website picture again. Jodie was wearing the charm bracelet with the entwined letter Js. She hadn't noticed it before. She didn't know what to make of it. Could Bert be right after all?

Tom met a solo dancer from the state opera ballet company and was crazy about him. He stayed over whenever Tom did. She liked Vassily a lot.

"I want to see you dance." That suited Tom perfectly, and it was a great opportunity for them to be seen together.

"I think there will be something for both of us to enjoy."

"Tom, I trained as a dancer. I'm well aware of dancer bodies and I never even looked twice at them."

This time, to her surprise, it was different. It was a classical ballet and the beautiful legs on point stretching from under the tutus did indeed send signals to her crotch. What would it be like to lie on top of a ballerina and have her wind her gorgeous legs around her back? She had to have a swim when they returned home and make use of the water jets. It was eminently more satisfactory than her experience with Magdalena.

***

Throughout June, she worked long hours with Bert, putting together the new album. This time, they would record all the songs in English, and in addition about half in German, so that there would be a national and international version ready for release. The USA distributor was still holding back on the previous album, but it had been very successful in the UK and went quite high in the charts there. The next one was eagerly awaited, or so she was told. She had not yet confessed to Andreas that the new one would be completely devoid of anything resembling folk music. She was aware it would probably mean the parting of their ways. The thought made her equally panic stricken and overjoyed. Or maybe he would swallow his pride and continue raking in his share of her earnings. The thought brought her back to the divorce, and the possibility of losing money to Thorsten. A plummeting feeling in her gut made her nauseous. Then the call came from Magdalena.

"Congratulations. You are a divorced woman, and no longer Mrs De Luca. And it went in your favour. You only must pay him the costs agreed in the original settlement. Even so, he won't be poor for a while."

"Unless he blows it all on another ridiculous car with a front like a penis extension."

"My husband has one of those too. A red one, would you believe. I suppose we have to accept responsibility." It was a relief to be able to laugh with Magdalena.

"Au revoir, Juliette. I wish you all the best. I hope it works out for you, and I think you know what I mean. She is gorgeous."

***

Juliette phoned next door and rushed over with two bottles of Dom Perignon. The door was opened by the new nanny, Margarete, who did a double take.

"Oh, I didn't know. Miss Simon, what a pleasure."

"Hello…Juliette, please. I'm sure we will see a lot of each other." It was slightly flirtatious she realised even as she said it, but there was no response in Margarete's eyes. *Thank god, that's all I need.*

"Let me show you through."

"It's fine. Thanks. I know the way."

Marie and Arabella were each cuddling a baby. Arabella had blonde Clara on her lap, and Marie the raven-haired Anders.

"Shhh, they've just been fed. I'm weaning them, and it seems to be working. We are down to just one feed a day."

"I'm getting fed up with sharing my wife's glorious breasts with these two. I want them back exclusively."

Marie shook her head, but neither was embarrassed. Juliette envied them. She would love to be free to talk about Jodie like this in public. The thought came from her subconscious as it often did. As if Jodie was with her. As if they were still lovers. She felt a deep ache in her chest.

"I'll call Margarete to put them to bed. Here, take your goddaughter for a moment." She carefully put Clara into Juliette's arms and left the room.

"They are really growing. She's much heavier than the last time I held her."

Marie looked down at Anders. She had never looked so beautiful. She had her figure back and was slim and lithe; only her breasts were even more voluptuous than they had been. Juliette had always had a slight crush on Arabella, but now she looked at Marie and wondered what it would be like to be made love to by her. Her core reacted. Most of her adult life, she had gone out of her way to avoid sex. Now, she missed it terribly.

Arabella came back with Margarete who held a double carrying cot. The sleeping babies were put side by side and taken out.

"I come bearing gifts."

"What are we celebrating?"

"Mrs De Luca is no more."

"That's wonderful. I'll get glasses." Marie hurried out, both Arabella and Juliette looking admiringly at her long legs. She came back with glasses and a bowl of crackers.

"This is a double celebration. It's my first alcohol for months and months. And it's Dom Perignon. What a luxury, and how appropriate. I'll just have a couple of sips. I'm sure it won't do any harm now."

They toasted each other, Marie closing her eyes in sheer bliss.

"No mothers?"

"No, alone at last. Margarete is outside in her apartment at night, and I can make this one scream with pleasure again."

"You go too far sometimes, Bella, but on the other hand…" her eyes twinkled. "Both our fathers finally put their collective feet down. All four will be over again in September, when Margarete has her holiday, but until then we have the house to ourselves. Except for a few days when Suzanne and Beth come to visit, but that's different. In fact, things are going so well, that I'm going to begin singing again in November. Just two recitals, but it's a start."

"Does that mean you can appear in my New Year show again? I was praying it might be possible."

Arabella and Marie looked at each other. "I don't see why not. Let us know the exact date. Bella's calendar is so full."

"If you let me know when you are available, we can fix it now. I am still flexible within a week or so."

Arabella opened her phone. "I can do the second week of December."

"That's perfect. It was the original plan. Can you block it off?"

"Done."

Marie looked at her. "So…let me confront the elephant in the room. Will Jodie be there too?"

"No, I'm afraid not."

"Why not?" Arabella blurted out. "She told us her album would be out in October, and it would be perfect to present her. You know the success she had last year."

Juliette shook her head. "Are you in contact with her?"

"Of course, we are. She is our friend."

"Then you'll know she is now together with Laurie Porter."

They looked at each other. Arabella shrugged. "Not as far as we know. She certainly hasn't said anything other than that she is writing new material for her."

Juliette didn't know what to say, but she felt a surge of hope, even if she refused to acknowledge it. "She's made clear that it's over between us. I don't think I could bear to have her as a guest on the show. The recording days nearly killed me last year. The distraction of having Jodie there but not with me, would make it impossible."

"You know best."

***

She giggled inwardly when Marianne, the new backing singer, was introduced on the first of two rehearsal days before the album sessions began. She was a small, vivacious, curvy, cuddly woman with red hair and large green eyes, and more not Juliette's type would be difficult to imagine. *Someone somewhere finds her really hot, but not me.*

She was as good as Claudia promised she would be, and with her leading the group, they made a great sound. Bert was delighted. Juliette's songs were getting increasingly complex, and a lot more was required of the group than when she sang basic folk music.

There were twenty songs to record. *Heartbreak* would be the single. She also decided to sing the old Springfield/Westlake classic *Losing you*.

Bert and Arabella wrote her nine new songs, ranging from ballads to up-tempo numbers. She had seven songs from other writers, and Bert orchestrated the two melodies Jodie sang in the New Year show. She sang them in a higher key, and the full orchestration made them virtually new songs. Eight numbers were originally written in German, and these had to be recorded twice, so she had twenty-eight tracks to complete. There were four days scheduled, and a reserve fifth, and Juliette knew it was going to be tough. She did everything possible to ensure her voice was fit.

Tom always insisted on a complete track first, then corrections, and every time she had that first track down, she breathed a sigh of relief. *One in the bank*, as Bert liked to say.

Sadie watched her every interaction with Tom with wide-open eyes. They played up to the full. At least she knew that when Sadie reported it to Jodie, she wouldn't believe a word of it. Even this tenuous connection made her feel warm.

The first two days went exceptionally well. She completed a record seventeen songs, and they were well ahead of schedule. Eleven to go, but they were some of the most difficult.

When she woke up on the third morning after a restless night, her throat felt scratchy, and her vocal cords were tired. She drove to the studio and attempted *Heartbreak*, but her condition as well as the emotion of singing the song was too much for her, and at the most a half of the first take was just about passable.

"Bert, there's no point. I'll only do more damage to my chords if I go on forcing."

"Agreed."

She called Andreas. "I need to go to see Doctor Post immediately." She was the leading throat specialist in Munich, much frequented by opera singers. "Send a car as well. I don't feel like driving myself."

Doctor Post did a thorough examination. "Just tiredness. If you keep quiet for twenty-four hours, and I mean complete silence, and gargle with this, and inhale as well, you should be alright tomorrow afternoon. The chords are a bit red, but there is no infection."

Juliette sighed with relief. She was driven home. Tom would bring her car back later. Arabella who had been at the session helping Bert and playing the piano when necessary, texted to ask how things were going and she texted back the diagnosis, apologising for not calling her. Ten minutes later, Marie was at the door, helped her prepare the inhalation, and made her lie down on the couch with a woollen scarf around her neck, a hot water bottle on her chest and two thermos flasks of her special tea within reach. An opera singer knew better than anyone how to treat the condition.

"Rest. Try to sleep. It's the best thing of all. If you give me a key, I'll let myself in later to make more tea and see how you are."

Juliette wanted to weep. If Jodie was the best thing that had ever happened in her life, living next door to the Cooper-Nymans ran a close second.

She woke the next morning feeling much better. Tom drove to the studio with the good news. Bert would utilise the morning session to lay down orchestra tracks in case they couldn't finish, which Juliette could then dub over. But she hoped it wouldn't come to it. She had no flexibility to interpret when she had to sing to a finished track.

A car collected her. She needed all her strength and driving through the late morning traffic in Munich sapped it. If things went well, the orchestra had agreed to an hour's extension. She managed to finish four songs, and her voice held up.

With seven songs left, and a day remaining, it now looked possible to finish the album.

She began the last day with Jodie's songs. She summoned every ounce of professionalism she possessed and tried to banish the lovely face from her mind.

She knew they were good when she finished. She then sang *You don't own me,* the great feminist song from the sixties, which was unfortunately just as pertinent in the third decade of the twenty-first century. She would have loved to change the line *Don't say I can't go with other boys* into *girls*, but she sang it only to herself. After a further two easier numbers, they broke for lunch. She had only three songs left, but they were the most difficult. Her voice was fragile, but it was there.

Marie had asked her the day before if she could come to the session. Arabella was now away again, and she was starved for a breath of show business after so many months of baby care. She arrived with another thermos of her secret tea, which really did do wonders for the vocal cords. Marie ordered Juliette to keep silent for the full hour's break and she rested on a couch in the control room. Marie spent her time wandering around the studio, talking to Bert and the backing singers, so as to ensure Juliette did as she was told. Her eyes were sparkling. It was obvious how she longed to get back to work.

Juliette drew a deep breath as the orchestra returned and tuned. The first number went well. Only two to go, *Heartbreak* and *Losing you*. Marie was in the control room with Tom. She came into the studio and went over to Claudia, Sadie and Marianne.

"Mind if I join you?" They looked at her open mouthed.

Bert grinned. "We can't pay you." She rolled her eyes.

Tom's voice came from the control room "How am I going to balance that?" He was smiling. "Bert, once through with everyone except Juliette please."

Marie hadn't really warmed up her voice, but she sounded glorious all the same.

"Not one decibel more, Marie, and we'll be fine."

Juliette had sung through *Heartbreak* often while learning it, and she could now maintain some distance to the text. The version she put down was moving and powerful. The orchestra applauded.

Now, she had only *Losing you* to get through. Again, it was a so-called big number with luscious orchestral and backing singer sound. It was a blessing in disguise Marie was there to plump up their contribution. Juliette had chosen the song because of the lyrics. She poured all her love for Jodie into her singing. *No... I'll never forget her, even if I've lost her.*

At the end, the tears were running down her cheeks. She needed vocal rest again, but she had got through and finished the album. She also had her new single. Everyone hugged everyone else. Tom brought in cases of beer and pretzels and there was a spontaneous party. Life was good. Her friend Marie was at her side. It would have been perfect if Jodie had been there to share it with them.

***

The month of August was hot. Tom and Vassily, who were both on holiday, decided not to go away. Why should they when they had the luxurious lakeside house to enjoy? They spent their days sunbathing, boating and swimming. Sometimes, on days when Arabella was away conducting, Marie and the babies joined them in the garden. There was now a gate in the hedge.

Every evening, the men cooked for Juliette. She had to work most of the time. The final preparations for the tour filled her hours with meetings and costume fittings and for the last two weeks of the month, with rehearsals in a studio in Munich. She decided to steal three dance numbers from the last New Year show, but there were still three new ones to learn. She also had to fit in a photo session for the cover of the album, which needed to be rushed out in time for the tour. The promotion video would be filmed during final rehearsals. For the album cover, she decided on a daring photo of herself kissing another figure in long shot under a tree. Vassily with his shoulder length hair would model the second figure. She wanted it to be impossible to identify whether the figure was a man or a woman. It was meant as a snub to the paparazzi who had taken the picture in the park. Only Tom, Vassily and she knew this. She was delighted with the shot she chose. She hoped Jodie would see it.

***

The tour began in Innsbruck. It was not far from Starnberg, a good hour's drive over the Alps, and as she preferred to sleep in her own bed and not in an overwarm and noisy hotel suite in the Innsbruck old town, she was driven back and forth for the final five rehearsal days. She would be living in hotels for the next six weeks, so any chance to be at home she grabbed with both hands.

It was an intensive five days, during which nobody except the orchestra looked at their watches. There were numerous technical problems and tempers often frayed. Juliette had a reputation for friendliness to maintain, and she had several times to dig her fingernails into her palms in frustration. She had grown them longer again. She had no inclination for another sexual adventure, so had no need to keep them trimmed.

Her parents arrived two days before the first concert, but they discreetly kept out of her way and were looked after by Vassily. Tom was with her all week, not just for the sake of appearances, but also because of his expertise in all things relevant to the sound system. As the tour repertory consisted of many of the new songs, his advice was invaluable, as he knew the numbers inside out.

At last, it was the day of the concert. She was driven over early, so early that fortunately not more than fifty fans had gathered in front of the hall.

Compared with many of the later dates on the tour, the venue was small, but it suited Juliette to ease in slowly. There was seating for around three thousand people.

The LED walls were installed, and the hydraulic lift which brought her on for her first entrance also functioned here because the stage contained a lift used for bringing on grand pianos. The lighting effects would be much more spectacular in the larger venues, and there were no pyrotechnic effects allowed for fear of a fire breaking out in the wood-clad auditorium.

As she came up on the lift, the wall of sound which greeted her was surprising for this rather staid corner of Austria, and it got even louder as the show progressed. She saw that a lot of her fan base had travelled from other parts of Europe. It was important for them to be at the very first show. Most of them would see it at least once more.

Everything mechanical worked, and Juliette was full of energy. She began the second half with *Heartbreak* and finished the show with *You don't own me*. Andreas was biting his nails about this. He had slowly come around to half supporting her on her change of musical direction. He had no choice. He could stay or he could go, and Juliette's increasing popularity, albeit at the cost of losing large numbers of her original fans, convinced him it would be plain stupidity to leave a buoyant luxury liner, instead of the sinking ship he had been prophesying.

Jamie designed her another tux, breathtakingly elegant. Wearing it with high stilettos and a bow tie, she heard a collective sigh when she walked out for the final number. One day, she would have the courage to replace *boy* with *girl*, but she was not ready yet.

The applause shook the building to its foundations. As an encore she sang one of her greatest hits. She owed that at least to the older fans.

There was a party for the crew and the team backstage. Arabella and Marie were there, and as Suzanne and Beth were staying with them, they were too. For the photographers, it was a sensation. Innsbruck had never seen anything like such an array of stars on one evening. Juliette had to spend an hour with the fans in the foyer, but her parents and guests waited for her. They were signing autographs too.

Vassily and Tom had gone on ahead to prepare food, and when the group arrived home, they sat outside under the rose covered pergola on the terrace until dawn became visible in the form of silvery fingers on the still waters of the lake. Giuseppe was busy with his camera snapping photos. Everyone wanted copies, and he promised to send them. When Juliette finally climbed into her bed, exhausted but still running high on adrenalin, she turned on her phone. There was a text: * 'Toi toi toi. I know you will be fabulous. I wish I could be up on stage with you. I miss the girls.'

Only the girls? Or did that include her? She kissed the little monkey and eventually slept.

***

The day was free, before two more sold out shows in Innsbruck, after which everything would be transported northwards to the next venue. Anna-Maria brought her a cup of coffee in bed at one o'clock when she asked to be woken. She had seen little of her parents, and she wanted to spend at least the rest of the day with them.

The weather was still wonderful, and they sat or lay in loungers outside, talking sporadically and dozing in the warmth. Andreas emailed through that the reception so far was positive, although the folk magazines had not reviewed the concert. Instead, she was reaching the more serious newspapers and magazines. She was universally applauded for the feminist stand at the end of the show.

She asked to see Giuseppe's photos. There was one of Arabella, Marie, Suzanne, Beth and herself smiling at the camera, although Juliette saw a hint of sadness in her own eyes. *Do I often look like that? Probably.* Despite all the positive things in her life, her basic mood was melancholic. She was not getting over Jodie at all. She functioned, but that was all. She remembered Marie saying that she had merely existed for a year without Arabella. She empathised completely.

"Papa, send me all the photos when you have time. This one immediately please."

Her phone pinged. She rerouted the photo, with the text: * 'Someone is missing here, and that someone is sorely missed…by everyone.'

***

The *Heartbreak* single went straight to number one in the charts. The album was released on Juliette's birthday, September the twenty-seventh. The first concert in Cologne was to take place the following day, and that evening she was booked to make a return appearance on the talk show from the previous year.

She stayed in the same hotel in Cologne, and she thought it was probably the same room, though as she lodged in so many hotels, she couldn't be sure. They tended to blur into each other. But she remembered the sex perfectly. It was the first time she and Jodie climaxed together. The memory aroused her instantly and she showered and tended to herself, whispering Jodie's name as she came.

"So, here you are again, almost exactly a year after your last sensational visit to us."

"Yes, thank you so much for inviting me again."

"We could hardly resist after the ratings last year. Is it my imagination, or are you less present in the boulevard press than you were back then?"

"That's correct. After my divorce, I made a conscious decision to reduce interviews. Living, so to say, in my fan's kitchens, didn't help my marriage."

"After the news of your separation, you were on all the front pages for what felt like months."

"It was only weeks, but to me it felt like years." The studio audience laughed. "And that's when I resolved to be less in the public eye."

"You are now in a new relationship?"

"No comment."

"Ah, I see. Alright, let's talk about your new show, which you are presently touring. It finishes on a very feminist note, and what sounds like a rebuke to your fans for their voyeurism."

"I sing an old song, from the early sixties, but it's as relevant today as it was when it was written. I did not commission it to reprimand my fans, but if it helps to get across the message that I have the right to some private life, then so be it."

"Last year, you told us you might eventually venture into musicals. Are there now plans for this?"

"It's too early to say. But in my next New Year show, I will be featuring segments from three musicals. I love the genre, and I love performing them."

"Tell us some details."

"Oh no, you will have to wait for that. Watch the show."

"Juliette Simon, thank you for being here. By the way, the politician you accused of having criminal energy resigned soon after the show. You were right."

"Don't scare me. I hope his criminal connections aren't with the mob."

"I don't think so. I believe he is selling trucks somewhere in South America."

The audience laughed and applauded.

"We'll be hearing from you at the end of the show with your new single, which is also the title of your album released today. And by the way, happy birthday from all of us here." The studio audience stomped their feet.

She sang *Heartbreak* without a hitch. She drank a pina colada in the hotel bar with Bert and her backing girls, before sobbing herself to sleep. Three days later, the album topped the charts.

***

The first part of the tour came to an end. At the last of three concerts in Berlin, Juliette threw a party for the crew and team. She had grown attached to them all, and they had had good times together. Her constant companion was Bert, and Tom if he came up to visit. They often ate together. Sometimes, she invited Sadie, Claudia and Marianne to join them as she promised. Sadie always had the table in stitches, and Juliette grew to appreciate Marianne's more subtle humour. Sadie offered information about Jodie unprompted. She was on a short tour again to promote her album, which would be released the first week of November. She had written a new song for Laurie Porter, which would be released as a single.

"Will Jodie be coming back as a guest on the New Year show?"

"I'm sure she is much too busy in the States. That's where she has the centre of her life now."

Bert looked at her disapprovingly. "Juliette, I do think she should be asked. The public would be thrilled to see her again. And you would get enormous credit. You did give her the breakthrough opportunity, after all."

She shrugged and changed the subject.

It was the end of October when she got back to Starnberg, but she had no opportunity to rest, other than trying to sleep more deeply in her own bed. She had a huge deficit after, with indifferent success, attempting to adapt to a series of hotel beds. But the planning for December was in full swing, and she had to bite the bullet and get what rest she could when she could. She had been regularly taking half a sleeping tablet. With will-power accumulated over years of physically pushing her body past the pain barrier, she weaned herself off them.

The New Year show would have to be bigger and better than the last two. It was a strain, not only for her, but for the whole team. She had many meetings to attend, and decisions to make. Jamie was already designing costumes. As she said in the Cologne interview, she wanted segments out of three musicals. For the first time, there would be entire scenes, with dialogue, and she would be very careful to limit the dance numbers after what happened the previous year. She would continue to dance, but intended to cut back, hopefully subtly enough that it wouldn't be noticed. The dancers now had an extra number to themselves, and she invited Vassily to bring a group from the state opera in Munich. They planned to dance a choreography to Beyoncé's *Diva*. Much as she would rather see some classical ballet, she knew it wouldn't work within the context of the show.

Andreas sat at the head of the long table in his office. "Have you made a final decision about the musicals?"

"*My Fair Lady*." He looked pleased. "*Pretty Woman* and *Wicked*."

He sighed. "They are not really that well known. The public can't sing along."

Juliette rolled her eyes. "*Pretty Woman* is an ingenious variation on *My Fair Lady*, and one of the best loved films ever. I think it's a neat idea. And *Wicked* is hardly an unknown musical. What child doesn't know the *Wizard of Oz*?"

Bert nodded. "I think they are great choices."

Andreas sighed again, pursed his lips in the way, after Sadie's impersonation, always made Juliette want to giggle, and moved on. "What about Jodie Sanchez?"

"What about Jodie Sanchez?"

"There's tremendous interest in her. Can't you ask her to be in the show?"

"She lives in the States."

"Juliette, there are intercontinental flights, you know. She and Cooper-Nyman were the big hits last year." *No thanks to you.* Sometimes, she loathed Andreas Meyer.

"I've already booked Marie and Arabella. You know that."

Andreas wouldn't let go. "Are you angry with her for leaving the backing group? I just don't understand why you are fighting this. You were good friends."

"Not anymore, unfortunately."

"I am going to go against you on this one. I'm going to enquire about her availability."

"Do it then." Juliette was convinced Jodie would say no, even if she had time, which she almost certainly didn't.

The answer came back in the affirmative. She was thrilled and terrified. It would need every ounce of her professionalism to carry her through the show taping, seeing her and having to interact with her, but not to make love to her.

***

The musical excerpts required more rehearsal than the previous years. The casts were bigger, and the dialogue scenes needed to be well rehearsed. A studio was made available a full week before the taping took place, again in Munich. The casts were a mixture of musical singers and TV actors. No expense was spared to get the best available, although as Andreas remarked, nobody charged an exorbitant fee. The publicity they received from appearing in front of a Europe wide audience of many millions ensured that.

Juliette was dialogue word perfect before rehearsals began, as was usual with her. She left nothing to chance and was a perfectionist. She sensed a couple of the actors were patronising, until she convinced them in short order that her acting abilities were equal to theirs, and they sure as hell couldn't sing and dance like she could. She felt the respect grow.

The dancers arrived, and Juliette spent three days with them, this time not pushing herself, so that on the day they moved into the arena and onto the set, she was pain free. Her back was holding up well, as was her knee, which she had professionally strapped from the first dance rehearsal onwards. She was massaged by the physiotherapist twice a day.

Martina was happy. "Juliette, there is no comparison with last year. Unless you fall, which we don't want of course, I think you will come through this year without problems."

The day was spent running through the dances and her own musical numbers with the orchestra and her backing singers. She concentrated hard, but at the back of her mind was Jodie. Jodie would arrive tomorrow for the rehearsals with all the other guest artists. She felt sick with apprehension.

It was a tiring day, which was fortunate, and she fell into an exhausted sleep after being terrified that she wouldn't. Her heart sank as she woke, and the day ahead loomed in her conscious. She cursed Andreas once again for his insistence on inviting Jodie. *I'm going to look at her like a lovesick puppy, and she is going to be a sophisticated star and laugh at me.*

The large black Mercedes collected her at eight o'clock. Tom and Vassily drove in with her. She didn't want to be alone, and the fifty or so diehard fans waiting would get to see her and Tom together. Quite what they made of Vassily she didn't know, and she didn't care anymore, but the photos which would appear on thousands of Facebook pages would belie any other rumours likely to be fabricated when she hugged this or that guest star. It was so enervating to be forced to deny silly stories.

She was in her dressing room long before anyone else arrived. She looked at the plan. Again, for reasons of economy with moving and tuning the grand piano, Arabella, Marie and Jodie were scheduled to rehearse consecutively at three o'clock.

She had her first massage of the day. "Juliette, why are you so tense? You haven't been like this all week."

"Oh, you know, it's getting close to show-time, and there are a lot of egos to contend with today." She wore a black designer training outfit, which fit snuggly to her body. Petra came in and pinned her hair up off her neck. She would be working up a good sweat over the day.

At twelve, the first guest artists began to rehearse. She sang duets with several of them, and as she had to rehearse her introductions as well, she barely left the stage. When she had a small break as a band took over, she moved into the arena and sat with her feet up on a chair in front of her. She started in surprise as a hand reached from behind her and handed her a water bottle. At the same time, she smelt her scent. She felt a jolt in her clit, as she turned round, to see enormous dark brown eyes looking a little tentatively into her own. Instinctively, she moved towards her, but Jodie leaned back.

"Careful, people are watching."

"I want to hug you, and if you don't object, that's what I'm going to do. It's perfectly natural."

"Sadie's watching."

"Sadie is the last person who is going to think anything is odd. Please let me."

Jodie stepped towards her, and they wrapped their arms around each other. Juliette held on for as long as possible. She wanted to cry. There was a huge lump in her throat.

It was Jodie who broke away. "Are we really ready for this again?"

Juliette sighed. "No, I'm sure you aren't. I'm sorry."

They were interrupted by Arabella and Marie, who fell on Jodie. Juliette stood aside and she had time to take her in. She was more beautiful than ever. She wore dark brown skinny jeans, with tall riding boots, and a brown slim-fitting roll neck, stretched across her breasts. Her hair was slightly longer and gleamed with a blue sheen in the stage lighting. Juliette's thong was immediately uncomfortably damp. *What the fuck am I going to do now?* An excited Sadie and Claudia joined them, and Bert jumped down off the stage too. The band up on the stage was incredibly loud, so the group did not disturb them. Juliette felt like an outsider, until Jodie looked at her. For a second, she saw the lust in her eyes.

Two stage managers with headsets and tablets approached the group and escorted Marie, Arabella and Jodie to their dressing rooms. The band finished, and Juliette took a deep breath before going to rehearse her next introduction and sing the following duet. She was trembling.

Then, it was time for the piano to be wheeled on. Jodie sang first, two new numbers from her album, followed by a Schmidt/Cooper composition, which neatly introduced Marie and Arabella. That was the plan. This year, the acts would follow each other on the second day, and more or less top the bill. They sang two numbers from their new album, and Juliette joined them to duet with Marie on one of her own previous hits. She thought they were finished, but Jodie walked back on and squeezed next to Arabella on the piano stool. Fourhanded, they played the introduction to *Heartbreak*, and Juliette began to sing it, with Marie singing the harmony. At the end, the orchestra applauded, and the disembodied voice of the director spoke into the empty arena. "Is that a change of plan? I like it. We should keep it. Bert, can we replace the solo version of *Heartbreak* with something else?"

"If Juliette is agreeable, it's no problem. We have three reserve numbers already rehearsed with the orchestra."

"Juliette, what do you think?"

"Yes, I'm fine with it."

"Then let's move on. We are a little behind schedule. We must do all the musicals before we finish tonight."

The technicians removed the piano, and the group stood chatting for a while longer, until Marie moved them away. "Come on, we're in the way here. Jodie, do you want us to drop you anywhere, or are you staying here?"

Jodie looked at her. There was a slight questioning look in her eyes. Juliette shrugged her shoulders and looked towards the main stage.

"No, I won't stay. I remember how it was last year. Juliette has no time to breathe. And I have a full day tomorrow with meetings of my own. We'll all see each other the day after tomorrow."

Marie squeezed Juliette's arm. "Goodbye, darling. Take care of yourself. Your godchildren need you." And they were gone. She felt bereft. She shook herself and continued the rehearsal.

That night, she again took half a sleeping pill. *This cannot be a go-to solution. From now on, only on intercontinental flights.* But she knew a gorgeous face was going to stop her sleeping if she didn't and she couldn't afford the distraction.

***

The first day of taping went almost too perfectly. No dancer slipped, and the guests rarely wanted a second take. Instead of only the planned *My Fair Lady*, they would also have time to record *Wicked*, which meant that the second day would be more relaxed.

The costumes for *My Fair Lady* were based on the film version, though Jamie had subtly updated them. They played the long dialogue scene between Higgins and Eliza and the number *Rain in Spain*, followed by the *Ascot gavotte*. Then one of the guests sang *On the street where you live,* and they went into *I could have danced all* night as a fully choreographed number.

While a band played, Juliette was changed into her wig and costume for *Wicked* in which she would sing two numbers, and dance in a third. The change was remarkable, as she had a long black wig and a green face. The audience gasped when she came on to sing two numbers from the show, *No good deed* and *Defying gravity*, where she had to fly above the heads of the audience. She had done it many times in her shows. It was not a problem and they needed only one take, despite the technical complexity. Juliette had a phenomenal head for heights and was fearless as she swooped high across the arena.

The applause for *Wicked* was almost more enthusiastic than for *My Fair Lady*. It was the last take of the day, and Andreas waited in her dressing room when she got back. She sat in her make-up chair, slightly out of breath, but free of all but a few minor aches and pains.

"Well, Andreas. Am I allowed to say *I told you so*? She mimicked his nasal voice. My audience is changing. They want something new. They are more inquisitive."

"I can't wait to see what you think up next year."

Juliette was silent before she spoke in a quiet voice. "Petra, I know I can count on you. On your discretion, I mean."

She nodded.

"There won't be a next year, Andreas. This is the last one. I know when to get out when I'm on top, and there is too much pressure attached to these TV entertainment extravaganzas. I hope they are going to write that it's *even better than last year*, but I would be content with, *she maintains her high standards*. There is a limit to what I can do with this type of show, and they demand too much of me, my time and my energy. Someone else can breathe new life into this rather creaky format."

"You're not thinking of retiring, are you?" The colour left his face, and he sat down on the couch behind her.

She laughed. "No, but I might well go in another direction. I don't know yet. It's dependant on what happens in my private life."

"But Tom…"

"Will probably marry Vassily. I'm talking about *my* private life, not Tom's. And that's all I have to say on the matter."

***

She woke feeling tired but not exhausted. What a difference to last year. She was in early for her massage. Martina was nearly through pummelling her, when there was a knock on the door.

"Who is it?" She was irritated. It was common knowledge that she was not to be disturbed unless there was an emergency.

"Jodie."

"Come in." The physiotherapist went to pull a sheet over her naked back, but Juliette stopped her. Jodie walked in with a cup of steaming coffee and a sandwich.

"Oh, Jodie, thank you so much."

"You are thinner than you were. I'm sure you don't eat enough." Jodie's eyes narrowed as she looked up and down her naked back, and she swallowed hard.

"I do, but I exercise it all off."

"Really?" The atmosphere was charged. Martina finished and washed her hands. "Just lie there for five minutes before you get up. I'll see you in the break." She left.

There was silence in the room. Jodie put the coffee and sandwich on the table. She nodded towards the door. "Shall I lock it?"

"I think you had better." Jodie walked across and slid the lock. Juliette sat up and wrapped the sheet around herself. Then they were kissing frantically, moaning into each other's mouths. Juliette spread her legs and Jodie slipped between them.

"Oh, my darling, my love."

Juliette was brought to her senses by a knock.

"Who is it?" She croaked.

"Petra."

"Two seconds." She threw on a bathrobe. Jodie sat in a chair and raked her hand through her thick hair. Juliette unlocked the door. Petra looked puzzled.

"Sorry, Petra, people were bothering me. Jodie brought me a coffee."

"Hi, Jodie, it's great to see you again. Are you staying long?"

"Just until after Christmas. Then I must go back to New York to promote my album."

Juliette's heart sank. For a few minutes, she had let herself think that Jodie was back for good. But of course, she couldn't be. She lived in New York. She had also forgotten about Laurie Porter. She felt slightly sick.

Jodie stood up to leave. "Juliette, I'll see you later out there. Toi toi toi for everything today."

"You too. Thanks for the coffee."

"Isn't that sweet?" Petra began to lay out her materials. "She's a star herself now, but she still brings you a coffee and sandwich. She's an adorable person, and she doesn't seem to have changed a bit."

"I'm afraid she probably has though. She's grown up."

***

"Perhaps some of you remember back to the show last year, when I introduced a girl or rather a young woman who was part of my backing group." The screaming began. "I see, then I don't really have to say any more. That young woman went to the States, and found fame and probably fortune, I haven't asked her that," there was a roar of laughter. "She not only sings her own songs, but she also writes for others, Hollywood stars among them," she couldn't bring herself to name names. "Ladies and gentlemen… Jodie Sanchez."

Jodie came on and took her place at the piano. She had grown enormously in confidence and sat tall in her steam-punk-corsage with long slim black pants and stilettos. The audience whistled and stamped and waved banners. She introduced the third number herself and then waved Arabella and Marie onto the stage. They looked breath-taking in short leather skirts, Marie in stilettos, Arabella in boots. Marie wore a feminine blouse, Arabella her trademark waistcoat. The roars of applause shook the building after these two acts, and when Juliette joined them for *Heartbreak*, the applause wouldn't stop. The director made a snap decision and called a break, an act earlier than planned.

They walked off arm in arm, Juliette relishing the nearness to Jodie.

"I'm afraid you all have to hang around until the end, but luckily, it's not as long as we thought, as we managed to get two of the musicals taped yesterday."

"It's not a problem. We have a lot to catch up on, unless Jodie wants to watch the rest."

"I definitely want to see the musical."

"It's right at the end like last year, though this year, I don't need emergency surgery to get out there."

She had her massage anyway. It helped release some of the tension. All she could think about was kissing Jodie. Her soft lips, her sweet breath tasting slightly of coffee. She squirmed into the massage table; thankful she was wearing her thong. Her arousal would give her away to Martina. She hoped the scented massage oil disguised the smell from her sex.

The last segment began. The first couple of acts had it tough. The audience was quieter. Vassily and his ballet company brought back the cheering. The number was entirely unexpected, and the response was more than enthusiastic. The fans responded ecstatically to the beautiful bodies in tights and the graceful and athletic dance combinations. Juliette's own troop of dancers watched from the side and screamed the loudest.

The last part was *Pretty Woman*. It was lavishly staged with dancers and chorus. In the character of Vivian, Juliette sang the show duet *You're beautiful* with the actor playing Edward, followed by her solo *Anywhere but here,* then the duet *Long way home*, followed by her big number *I can't go back*. They finished with the duet and ensemble number *Together forever* which had some cheeky musical quotations from Verdi's *La Traviata* written into the orchestration. Now, Marie, Arabella and Jodie watched from the side, and cheered loudly when they heard it.

While the orchestra played other melodies from the show, she changed into her tux, and went out for the traditional last number, which was her biggest hit, now five years old, but the song she was most associated with. The audience danced and sang along, and the artists gathered behind her on the stage. The usual gold glitter rained down, the balloons tumbled from the arena roof, and they toasted in the New Year. As she had last year, Juliette manoeuvred herself between Jodie, Marie and Arabella.

"I need to speak to you," she whispered into Jodie's ear. She knew her microphone was most probably live, but it wasn't an incriminating question. Jodie nodded.

They left the stage, and she thanked the crew. They would have their own party. She and the other artists were expected in the huge foyer to meet and greet the fans. Juliette changed quickly into slim jeans, boots and a loose black silk shirt. Petra put her hair into a chignon. Tom collected her, Andreas joined them, and they walked into the foyer to face the masses. Tables were dotted all over the huge space, with artists' names on them, and the ushers were standing by to direct people out as soon as they had their signature. It was a well-organised system, but Juliette knew she had an hour and a half ahead of her. The two most popular guest acts, Jodie and Cooper-Nyman were placed further away from Juliette's table, in order to avoid a complete traffic jam.

"Tom, take me over to Jodie quickly. I need to say something to her." They did a left turn before she reached her table, and she waved to the waiting fans, signalling two minutes, above the din. Jodie saw her coming and stood from her table, signalling the same. Tom stood guard, out of earshot.

"Come home with me tonight."

"I thought you would never ask."

Juliette needed half an hour longer than anyone else, and all the guests left, calling a cheery goodnight. Only Tom, Vassily and Jodie were left, and they stood out of the way while Andreas was at her side and helped her. At last, it was over, and she staggered a little as she stood up.

"My hand is good for nothing tonight," she said shaking it to get the blood to flow again. "Good thing I've got a left one that works." Jodie looked away, hiding a grin. Juliette had trimmed her nails again three days ago, and worn false ones for the shows, but these she had removed before coming to the signing. It was much easier to scrawl her name a thousand times with short nails.

The Mercedes waited. Vassily sat in the front, Tom, Jodie and Juliette in the back. Andreas waved them off, along with the hundred or so fans, who were still waiting to catch a last glimpse of their idol.

As soon as they were under way, Tom said, "Could you drop us off at my apartment please?" He gave the driver the address.

Juliette squeezed his leg. "Thank you."

They were soon alone on the southbound motorway. Neither of them spoke much, being too aware of the driver. But as soon as they were inside the front door, Juliette took hold of Jodie's hand and pulled her up the stairs and into the bedroom, stopping only to draw the curtains before she pushed her onto the bed and fell on top of her. They clawed at each other's clothes, throwing them all over the room, until they were both naked.

"Your soft skin. I can't bear it. I want to drown in you."

Jodie drew her hand across Juliette's sex. "I think I'm the one who's going to be drowning."

Juliette ground her hips into her centre, pushing her legs apart. She felt the slick arousal coating her own pudenda. "That's the pot calling the kettle…"

"Shhh," Jodie silenced her by pulling her head down and giving her a bruising kiss. Juliette supported herself on her arms and dipped her head to take a breast into her mouth, gently sucking, then biting. Jodie yelped.

"That's for being unfaithful."

Her eyes widened in surprise. "Let's take a rain check on that remark and revisit it later."

She put her fist between Juliette's legs and pushed them apart. She was so wet; her arousal was glistening on the inside of her upper thighs. Jodie drew her finger up her folds and brought it up to her mouth to suck. Juliette moaned and crashed her hips down onto Jodie again, then moved her left hand down and pushed into her. Jodie's hand went back and entered her and started thrusting. In less than a minute, they both threw their head back and shouted each other's name as their climax hit.

They lay in each other's arms, pressed so tightly together it was difficult to breathe. They were desperate to hold each other so that there wasn't a millimetre of space between them.

Jodie reached down and pulled the cover over them. "It's good to be home."

Juliette squeezed her and bit back the question, *but for how long*?

***

They made love for hours, relearning each other, being gentle, then rough, then gentle again. At last, they slept, and woke late the next morning. They made love again and talked for the first time.

"What's with the unfaithful bit?"

Juliette's heart sank. "I don't really want to know, do I?"

"Juliette, what are you talking about?"

She didn't answer for several seconds, then whispered, "Laurie Porter."

"What about Laurie?"

"Do you actually live together?"

"No, why should we. I write songs for her. She lives in LA and I live in New York."

"And you're not going to move to LA?"

"No. Nowadays, we have the phone, emails, Skype, Zoom, Dropbox, and all manner of communication methods. I can play the piano in New York, and she can sing along in LA." Jodie was shaking her head.

"She's not your new lover? But the photo…on her website…of you both…I thought…"

"Oh Juliette…it's not a selfie, is it?"

"No, I don't think so."

"Then somebody took that photo?"

"I suppose so."

"Her personal trainer, and live-in-lover took the photo, you idiot! They are very happy together and are getting married in March. Don't you read the gossip magazines?"

"No, I've stopped. After the Thorsten break up, I swore I would never look at one, ever again. So, you mean you don't have anyone?"

"I wouldn't say that."

A tear formed itself and ran down Juliette's nose. She sniffed.

"How can a *powerfrau*, a superstar, a creative genius like you be so dense? I have you. You are the love of my life. I know we can never be together properly, but I don't want anybody else." They kissed, and snuggled, holding each other tightly.

"Wasn't there anyone in the States? You are so young and so beautiful. You must be chased all the time."

"You know what it's like with fans. Right at the beginning I did give way…once. She looked like you. And I was still hurt about being sent away. I didn't feel good about it though. Luckily, I was on tour, and left the next morning. And you?"

"Also, just once. My divorce lawyer. A CEO type in pencil skirt suit with heels so high she needs a parachute. I was so sure you were in love with Laurie, and it hurt so much."

"Was it good?"

"She could only get off with a strap-on. No, it wasn't at all good, not for me at any rate."

"A strap-on? Is that what you are into now? Shall I fuck you again?"

"Yes please."

***

Jodie had to drive into Munich the next day. Her agent was coming down from Berlin to meet her, and she needed to check out of her hotel.

Anna-Maria and Giuseppe arrived for their annual Christmas visit. They were overjoyed to see Jodie.

"My daughter has been so unhappy. Please say you are staying this time."

"Mamma, it was my fault she left. Jodie has a big career in the States. She has to go back."

"But you are at least together again?"

"Yes, I think we are together again."

They had a quiet Christmas Eve, with a visit to midnight mass, before Christmas day lunch with the Cooper-Nymans. Except for Fredrik and Mats, the same group assembled. Two rather frail women were unknown to Jodie and Juliette. Clara was Arabella's grandmother, and she and her friend Mia with whom she lived were treated with great affection, particularly by Marie.

The twins were new this year, of course. Marie had been heavily pregnant the previous year. Margarete, the nanny, was given the holiday period off, as the grandparents were only too happy to look after the babies. Little Clara was beginning to walk, and her wobbles as she held her arms out either to Arabella or Marie were adorable. Her twin was still crawling, but he could cover impressive distances. Marie was already talking to them in Swedish, Arabella in English, and Margarete took care of the German. Juliette and her parents cooed at them in Italian and Jodie joined in in Spanish. It was like the tower of Babel.

When the babies were taken off for their afternoon nap, things quietened down a little. Suzanne and Beth monopolised Jodie, wanting to know everything about her life in the States. To Juliette's surprise, she heard her say that she was living with her parents in Manhattan. She presumed she would have her own apartment. The news made her feel a little more secure. Despite Jodie's protestations to the contrary, she couldn't quite rid herself of the picture of an attractive fan lying under her, writhing with pleasure. She felt herself get hot at the thought, as her voyeuristic tendencies hit her core.

It began to snow hard, and Suzanne and Beth left to drive back to Munich, where Suzanne had a performance to sing the following day.

They exchanged gifts that night. Jodie gave her a set of luxurious sweatbands for her wrists and a headband, all embroidered with their double letter J logo. Juliette had a present she had had crafted but didn't know if she would ever give her. It was a charm, a gold and bejewelled copy of the little monkey.

They had one more day together before Jodie left. Juliette wanted to take her in every room in the house, but the presence of her parents made that impossible. They spent as much time in bed as they could, but also enjoyed Anna-Maria's cooking and spending time with her and Giuseppe.

After a last bout of morning sex, Juliette sighed.

"I'll drive you to the airport."

"No, don't. People will recognise you and the rumours will start again."

"I. Am. Going. To. Drive. You. To. The. Airport."

It had snowed steadily since Christmas Day. The motorways were clear, but Juliette was glad of the four-wheeled drive SUV. They arrived at Munich Airport.

"Just drop me off."

"No. I'm coming in with you."

Jodie sighed. "You know what will happen."

They took a piece of luggage each, and checked Jodie in. Heads whirled all the time, but Juliette made sure to catch no one's eye, and they were left alone as they walked to the gate. There was no queue, so Jodie would be able to walk straight through. They stopped.

Jodie looked at her with tears in her eyes. "Goodbye. Until soon I hope."

Juliette took her into her arms and kissed her open mouthed. They pressed their bodies together. "Goodbye, my darling. I love you so much."

They parted, and with one last wave, Jodie was gone. Juliette hurried back to her car before the tears overwhelmed her.

**

Her life had changed for the better. Jodie's absence was like a permanent ache, but now they were in daily contact. There had been no repercussions from the airport kiss. Either they hadn't been photographed, or people respected her privacy. As human nature couldn't change that fast, Juliette supposed they had been lucky enough to dodge photographic evidence.

The second part of the tour began at the end of January and was even more gruelling than the first part had been. Every arena and concert hall played to capacity, and two extra dates were squeezed in. She only got back home once for two days, which she spent in bed. Tom and Vassily looked after her. She loved them dearly and was happy to see Tom so much in love.

When she got back on the tour, she needed permanent massages, before and after each concert, but her back and knee were tenuously holding on. Finally, the concerts in Zürich, the penultimate date, were over and she could check out of the hotel and return home. It was a relief. Now, there were just the three concerts in the vast Olympia Halle in Munich to get through. It seated over fifteen thousand, and all three concerts had been sold out since the autumn.

Jodie wished her luck for the first two concerts, but then Juliette didn't hear from her. She was slightly concerned but forgot as she concentrated on making the last show on the tour something to remember.

It was almost over, and she would leave the stage to change into her tux while Bert and the orchestra played a medley of her hits. She caught a movement on the side of the stage, and there were some screams and cheering from the audience on her right. The orchestra were fumbling with music, and Bert gave the downbeat and began an introduction to a song she barely knew. Jodie walked to the piano and began to sing Laurie Porter's number one hit *Try to be brave*. Juliette leaned over the piano, only rushing from the stage when it was nearly over, and managing a thirty-second change into her tux. She came back on as the number ended. The audience went wild. Jodie walked to the front of the stage, and they hugged.

"This is as much a surprise to me as it is to you. For the few people who don't know who this is, Jodie Sanchez just sang the hit she wrote for Laurie Porter." There were cheers and shouts. They stood holding hands and gazing into each other's eyes until Jodie left the stage. She remained just out of sight of the audience.

"What a high point to end on. Bert, I'm going to ask you later how you managed to rehearse the orchestra without me knowing." The audience laughed and cheered.

"Well, this is the last concert of the tour. I thank you all for being here, and especially those of you who have been to more concerts than just this one. I guess you must have enjoyed it." There was frenetic applause. "But now it's time for the final number." A collective groan went up.

Bert launched into *You don't own me.* Juliette didn't hesitate as she sang the word *girls* instead of *boys,* even if it no longer rhymed. She heard gasps from the arena. When the song ended, she took a deep bow and kept her head down until eventually the cheering stopped.

"Ladies and gentlemen, for two years I have lied to you, and I have lied to myself for many years longer. I apologise…deeply." There was a murmur, which grew into a roar. She held out her hand to quieten it.

"The time has come to tell the truth. I thought I never would be able to. I thought my career was more important to me than anything else. I do love it, and I love you all, but it's not enough." She paused. She turned to the side of the stage and extended her arm. Jodie walked slowly towards her.

"This is the woman I'm in love with. I intend to spend the rest of my life with her."

***

Epilogue

Eighteen months later

They boarded the flight from JFK to Munich and sank into the first-class seats.

"It was great, but I'm so glad it's over." Juliette had completed a six-month run of *Chicago* on Broadway. Combined with the six months in the West End, with barely a month in between, she was away from home for over a year. The London part was hard. Jodie was in New York for most of it, but for the Broadway months, they were together. They rented an apartment in a brownstone on the Upper West Side, overlooking the Hudson.

But now, they were both going home. Jodie promoted her album on a tour during Juliette's London run, but she had more and more come to the conclusion that performing didn't really interest her and being separated from Juliette wasn't worth it. She was now an established songwriter, with a string of hits with various artists to her credit. And for that she needed at the most a piano. There was nothing to prevent them from being together the whole time.

Tom and Vassily met them at the airport with a small transporter. After six months in New York, they had accumulated a lot of luggage, and Jodie brought most of her possessions with her. Her books would be shipped. Someone, probably Andreas, tipped off the press, and there was a horde of photographers waiting as they emerged from the baggage hall. Juliette took Jodie's hand as a microphone was shoved under her nose.

"Miss Simon, are you back for good?"

"I can't answer that, but we will be at home for several months, if not longer."

"Are you ready to announce a new album? Your fans are getting restless."

"Yes, I'm going to record an album of songs written by Jodie Sanchez, Bert Schmidt and Arabella Cooper. All completely new."

"And will you tour again?"

"No. There might be some concerts and some TV appearances, but I will not tour the big venues. I have other plans."

"There is a rumour about a TV series."

"No comment."

"Miss Sanchez, will you be staying in Munich?"

"Not *in* Munich, no."

"Darling, don't tell them where we live."

"It's not the best kept secret, Miss Simon."

"I know, but the whole world doesn't have to know. Come on, ladies and gentlemen, give us some privacy."

"Are you both happy?" They looked at each other and kissed. The photo made the papers the next day.

***

The late September weather was unexpectedly glorious. One of the deck tables under the big tree in the Cooper-Nyman garden was full of people eating and drinking delicious food and wine. A pretty young girl walked down from the house carefully carrying a large cake, which she placed on the table in front of Marie.

"Leonie, it's beautiful. Thank you so much. Suzanne and Beth, Leonie is Wiebke's daughter. Did you really decorate it yourself?" The girl nodded, blushing attractively. "Stay and eat a piece with us."

"No, I shouldn't. Mutti… I mean Mama… needs me in the kitchen but thank you." She had a surprisingly deep voice, which broke a little on some words. It was sexy.

Juliette jumped up and kissed her cheek. Jodie gave her a high five. Leonie blushed a deeper pink.

"I'm sure we won't manage all of it. You can have some later." The girl turned and left.

"She's going to break hearts as she gets older." Suzanne watched her appreciatively. Beth gave her a warning glare. The others sniggered. The girl increased her pace and ran up the steps into the house.

Marie took the large cake knife in her hand. "Juliette, look at the detail. It's your birthday cake."

They all studied the design. There were four platinum and five gold discs surrounding a Tony award, which she had won in New York for *Chicago*. All crafted out of fondant.

"Someone photograph it before I cut." Jodie took several photos, from different angles.

"Happy Birthday, Juliette."

They toasted her.

"Mmmm, it's good. What a wonderful birthday cake. Thank you both so much. I'm going to eat two pieces and then waddle straight to the gym to work it off."

"I can think of a better idea." Jodie snatched another piece.

Juliette rolled her eyes. "You have a one-track mind."

Suzanne patted her stomach. "Beth, please don't say anything. I know." She was nearing fifty and had given up the trouser roles, which made her so famous. Now, she was singing and playing older women, with as much success as she had in her *boy* days. She was a little heavier than she had been but was still a remarkably attractive woman. "I haven't slowed down in the bedroom yet as you well know." Beth took her hand and kissed the palm.

"Don't do that now. Save it for later. Having said that about slowing down, I, or rather we, have news. I have been offered a Professorship at the Music University here in Munich, and I'm going to accept it. I have to start planning for when I can't sing anymore, and this post became vacant, so I jumped at it."

"You mean they jumped at getting you onto the staff." Beth poked her in the ribs.

"Will you get an apartment in Munich?"

"No, that's our other news. We've found a lakeside house about three kilometres from here. We will be moving down from Berlin. Beth has been contacted by a failing agency in Munich who need her expertise, so she has an interesting job to keep her busy. But the main reason for the move is so that I can see my godchildren growing up."

Marie leaned over and hugged her. "I'll have them with me next year in Bayreuth." She and Suzanne would be singing Elsa and Ortrud in a new production of *Lohengrin*. Wagner fans worldwide were already salivating. Marie's voice had become even richer since the birth of the twins, and she was now the most sought-after soprano of her generation in Wagner and Richard Strauss roles. She had offers and enquiries about her availability for the next ten years. It made her dizzy to look at her calendar.

"No, oh no, you won't have them all the time. When I'm here at home, they will be with me."

Marie snorted, "*When* you are home."

"Just be patient for another two years, my love." It had been announced Arabella Cooper would assume the music directorship of the state opera in Munich, the first woman and the youngest conductor ever to hold the post.

"Talking of patience, although the children are my world, I am rather looking forward to next week. My parents are coming from Stockholm to collect them and fly them over to Wales for a week. A week of bliss for all the grandparents coming up."

"And for us too, I hope." Arabella reached over and ran her finger down Marie's cheek.

Marie looked at her lustfully. "I want to f…make love to my wife uninterrupted. They wandered into the bedroom recently at a most inconvenient moment."

Arabella made a face. "Anders was really upset. *Mama, why are you lying on top of mummy and hurting her? She's groaning.* That put paid to an orgasm I'll never get back."

"Mama, mummy," the twins were playing down by the water, supervised by Margarete. They ran up the garden and hurled themselves onto their mother's laps. Anders still looked like Arabella with his black hair and blue eyes, and to everyone's astonishment Clara looked increasingly like Marie, with her ash blonde hair and grey eyes. It was difficult to believe that she wasn't her blood mother.

"Juliette, when are you going to start Italian lessons with them? And, Jodie Spanish."

"Poor kids, they will be so confused."

"We are not confused, are we Anders?" The little boy shook his head shyly.

"You should hear them speaking to each other when they think nobody is listening. They speak Lingua Twin, and neither of us understand a word."

"Juliette, when do you begin filming your series?"

"In three weeks from now. There will be six ninety-minute episodes, and if it's a success, there is an option for a second run."

"And will you be singing in the role?"

"As a ruthless prosecution lawyer? Are you kidding? No, I have nothing to clutch onto except my acting talent, which I hope I have enough of. Otherwise…"

Jodie took her hand. "Nobody doubts you for a minute. You will be fabulous."

The sun sank slowly behind the Alps, the first snow on the tips glowing pink. The lake was streaked with gold.

Arabella proposed another toast. "To us all, and to our friendship, and to the best neighbours anyone could ever dream of." They raised their glasses and drank.

***

They had had lazy sex after returning home. Jodie brushed her fingers across the soft skin of Juliette's perfectly flat and muscular belly. Juliette worshipped Jodie's golden brown tanned body.

"How did the costume fitting go yesterday? I forgot to ask you."

"Predictable I suppose. I wear pencil skirt suits, starched shirts with high collars and stilettos that are going to kill me after a full day's filming."

Jodie attempted to swallow. "I insist that you come home in your costume some days," her voice croaked.

"Really?"

"Yes, really."

"Darling, do you want *me* to buy the strap-on?"

"Maybe you should."

THE END

Ingram Content Group UK Ltd.
Milton Keynes UK
UKHW020608140723
425125UK00006B/258